SAVING MY SOUL

A SECOND CHANCE MMA ROMANCE

SECOND CHANCE CHICAGO SERIES

GINA AZZI

Saving My Soul

Copyright © 2020 by Gina Azzi

All rights reserved.

This is a work of fiction. Names, characters, businesses, places, events, locales, and incidents are either the products of the author's imagination or used in a fictitious manner. Any resemblance to actual persons, living or dead, or actual events is purely coincidental.

1

HARLOW

"I got this. I'm good," I tell my reflection, squaring my shoulders and fluffing my hair at the roots. I give myself a final once-over, leaning closer to the mirror to check that my eyeliner isn't smudged before stepping back, satisfied.

I catch my fingers fiddling with my nose ring the way I always do when I'm nervous. It's my tell and I hate it.

Yanking my hand away, I grip the bathroom vanity and let out a slow breath.

I'm not nervous. I'm good. I'm good!

I curled my honey-blonde hair so it falls softly around my face. My eyes pop with the new eyeliner I bought at the airport and my lips are painted in my favorite shade of hot pink: Candy Kiss.

"You're an independent woman," I remind my reflection, nodding to solidify the claim. "You're in a stable relationship, your career is on track, you're…put together." I roll my eyes at how lame that sounds, turn away from the mirror in the W Hotel's luxurious bathroom and step back into my hotel room.

An image of the other half of my stable relationship,

Bryce Hawke, fills my mind and I smile, my fingertips pressing against my lips.

I'm not nervous; I'm excited. That's all this is.

Two weeks ago, when we were shopping in Beverly Hills, Bryce pointed out *the* engagement ring. A flawless, three-carat, princess cut wonder that he said would look "perfect" on my ring finger.

Sinking to the edge of the bed, I savor the butterflies fluttering against my ribcage.

I'm just excited.

Not at all nervous about being back in Chicago and seeing *him*. Connor Scott.

Nope. Because I'm good. Bryce and I are good.

So what if my breath doesn't catch when Bryce enters a room the way it always does with Connor? Who cares if my skin doesn't tingle from Bryce's glance alone like when Connor turned his eyes on me?

I'm not twenty-three anymore. That passionate, intense, so-hot-I-could-burn-to-ash fascination isn't healthy for what I want now.

Stability. Commitment. A family.

Connor Scott never indicated that he was capable of any of those things.

My phone chimes with a message and I swipe it off the nightstand. Bryce must be checking on me. Disappointment swirls in my stomach that it's not him, but it quickly morphs into excitement when I read Zoe's name.

Zoe: Hey! Are you almost here?

Me: Yes! Leaving hotel now. Can't wait to see the birthday girl!

Zoe: You could have stayed with us.

Me: I flew in at the butt crack of dawn.

Zoe: (eye roll emoji) Maddie is so excited! Don't be

alarmed if she approaches you with scissors... but DO NOT cut her hair. She's extra when embracing the Dora theme of her party.

I burst out laughing, imagining the daughter of my closest girlfriend Zoe and my former boss, Hollywood hotshot Eli Holt, sneakily trying to cut her hair to look more like an animated character. Kids are mischievous, but any offspring of Eli is bound to give Zoe a run for her money.

Me: Got it! She's hilarious. See you guys soon. Anything I can bring?

Zoe: Just yourself.

Shouldering my purse, I pick up the large shopping bag holding Maddie's neatly wrapped birthday gift. A balloon is tied to the handle and I grin at the big number three bouncing in the air. I step into the hallway and head for the elevators.

Wanting to surprise my "niece" on her special day, I took the red-eye from L.A. so I could arrive at her party before her friends show up.

If I happen to also arrive before her "uncle," Eli's best friend Connor, well, that's just icing on the cake and not at all why I chose a damn red-eye over a full night's sleep.

I slip into a taxi and relax against the backseat. I try to remember the last time Connor and I spoke. Not counting greetings or superficial platitudes, it's been more than two years. Since then, I've paraded around the L.A. party scene with a multitude of men, desperately trying to replace Connor's touch with one that would make me feel whole instead of empty.

No one has ever come close. Except Bryce.

"Thank you." I slip the fare to the driver as I slide out of the cab and square my shoulders in front of Eli and Zoe's gorgeous, contemporary home.

Glancing down at my designer threads that artfully show

off the svelte figure I've literally worked my ass off for, I blow out a deep breath and enter the beautiful home.

Maddie's squeals pierce the foyer. Footsteps rush the door. Her face opens like a sunflower when she sees me, sprinting straight for my legs and knocking me back a few steps. I teeter in my four-inch heels, grabbing the doorframe to catch myself.

Laughing, I wrap Maddie in my arms, holding her tight.

My heart aches in my chest as I breathe in her sweet scent. "I missed you, Ms. Madison Ann."

"You're here!" Zoe exclaims, appearing behind Maddie.

"I'm here," I grin at her, kissing her cheek in greeting.

"You're the first one!" Maddie tells me.

"That's because I'm the best one."

Maddie giggles before slyly asking, "What's in the bag?"

"Madison Ann," Zoe scolds her daughter.

"Just the best birthday gift in all the land." I crouch down until I'm eye-level with Maddie, the present in between us. "Want to add it to your gift table?"

Maddie's eyes glimmer and she smiles, her dimple popping. The perfect mix of Eli and Zoe, Maddie's got her father's charm and her mother's sweetness. Basically, telling her no is impossible and giving in to all of her demands is the only answer. At least, as her auntie.

"What do you say?" Zoe prods Maddie.

"Thank you, Auntie Harlow." My sweet girl winds her arms around my neck for a quick hug before grasping the balloon string and pulling the gift into the living room.

"She's too much," I laugh, standing up.

"She's definitely that," Zoe agrees. "Come on," she curls her arm around my waist, steering me toward the kitchen. "Let's get you a drink. It's been too long since I've seen you."

"Way too long," I agree. "Are you coming out to L.A. for the *Reckless Waters* film premiere?"

"Of course," Zoe waves a hand. We stop at the kitchen island and she fixes us mimosas. "I'm so proud of Eli. He's really excited about this film. It's going to be interesting to watch it with a more technical eye, instead of drooling over Eli's abs."

I snort, rolling my eyes.

"What?" Zoe laughs. "He has hot abs! But as much as I love seeing my husband on screen, he's much more content in the director's chair. Co-directing is definitely a new challenge for him and I like seeing him so excited about a project again. Will you be there? With Bryce?" Her eyebrows raise and a wide smile crosses her mouth.

"Yes!" I clasp her hand. "Fly out early. We'll spend time together before the premiere."

"Oh, thank God! I'd love to. We can sit together too."

"Absolutely." I clink my glass against hers before taking a sip. I hope Bryce hasn't already committed us to a seating arrangement. He usually tries to capitalize on these opportunities to shore up support for a role he's considering or get a pulse on some issue circling in the industry. But to sit with my friends—

"Low," Eli's voice cuts through my thoughts. I turn as he enters the kitchen.

Eli Holt has been a Hollywood megastar since the moment he exploded on the scene six years ago. But now, dressed in ripped jeans and a casual gray T-shirt, he looks happier than ever before, including the night he won a Golden Globe for his performance in *Dangerous Devils*.

"Dad life suits you, Eli." I smile as he pulls me into a big hug.

"Jesus, it's been too damn long. You should visit more

often." He leans back, peering at me. "You know, if you can pull yourself away from the bright lights and Bryce's ego."

"Eli," Zoe warns.

"What?" My former boss, turned friend, turned family, shrugs. "His giant head isn't a secret."

"Who has a giant head?" Maddie asks, zooming around the corner.

Eli catches her and raises her over his head. "Actors. They are the absolute worst, Maddie."

"I thought you were an actor, Daddy."

"You thought wrong, Princess. I'm the tickle monster." He shakes her, tickling her like crazy, as she erupts in laughter.

While Eli runs Maddie through the first floor of the house, I try to shake off the bubble of doubt caused by Eli's words. It's no secret that my friends' acceptance of the news of my dating Bryce was lukewarm at best. While Zoe has actively tried to form a friendship with Bryce over the past year, Eli's complete dismissal stings, especially since Bryce starred in *Reckless Waters*. Sipping my mimosa, I swallow the champagne, now tinged with bitterness, and turn my attention back to Zoe.

"Don't mind him," she says gently. "The most important thing is that you're happy."

"Right." I smile, placing my glass on the counter. "And I am. Happy."

"Good." My friend grins but the light in her eyes dims, as if she doesn't believe a word of it.

My mouth drops open to explain how Bryce and I are moving forward in our relationship, even talking marriage, when a voice cuts through the air, causing shivers to skate up my spine.

"Where's the birthday girl?" A deep rumble echoes through the foyer as the front door closes.

Connor walks into the kitchen, birthday gift in hand. My gaze connects with his. At his startled expression, my stomach sinks and twists. Did he think I wouldn't come to Maddie's birthday party? Is he happy or disappointed that I'm here?

A strange mixture of shame and doubt coats my veins at Eli's rejection of Bryce. The offsetting emotions deepen under Connor's scrutiny.

Confusion swirls in my stomach as I blink and look away.

"Hey," his voice rasps and I shiver again. Coarse like gravel, smooth like whiskey, and sexy as sin, Connor Scott unleashes a million butterflies in my stomach and twists my thoughts into knots.

With one word, he makes me question if my reactions to Bryce are ever this visceral. Guilt burns my chest and an unexpected sting of tears forms behind my nose.

I let out a slow exhale, trying to shore up my resolve to 'act normal.' But some things never change, and my body's natural pull toward Connor is one of them.

"Connor," Zoe steps forward to hug him hello. "Drink?"

"Just a water. Thanks, Zo," he responds, his gaze still locked on me.

I clear my throat. "Hi."

Connor nods, taking a swig of water.

"I just want to check on a few things before everyone arrives," Zoe explains, leaving the kitchen.

The moment she does, the air seems to constrict.

Connor leans against the countertop, crossing his ankles. He's calm, at ease, normal. "How's it going?"

I wrap my fingers around the stem of my champagne flute, just to have something to do with my hands.

I'm good. I'm good. I'm good.

My heart hammers so loud I wonder if he can hear it. My palms grow clammy. The cool facade I've spent two years perfecting begins to crack.

"Pretty good," I manage to breathe out, relieved when my voice doesn't squeak.

"It's been a minute," Connor comments.

"Yeah," I nod. For the past two years, I've only ever seen Connor at events like this, for Maddie, or for Eli. But we've rarely spoken and we definitely were never in a room alone together. My awareness at his proximity spikes and I offer a small smile, genuinely happy to see him.

My phone beeps in my purse. I offer a sheepish grin as I pull it out. This time, I'm sure it's Bryce. The second my hand connects with my cell, it's like the unleashing of a tsunami. The beeping is incessant, chimes going off as all of my apps pour out a barrage of information.

The image that pops up on my screen chills my blood to ice.

A photo of Bryce, shirtless, his abs rippling, sweats low on his hips, pressing his mouth against a raven-haired beauty with a thigh gap glares at me.

The headline: *Hollywood's Golden Boy Caught Red-Handed*

What the hell?

My chest constricts, caving in on itself, until inhaling is a struggle.

I falter, confusion and hurt and a keen sense of betrayal exploding in my veins like landmines. My temples pulse, my heartbeat echoing in my eardrums. Shivers crawl up my arms, but the back of my neck blazes with heat. I feel sick, my stomach churning dangerously as I try to process my life falling apart on social media. Choking on the intensity of my emotions, I shake my head in disbelief, staring at my trembling fingers as I scroll through the other photos.

There are so damn many of them. Of Bryce and this woman touching, embracing, kissing.

But worse than that is the familiar intimacy between them. This isn't a one-time thing but something with real emotions and feelings and… truth.

My stomach twists painfully as a neon sign blinks in my mind: Bryce is cheating on me.

Not good. Not good. Not good.

"Low? You okay?" Connor's fingertips land in the small of my back.

I flinch even as I lean into his touch.

He moves closer. His cologne rolls off of him, heady and intense and familiar.

Nausea rolls in my stomach as a snowball of unshed tears burns my throat. How could Bryce do this to me?

I stagger back a half-step, my shoulder blades hitting the wall of muscle behind me.

Connor inhales sharply as I melt into him, letting his strength absorb my shock.

"Oh, fuck. I'm sorry, Harlow," he murmurs, his breath skating over the shell of my ear, as he peers over my shoulder at the images on my phone.

My head pounds, my body shakes. Standing in Zoe and Eli's kitchen, the life I had been crafting so carefully collapses like a house of cards. With Connor at my back, I feel exposed. I couldn't be more embarrassed and wish I had learned of Bryce's infidelity in my own kitchen.

The thought confuses me and kicks up the shame stirring in my stomach. Fight-or-flight seizes me and I drop the phone into my purse, pulling it straight off the counter.

"Harlow?" Connor spins me around, his hands gripping my shoulders.

Keeping my gaze averted, I shake my head. "I need, I just, excuse me, please." I step around him and escape to the bathroom.

As soon as the door is locked behind me, the tears come. Humiliation streaks down my cheeks as I lean over the sink, my stomach clenching, my hands shaking.

How could he do this to me? How could he hurt me likes this? How could he get caught? Why does Connor have to witness me fall apart?

Why am I not enough?

The tears fall faster, harder. I bite my lip to hold in a sob.

I flip on the faucet, slide my hands into the rushing water, and close my eyes. Unsure if I'm more upset over Bryce's deceit or Connor seeing it unfold, I hang my head and wash my face, ruining the make-up I had painstakingly applied an hour ago.

The doorbell rings, and voices fill up the house with chatter.

I regulate my breathing, staring at myself in the reflection of the mirror and hating the insecurity pouring from my eyes.

Most of all, I despise that Connor saw it too.

2

CONNOR

L oitering in the hallway like a creep, the muffled sounds of Harlow's sobs rip through me.

What a fucking dick. I hate men who can't just be straight up. You want to fuck around? Don't be in a serious relationship. You want a constant in your life? A woman to make your house a home, a woman you can slide into bed next to every night? Then be worthy of her.

Besides, who in their right mind would step out on a woman like Harlow?

My hands clench into fists as I pace the hallway, unsure what the hell to do. I hate that Low is hurting. Fucking hate it. But I also can't pretend like I haven't been the cause of her hurt in the past. I can't ignore the fact that me seeing her fall apart is embarrassing for both of us. Her, because she doesn't want to lose face in front of me. And me, because I don't want to cause her anymore grief.

For months, our hooking up was casual, fun, and so damn hot I craved it, *her*, more than any other woman. But when she told me she wanted more — the feelings and future of a real relationship — I pulled back. I knew if I didn't end it with her right then, she'd shrink her world to fit into mine. Harlow Reid is meant to do big things. Staying in Chicago to be the girlfriend of a has-been MMA fighter isn't one of them. Still, I had no idea that ending our thing would spur her to disappear from my life overnight. Or that she wouldn't talk to me unless she absolutely had to for the next two fucking years.

A whimper sounds through the door, and I wince.

I can't just walk away. Not when the sounds of her sobs are ripping through my chest. Not when the image of her with tears in her eyes, her shoulders curving forward, is glaring in my head.

I don't know what the protocol is when a woman you care for is hurting because another man did her wrong, but I know I'm about to break ranks.

Posting up against the wall opposite the bathroom, I give Harlow a few more moments to herself. Where she's concerned, walking away has always been my default mode. I'm consistent like that. From the first time I saw her, bright green eyes, an infectious laugh, and a presence that charged the air with energy, altering the atmosphere of any room she entered, I knew she was too damn good for me. We never had a chance.

Harlow could be a Hollywood darling. She deserves it.

And me? I'm a washed-up, nobody who relied on my street smarts and my fists to get to the ripe old age of thirty-one. Glancing down, I scoff at my split knuckles, calloused fingers, and misshapen hands. Too many fractures. Too much temper.

Reckless, determined, and demanding, I'm absolutely nothing like Golden Boy. But I always knew Harlow would end up with someone like him. I was the dark, mysterious, alpha she killed time with in her twenties. Girls like Harlow don't end up with guys like me. At least, the smart ones don't. And Harlow's one of the most intelligent people I know.

Her crying subsides on the other side of the door and some of the pressure in my chest alleviates, like helium escaping a balloon.

Harlow Reid. The one who got away.

Nope, the one you pushed away, you dumb ass.

When I entered Eli's kitchen and my eyes slammed into hers, I couldn't believe she was really here. Even though I never ask Eli outright about her, he's offered enough glimpses into her life over the past few months to bitch about the guy, Bryce Hawke, she's altering herself for. Eli had no problem telling me that Harlow's new love interest wasn't worth a damn.

"Self-centered and egotistical prick. I know the type. He's going to take everything from her and give nothing in return," my best friend ranted one night after Zoe expressed worry about Harlow's relationship.

The more serious their commitment became, the harder it was to avoid. Every fucking magazine in the grocery store checkout aisle advertised their perfect romance. I even bought a copy once because Harlow looked breathtaking on the cover. It was a candid. She still looked like herself — effortless, flawless, undeniably sexy — and nothing like the woman sipping a mimosa in the kitchen this morning.

Even before she received the message that made her cry, she was too stiff, too standoffish. Her hair is lighter, with more blond than the last time I saw her. She's thinner too, lean like all those California girls who look airbrushed even when they're trying to be real.

But worse than appearing every bit the L.A. socialite she swore she'd never become, was the way she looked at me.

Disinterested, almost bored. Like we've never shared a history. Like I don't know she has a birthmark shaped like a star on her right hip. Like I'm not the person who held her when she broke down after her mom checked into rehab for the fourth time. Like I'm not the man who can bring her to the brink of her goddamn sanity. Her aloofness struck a chord, squashing my party mood and filling my stomach with anger and disappointment. I hate that she looked *through* me without looking *at* me. I especially hate that I made it this way between us.

Pushing off the wall, a wave of frustration rolling through me, I step to the bathroom door. This is stupid. I'm not going to stand in the hallway, waiting for Harlow to decide if she wants to talk. She's crying at a three-year-old's birthday party, for fuck's sake. Clearly, she needs to talk to someone.

Right now, with Zoe greeting guests and Eli starting the festivities, I'm her best option.

I lift my hand to knock on the door when it swings open.

Surprised, I falter as she slams into me. My arms wrap around her to keep her from falling. Unexpectedly, she crumbles in my embrace, her strength leaving her as she sags against my chest.

Shit. The gleeful yelling of preschoolers grows closer. Without overthinking it, I walk Harlow backward into the bathroom, kicking the door closed behind us. We're no sooner concealed in the powder room than her tears start up again and I hold her tighter.

Harlow breaks apart in my arms. Witnessing her anguish causes my throat to close, until swallowing is difficult. Anger builds in my bloodstream. I'm furious at pansy-ass Bryce for causing Harlow pain. I'm pissed at the media for blindsiding her. But most of all, I'm angry with myself for not being enough for her when she asked me to be. Now, instead of drowning in her bright green eyes and hearing the music of her laughter, I'm comforting her as she collapses from the betrayal of the man she loves.

"Shh, you're okay," I whisper into her hair, my hand cradling the back of her head.

She hiccups against my chest and I smile, relishing the sound since it's the most real Harlow's been with me in years.

"I got you, Low."

"I'm sorry," she wails. "I'm ruining your shirt."

Snorting, I try to bite back my laughter. She must sense it because she pulls back, looking up at me with puffy eyes and a red-tipped nose.

I grin, "That's what's ripping you up? My shirt?"

Her eyes simultaneously narrow and fill with tears. I reach out and crush her back against my chest. "Let it out, babe. I promise not to sell your secrets to the tabloids."

She groans, smacking my ribs.

I hold her tighter. Little by little, she relaxes in my embrace. I don't know how long we spend hugging, but when I catch sight of us in the huge bathroom mirror, I like our reflection more than I should.

Petite in stature but larger than life in personality, Harlow still fits perfectly against me. Her blonde hair pops against the tanned skin of my forearms, a consequence of working odd construction jobs while trying to keep my gym afloat. While she's pristine, I'm flawed. Where she's outgoing, I'm introverted. But when we're together, everything slows and I hold onto the moment for as long as she'll let me.

Harlow pulls back, wiping the backs of her knuckles against her eyes. When she catches her reflection, she blanches. "I look terrible," she murmurs, reaching for her purse and pulling out a makeup bag.

I plop down on the closed toilet seat, silently watching as she pulls out compacts and tubes of gunk.

"What are you doing?" I ask as she dabs some goo under her eyes.

"Fixing my face."

"Your face looks better without all that shit on it."

She glares at me, tossing the tube onto the vanity. "I'm a mess."

She sounds defeated. Slumping to the floor, she rests against the wall and looks up at me. Vulnerability flares in her eyes. It's such a relief to see a real expression that I move to sit beside her, my legs cramping in the small space.

"Low, you're a lot of things, but you're never a mess." I place a hand on her knee. The smoothness of her skin sends a ripple of awareness through me.

Harlow Reid is all woman. Smooth, soft skin, curvy lines, and sweet angles. She's always been beautiful. Not just because of her looks — which are goddamn gorgeous — but because of her heart.

She rests her head on my shoulder, her pretenses from the kitchen disappearing. "My boyfriend cheated on me and the entire world knows."

I squeeze her knee.

"I was going to marry him," she admits, her tone unreadable.

Her confession rocks me to my core. A blinding type of anger — at Hawke, at Low, at my damn self — blazes, making my skin burn. "You were going to *marry* that limp dick?"

Harlow freezes next to me but I don't care.

"What the hell were you thinking? The Golden Boy? Really, Low? What'd you want to spend your life following him around until he bored you to death?"

"What do you mean?" she asks, her tone more curious than the defensive anger I expected.

I glare at her, my hand sliding up over her dress to rest on her hip. "Harlow Reid, you deserve a hell of a lot more than spending your life overshadowed by a man's ego. Golden Boy? He only thinks about himself, his career. If he cared about you, he would never put you in the position of learning of his goddamn infidelity in a fucking tweet."

"It was a blog."

"Whatever. He's a dick."

"I feel so stupid." Her eyes close and she settles back against the wall. .

"Why? He's the stupid one. He lost you."

"Everyone knows," she whispers, her fingers twisting her nose piercing the way she does when she's nervous, uncomfortable, or thinking through something.

"Who's everyone, Low? A bunch of people in L.A. you don't even care about?"

She whirls on me, her eyes blazing. "What do you mean, people I don't care about? It's been two years, Connor. You don't know me anymore."

"Yes, I do," I say without hesitation. "I know it's been a minute, Low, but I know you."

She scoffs, shaking her head. "I have a life, a career that I've built —"

"Overseeing losers who try to find love on airplanes in front of a camera?" I cut her off, referencing her position as host on some bullshit reality television show where contestants make absolute asses of themselves thirty-thousand feet in the sky.

Harlow bristles, jumping to her feet. "At least those people are trying, Connor. At least I'm trying. I put myself out there and yeah, I'm fucking humiliated right now. I'm ashamed and embarrassed and feel so damn stupid. Especially since of all the people in the world to watch me get cut off at the knees, it has to be you." She jabs a finger at me.

I sit up straighter, absorbing her anger and hating it at the same time. "Harlow—"

"No. You don't get to sit here, all sanctimonious, and judge strangers for trying to find love. Is that so horrible? To not want to spend your life entirely alone? I mean, fine, clearly I suck at it, but at least I try." With a grunt, she shovels her belongings back into her purse.

"Low, wait a minute." I stand, blocking the door. "I didn't mean you."

"Didn't you, though? What makes me any different than any of those people on the show? My life is imploding in real time for everyone to pick apart, just like them, and all because I want to believe that I'm enough for someone."

The hurt behind her words, coupled with her dejected expression, causes the second shockwave. She doesn't think she's *enough*? Jesus Christ.

I fight the urge to chuckle. The issue is that she's too damn much.

She narrows her eyes at me, as if daring me to laugh. As usual, she's got the reasoning all wrong.

I clear my throat, "I'm sorry."

"What?"

"I apologize."

"I know. I just, I wanted to hear it again."

I hold out my arms again, desperate to hold her. "C'mere."

"Connor." She shuffles from one foot to the other, her indignation burning out as quickly as it flared.

"I'm an asshole and I don't know how to do this, but I want to try."

"Try what?" she asks, a flicker of panic ringing her irises.

"To cheer you up."

A snort escapes her nose as a small smile tugs at her lips. "If that's your goal, you suck at it."

"You're smiling."

"I'm smirking."

"C'mere, Low."

Rolling her eyes, she steps into my embrace and I wrap her up tight, savoring the feel of her in my arms.

3

HARLOW

After a wildly successful *Dora the Explorer* birthday party, that included a real-life appearance by Boots, I feel calmer, more settled, than I did when I walked into Eli and Zoe's home this morning.

What started off rocky transformed into an easy familiar. The muscle memory of how things used to be, should be, took over, and I slid right back into the comfort of being surrounded by friends, by people I know have my best interests at heart, and letting them build me up as I crumble.

As Eli and Connor stuff streamers and confetti into trash bags, Zoe packs a bag for Maddie to have a sleepover at her cousin Ollie's house. Officially banned from clean-up duty, I pace back and forth on the back patio, my cellphone glued to my ear.

"It was one time. Sweetheart, I swear, she meant nothing," Bryce rushes to explain, a hint of panic in his tone.

"That's nice. You cheated on me with a girl who didn't even mean anything? You risked us for nothing!" I know on some level that whatever Bryce says tonight, he isn't going to win. I'm angry. Hurt. My pride shattered and lying in pieces in a gutter somewhere.

"Harlow, calm down. We can fix this."

I laugh. The sound is jarring and devoid of any humor. But the longer I laugh, the harder the emotions pour out of me until I'm standing under the moonlight, next to a beautiful pool, sobbing and giggling and wiping snot from my face.

"Harlow?" Bryce presses.

"Fuck off, Bryce. We're done. I don't want to 'fix this.' I don't even want to come back to L.A." I disconnect the call.

Plopping down on a pool lounger, I gaze up at the starry sky and wonder how I ended up here.

How did I? I was supposed to be planning my fairytale wedding, my own happily-ever-after after helping nearly everyone I know plan theirs. When is it going to be my turn?

My phone buzzes in my hand. When "Mom" flashes across the screen, I roll my eyes and ignore it. The last thing I need tonight is for her sharp words, rounded out with disappointment, to lacerate my open wounds. She'll try to convince me to forgive Bryce, watering down his infidelity to a simple lapse in judgement. She'll encourage me to consider the future, the financial and social stability a man like Bryce provides a woman like me. In short, she'll take his side over mine. I'm too raw, too wild, to absorb any more hurt.

"Harlow?" Zoe calls out.

I turn to see my friend standing just off of the patio, her hands clasped in front of her.

"Hey." I sit up, somehow managing a smile despite my sudden urge to scream profanities and hurl myself into the pool.

"I'm sorry Bryce turned out to be such a jerk."

I wave a hand dismissively but my words give away my heartache. "So am I."

Harlow sighs and tilts her head toward the house. "Want a drink?"

I nod and shakily stand from the lounger. Zoe slips an arm around my waist and pulls me close. Exuding warmth and strength, I let my friend hold me. I feel a tiny sliver of comfort spread through my chest.

Entering the kitchen, I step to the island where Eli lines up a row of hard liquor.

"Great. You guys are going to get shitfaced and have a grand old time while I'm on dad duty," Eli's brother Evan jokes, shooting me a sympathetic smile. He shoulders Maddie's overnight bag as the birthday girl runs into the kitchen.

"You can polish my nails, Uncle Ev!" Maddie attempts to jump on his back. "And Ollie's too!"

Ollie, Evan's nine-year-old son, blanches.

Eli smirks. "There's a chance her sugar high will wear off and she'll pass out on the car ride to your place."

Evan discreetly flips Eli off, bending down to give Maddie a piggy-back ride. "Alright you little rug rats. We're out." He waves to Eli, Zoe, Connor, and me.

"Happy birthday, Maddie," I say as Zoe walks Evan and the kids to the front door.

"Pick your poison, Low," Eli says, wincing when he takes in my tear-stained face.

"Tequila," I mutter.

Connor grimaces.

"Oh, come on." Zoe swats him as she waltzes back into the kitchen and grabs a handful of shot glasses. "Now that you're not training, you can drink with us like a normal person."

Eli slaps Connor on the back. "One of the perks."

"You're not in training?" I ask, confused. Connor's been a

UFC fighter for as long as I've known him, always gearing up for some kind of fight or competition. He's almost always in training, watching his diet, committed to intense workouts, and focused on the upcoming bout.

At my question, a strange tension tugs between the four of us. After a beat, Eli uncaps the tequila bottle and points at me. "Tonight, we're focusing on your heartbreak."

I gratefully accept the shot glass and toss it back.

My friends stare at me, more shocked than impressed.

"Fill it up." I hold the glass back out to Eli who pours wordlessly.

After my second shot, the brick that's been lodged in the center of my chest all day begins to crumble. I'm able to take my first deep inhale since I landed in Chicago this morning.

"Harlow, your phone is blowing up." Zoe shakes it at me.

On the screen, Bryce's name is everywhere.

"He's called four times since we came inside," she continues, alarmed.

"Pussy," Connor mutters.

"Dick," Eli chimes in.

"He should be here." Connor jabs his finger into the top of the island.

"Taken the first flight out," Eli confirms.

"Guys," Zoe warns.

But I tune them out and allow myself to grow numb to everything that is spiraling out of control around me.

My tears are starting to dry and in their place, anger blazes. . "He picked out a ring." I announce to the room, unsure if Bryce even purchased the ring he showed me. But right now, that's not the important part. The important part is that he allowed me to believe in a future he wasn't committed to living. He filled me with the hope for a marriage, a family, that he wasn't planning to follow through on.

"What?" Zoe gasps.

I nod. "It was three carats. Flawless. Princess cut. The band had—"

"How could he do this to you?" Zoe wails, starting to understand the depth of my heartbreak. On top of losing Bryce, I'm losing the dream.

Now, I'm forced to address the big black hole of my future with a confused question mark dangling over it.

"I didn't know you guys were that serious," Eli says slowly.

Shrugging, I pick up my shot glass and drain it.

"You're going to feel like shit tomorrow," Zoe cautions.

"I don't think I could feel worse than I do right now."

"Me either," Connor says, clinking a shot glass against mine before drinking it.

Zoe and Eli exchange a look, but I'm too exhausted from Bryce's bullshit and distracted by Connor's taking a shot to decipher it.

"Let's play Never Have I Ever," Zoe suggests.

"Jesus Christ," Eli murmurs, looking toward the heavens.

"Oh, come on. We're not going to talk any sense into them. Might as well join in and have some fun," Zoe tells Eli, pulling him onto a barstool.

Connor pours four shot glasses and places them in front of each of us.

"I'll start," I announce. "Never have I ever sat in the back of a police car."

Zoe snorts as Eli and Connor toss back their shots and refill the glasses.

"You suck, Low," Eli points at me as I wink at him.

"Never have I ever been broken up with in a tweet," Connor says, smirking at me.

I chuckle in spite of myself. "It was a blog," I clarify, even as I take the shot.

"Never have I ever gotten caught having sex." Zoe says.

Connor and I look at each other, a pregnant pause hovering between us. His eyes, cocoa and mysterious, burn with mischief.

Despite the fact that my heart feels like it's been fed through a meat grinder, I find myself smiling at him.

We both take our shots. Eli groans, throwing his hands in the air as Zoe claps and whoops wildly.

"Never have I ever cheated," Eli finally says.

None of us drink. The moment is sobering, causing some of the weight of the day to come rushing back.

We play a few more rounds before Eli and Zoe retire to bed.

But Connor and I stay up, the bottle of tequila between us. At some point, we stop playing the game and start talking.

"You are enough," Connor says suddenly, spinning the cap of the tequila bottle.

"Huh?"

"Before, in the bathroom. You asked why you aren't enough. You are, Harlow. You're too much."

I peer at him in confusion, the room starting to spin.

"I will never deserve a woman like you," he explains, gesturing between us.

"You're drunk," I blow off his honesty.

He shakes his head, reaching out to grab my fingers. "I'm an idiot."

"Already knew that one," I announce to the ceiling.

Connor chuckles but his hand grips mine, persistent, "Harlow, you're enough."

I blow out a deep breath, leaning over the table to stare into Connor's eyes. I don't know if I'm searching for his truth or mine but I fall into their endless depths, hypnotized by his sincerity and the sliver of vulnerability he's never shared with me before. "Why are you telling me this?"

"Because you should know that. You deserve everything, Low." His voice is low, husky, and so sexy I inch even closer.

"Connor, I—"

"I know."

"No, you don't," I shake my head, tilting it to the side.

Connor's hands settle on my shoulders, keeping me steady as I teeter back and forth on the barstool.

"You broke my heart," I admit, my confession shattering the air between us.

"I never meant to," he says solemnly, his words a salve to the wounds I've been carrying around since he shut me down two years ago.

"You were going to marry Golden Boy," he whispers, hurt heavy in his tone.

I nod, shimmying closer until his knee is nestled between my thighs and our mouths are inches apart.

"Would you care?" I ask, my heart thudding.

Connor's expression is tight, his eyes bleeding with honesty. He dips his chin, a jerky movement that belies the significance of his confession.

My hands lift until they rest on his cheeks. His stubble pricks my palms and I slip my hands higher, enjoying the friction against them.

Connor's eyelids drop to half-mast, one of his hands wrapping around my wrist, anchoring me to him. "Harlow," he says my name. A wish and a curse and a plea.

"Make the hurt stop," I say, desperate to feel the type of validation Connor can provide.

He sighs, his expression tortured. The strong muscles in his back bunch, causing tension to pop in his shoulders. He turns his face, pressing his cheek deeper into my palm. "Baby, I —"

"Shh," I cut him off. Emboldened by tequila and without a shred of dignity to worry about, I close the space between us and press my mouth against Connor's.

His full lips are soft against mine. But after a moment, his tongue slips in between the seam of my lips and meets mine in a long-overdue dance.

Heady, hungry, and overflowing with need, Connor kisses me fiercely. Like he isn't sure whether he wants to save me or consume me. My fingertips curl against his skin as his hands drop to squeeze my waist, kneading the skin under my dress.

Arching my back, my chest brushes against Connor's. My breasts feel heavy, straining against the flimsy material of my summer dress as my nipples harden.

I moan softly and Connor rips his mouth from mine.

"Fuck," he swears.

Our chests are heaving, panting breaths mingling in the space between us.

"Not like this, Low," Connor growls, sliding off the barstool.

He glares at me, his eyes darker than midnight. I shrink back from his intensity. He picks me up like a sack of potatoes and tosses me over his shoulder.

"Connor," I squeal, confused and delighted and delusional. I tap on his back, "Put me down."

"I'm putting you to bed. You're fucking dangerous, Reid." He declares, stalking to Zoe's guest room and depositing me in the bed.

The last thing I remember before sleep claims me is the warmth of Connor's touch as he brushes his fingertips through my hair and places a lingering kiss on my forehead.

Saying I couldn't feel worse was a big, fat, monumental lie.

When I wake in the morning, I feel like the Grim Reaper and a Salem Witch procreated. My head pounds. My mouth is too dry to swallow. Everything in my face feels swollen and out of place. My body aches and is simultaneously sweating and shivering.

"Motherfucker." I roll until I fall out of the bed, the floor rushing up to greet me. "What the hell?" I cry out, lying in a heap of limbs and twisted bedsheets on the floor.

The unfortunate events of the previous day slowly piece together in my mind. Cheating ass Bryce. Sexy as sin Connor.

Drinking all the tequila.

"Good morning," Connor chirps, suddenly kneeling beside me.

"Why are you here?"

"Wanted to make sure you didn't throw up and suffocate in your sleep."

"You're a gentleman."

"I wouldn't go that far." He slips his arms beneath me and lifts me easily.

The movement rattles my body and I groan.

"You drank too much," he adds.

"Thanks, Captain Obvious."

"You need to drink water."

"Stop talking."

"I missed your sunshine, Harlow."

"I haven't missed you at all."

He snickers.

"Why the hell are you so chipper? Shouldn't you feel like death like me?" I accuse.

"I didn't drink as much as you. Plus, I can handle my liquor better." He cradles me against his chest and strides out of the bedroom.

"What are you doing? Put me down." I clutch at his T-shirt, memories from last night muddling my brain.

"I'm on strict orders from Zoe to feed you and sober you up before Maddie comes home this afternoon. She wants to play with her new Barbie dream house with you."

I make a noise that sounds like an animal dying in the wild.

"That's what you get for showing the rest of us up with your 'best gift in all the land.'"

"I don't see her as much as you guys do." I backtrack to explain.

"Also your fault."

Bringing my hand to cover my face, I sigh. "Connor, I feel like death incarnate. Can you please go easy on me this morning?"

"Nope."

"What?"

"I can't. I went easy on you yesterday, babe. Today, we're piecing your life back together."

"'We?'"

"What, you think I'd just leave you to figure it out on your own?" He quirks an irritating eyebrow as if to say, 'look how well that worked out.'

"You mean like the last time?" I point out, mean-spiritedly.

But Connor is undeterred. His cocoa eyes gleam as he stares down at me. "I've learned a lot since then, Harlow. Haven't you?"

I grunt.

AFTER HALF A LOAF OF TOAST, strong coffee, and a hot shower, I feel more human.

"There she is," Eli grins when I enter the kitchen. "Zoe took Maddie out for lunch but they should be home soon." He explains as I glance around the quiet kitchen.

"Connor?" I ask.

"Went to check on his dad." My confusion must be evident because Eli continues, "He was diagnosed with Creutzfeldt-Jacob Disease."

My eyebrows pull together as I look at Eli, bewildered.

He sighs, scrubbing his palm over his face. "It's rare. Connor was rocked by the diagnosis."

"What is it?"

"A degenerative brain disorder. At first, Connor thought it was early onset Alzheimer's. Cameron's memory was starting to slip but it seemed to fail almost overnight."

"No," I shake my head. Images of Connor's dad, strong, resilient, and so damn proud of his son fill my mind. "What's the prognosis?"

"Not good." Eli clear his throat, pain twisting his features. "Seventy percent of those diagnosed pass within the first year."

"What? Are you serious?" My mind struggles to process such a staggering statistic. "When was Cameron diagnosed? How is Connor handling it?"

"About six months ago," Eli admits, regret heavy in his tone. "Cameron was diagnosed shortly after Connor lost his fight. It's been a tough year for him, everything he loves being ripped away."

Tears well in my eyes and I avert my gaze. The nausea

from my hangover fills my stomach but for an entirely different reason.

Connor's dad is going to die.

Connor doesn't fight anymore.

He hasn't alluded to either while I've been falling apart because Bryce and I broke up. Shame burns me from the inside out. Even though I know being cheated on sucks and I'm allowed to feel bitter about it, Connor is losing his dad. His career. His dream.

The realization hits me hard. For a moment, my heartbreak seems irrelevant. Instead, I'm left wondering how Connor is managing everything. I'm left questioning why he didn't tell me.

Eli pulls out a stool for me at the island. "How're you feeling?"

"Alive. Barely."

Eli snorts. "This is fucking role reversal."

"Yeah. I can't believe the amount of times I had to nurse your hungover ass back to health or pull you from random hotel rooms to make your call times."

"I was spiraling," he says, a rare admittance to his life before Zoe made it all better.

I shrug.

"You weren't going to marry him." Eli states, giving me whiplash with the change in direction of the conversation.

"Pardon?"

"Hawke. You wouldn't have gone through with it, Harlow. At least, not the Harlow I know."

I help myself to an apple and peanut butter. "What are you talking about?"

"Look, I get it. The allure of L.A. is hard to pass on. It's shiny and exciting. Every party is a scene and every restaurant is part of a wider trend. But, truthfully now, me and you, no bullshit, were you happy?"

Swallowing thickly, I blink at Eli, pausing.

In light of Bryce's cheating, moments of doubt that I buried, feelings of unease that I ignored, flicker to life.

I remember his late nights working. His beautiful co-star whose every whim he seemed to indulge. The way he makes every person, and mostly women, feel like they are the only one in the room, the center of his world.

"See?" Eli concludes, determining the truth from my silence.

Shoving a spoonful of peanut butter into my mouth, I plop down on the barstool. "What the hell am I supposed to do now?"

"Work for me again," he says like it's the most obvious solution in the world.

"What?"

"Work for me."

"As your assistant?"

Eli shakes his head. "Manager."

I stare at him, my mouth dropping open. "You're serious?"

"Yeah. To tell you the truth, I have a pretty great assistant even though he's not as good as you were. But I don't need an assistant as much as I need a manager. My life is split between L.A. and Chicago. My career is split between acting and directing. I need someone I trust to manage it all, to stay on top of things. Right now, it's becoming too much for my P.A. and things are starting to slip through the cracks."

I narrow my gaze at him. "Do you really need this position filled or are you just taking pity on me?"

"Both. I want you back on my team, Low. You never

should have left in the first place." He shoots me a knowing glance. My stomach twists.

Even though I never told Eli outright, he correctly deduced that the real reason I resigned from being his P.A. is because Connor broke my heart. When Connor ended our friends-with-benefits thing two years ago, I ran from everything that was tied to him. Including my job as his best friend's assistant.

"I haven't managed anyone's life since I quit being your P.A."

Eli chuckles, "I know. If you want to keep doing your thing in L.A., than do you. But if you're interested in running my life again, I'd love to have you back."

My head buzzes, my eardrums ringing loudly.

A job offer.

The opportunity is greater than hosting reality TV. It's a chance to build my career with tangible and transferrable skills. A long time ago, back when I started out as Eli's P.A., I dreamed of working in public relations. I wanted to help shape the careers of actors. Asking for the dirty deets about what went down between two strangers in an airplane bathroom seems galaxies away from that dream now.

I sigh. My stepdad Kent, a Hollywood producer, emailed me last night, offering to hook me up with a job offer on one of his films but I still want to pave my own way, without using his name to open the door or relying on it as my life spirals. "You're for real?"

"Yeah, Low. I'm for real. It's a shit-ton of hours. You'll have to travel between L.A. and Chicago a lot but since my life is rooted here, I'll need you to commit to a permanent move to Chicago." His eyes glimmer with mischief as he claps his hands together, rubbing them like the evil mastermind he is.

"You and Zoe concocted this, didn't you?"

Eli tips his head back and laughs. "You know it was all Zo."

"Jesus!" I jump from my chair, the reality of his offer hitting me in the face. I won't have to go back to L.A. with my tail between my legs. I won't have to go back to L.A. at all except in a professional capacity. Throwing my arms around Eli in gratitude, I smile. "Thank you, Eli. Thank you, thank you, thank you. You have no idea how much this means to me."

"You earned it, Low. It's about time you stopped letting Hawke overshadow you. It's about time you came home."

"Home?" I quirk an eyebrow. "I've never lived in Chicago."

"I know. But home is where your people are. And Harlow, the L.A. party scene was never your vibe," he flips his chin at me, "no matter how good a job you did at pretending to fit in."

Sighing, I sit back down on my stool. "Am I that obvious?"

"No, I just know you. Squeezing your ass into a size two and making your hair blonder doesn't stamp out your individuality. Dating Hawke doesn't change the fact that you hate small talk and forced socialization. You're too quirky, with your iced coffees in a blizzard and your nose piercing from when you were pretending to be a rebellious teen, to want that Hollywood glitz forever."

Shaking my head, I exhale. "I really tried to fit in."

"I know you did. But when you really fit somewhere, you don't have to try so hard. You've always been one of us, Low." He taps his water glass against mine. "Welcome home."

"Thank you for this chance, Eli."

"Don't thank me yet. The hours are brutal and I'm grumpy most of the time."

"I remember."

"And you start tomorrow."

I laugh.

Eli chuckles, tossing an arm around my shoulder. His voice sobers as he glances at me. "For what it's worth, I'm sorry he hurt you. I really am. But don't let him get you down. You're so much more than Bryce Hawke."

"He's Hollywood's Golden Boy."

"Pssh. Who fucking cares? You're Harlow Reid. You work for Eli fucking Holt. Hawke's got nothing on me." He drops his arm as I swat at him.

"You've always been modest."

Eli grins. "I've always been honest. L.A. can build you up as quickly as it can tear you down. But you've always been legit, Low. From the first day I hired you, when I barely could offer you a salary —"

"You bought me Taco Bell."

Eli laughs, "Because I fucking knew. Knew you were down for the adventure and not the glam. You cared about the films, not the noise. You still do. Don't let this thing with Bryce define you. Not publicly and especially not personally."

"Yeah, you're right." I nod slowly, digesting his words. Wrinkling my nose at him, I ask, "Do I really start tomorrow?"

Eli grins, flipping his chin toward the nearly depleted tequila bottle. "Want to drink to it?"

I flip him the middle finger as he laughs.

4

CONNOR

The Bulldog's cross catches the right side of my face, landing a punch that blurs my vision and causes pink-tinged saliva to shoot from my mouth.

Staggering back several steps, I regain my footing, sharpen my focus.

This is my last fight. In my soul, I know it. Now, I just need my dumb head to catch up. But I've never been the brightest crayon in the box and this, me taking on the reigning cruiserweight, Dan "The Bulldog" O'Brien, after my injury, my shortened training schedule, and thinking I can win, demonstrates the point.

It doesn't matter that I'll walk out of the ring with my wallet padded, win or lose. I need this win. My reputation depends on it to grow my gym. My soul demands it to prove that I did everything in my power to win this fight, that I'm ending my career at the top.

O'Brien comes at me again but this time, I'm ready. I unleash a powerful combination that throws him for a split-second. He responds with a crushing jab that knocks my head back, followed by a right hook that tosses me off-balance.

Reaching for the ropes, my fingertips glide past the vinyl coating the steel-cables and I hit the canvas with a thud. In an instant, O'Brien is on me. I dig deep, adrenaline coursing in my veins, humming in my temples, pounding in my chest. My head is spinning, my thoughts pulling in too many directions. His knee connects with my ribs and I lose the ability to draw in a breath.

I'm going to fucking lose this fight.

Lose everything I've spent my entire career working towards.

No.

Managing to twist away from O'Brien, I roll out of the clinch until we're both on our feet again. The Bulldog grins at me, his smile sinister, his eyes sharp. My head throbs, the colors around the arena bleeding into each other, the sound of cheering and yelling erupting in my eardrums and fading into a whisper. I try to shake it off.

This is it; the fifth round.

I can do this. I need to do this.

I start for O'Brien and connect with a Thai kick followed by a combination that he blocks before taking me down.

The arena buzzes in the background as everything around me goes black.

I awake with a start, cold sweat beading along my forehead, my hands clammy and clenched.

Fuck.

I blow out a ragged exhale, hoping my heart rate returns to normal. The sheets are twisted around my waist and I close my eyes, slowing my breathing.

Anxiety rattles in my chest as my nightmare recedes from memory.

Six months ago, I hung up my gloves for good after getting my ass handed to me. My career ended in a monumental loss and a punishing concussion. Since that night, my life has taken a drastic nosedive.

My reputation, shot to hell, had the fighters I trained looking at new gyms.

Pop's unexpected diagnosis with Creutzfeldt-Jacob Disease the following month rocked me to my core. Losing MMA hurt, but it was nothing compared to the realization that my days with Pop are numbered. With each passing day, he fades further away and I desperately cling to the parts of him I recognize.

Sighing, I pull myself from my bed even though it's barely light outside. I tug on the faded jeans and T-shirt I wear to the construction site.

Instead of sweating in the gym, perfecting my footwork and honing my strength to fight, I now sweat under the merciless sun clearing debris and hauling around building materials.

I know I should be grateful. I'm able-bodied. I'm employed. I'm healthy.

But it's real fucking hard to count my blessings when Pop is fading away and I'm helpless to help him, literally unable to save him.

Uselessness grips my neck like a noose, the same way it did the night I lost to O'Brien.

That night, drunk and hurting, I pulled out the magazine with Harlow's radiance beaming from the cover. I spent I don't know how long staring at the woman who would never be mine. Why not kick a dog when it's down?

She looked happy with Bryce. Even though it turned my stomach sour, I tried to be happy for her. I rolled up the magazine and put it away for good. After losing to the Bulldog, Harlow was just another loss to add to my arsenal of defeat.

Lacing up my work boots, I stand from my bed and exit the room. I can still taste Harlow's lips on mine. Feel her soft skin, breathe in her scent.

My heart rate ticks up as I recall everything about two nights ago. Telling her truths, absorbing her hurts, kissing her lips. For the first time in a long time, the heaviness that hangs over me like a perpetual storm cloud lessens.

This year has kicked my ass. Right now, though, Harlow being back seems like a silver lining.

I had no right to tell her I would help her rebuild her life. Being close to her will only blur the line I drew in the sand two years ago. Since then, nothing's changed. If anything, I'm worse for her now, with even less to offer, than I was back then.

I tear a banana off the bunch, toss it into my backpack, lock the front door behind me, and bound down the porch steps toward my truck.

Harlow's crestfallen expression and puffy eyes flicker in my mind, along with the hurt that laced her words when she asked the heartbreaking question: *Why am I not enough?*

There's no way in hell I'll be able to stay away from her again.

I can keep lying to myself and pretend I care because of our history. I've fucked her in every imaginable position overlooking the city lights of Los Angeles and Chicago. Or maybe it's because of our mutual friends and the overlap of our lives.

But that's all bullshit.

I can't stay away. A part of me, a bigger part than I want to admit, wants her more than my next breath.

She makes me feel something again. Something that isn't hopeless.

As soon as I pull down Eli's street, I see her. And, since my windows are open, I hear her.

"Give me everything you got, Maddie!" she hollers, bouncing from one foot to the other. Behind her, two orange cones are set up to create a goal.

Maddie places a soccer ball in front of Harlow and backs up, preparing to make her kick.

I pull into Eli's driveway and kill the engine.

Harlow's ass sways in my line of vision, her shorts so goddamn high up her thighs I can't look away. Her legs are tanned and shapely, her feet bare, her energy infectious.

"Kick it, baby girl!" she cheers as Maddie runs toward the soccer ball, her foot connecting and sending the ball straight toward Harlow.

Harlow's hands are up and even though she could easily catch the ball, she dives in the opposite direction, missing completely.

"GOOOOOOAAAAAALLLLLL!" Maddie screams, raising her arms in V for victory and running around the front yard.

"You're the next Abby Wambach!" Harlow announces. She stands from the lawn, wiping blades of grass from her perfect ass before turning to me.

The second her gaze collides with mine, she smirks and I know she caught me checking her out.

I dip my head to the side and feign casual. "I didn't know you played soccer."

"It's been years."

"Were you goalie?" I ask, skepticism heavy in my tone. My eyes scan her body, drink in her curves, and linger on the pucker of her mouth.

"Forward. Did diving in the wrong direction give me away?"

"Just a little bit."

Her grin widens, her eyes blazing. "I'll have you know that my team was badass. We almost one State my junior year."

"What happened? You trip over the ball?"

Her mouth drops open, indignation stamped in her expression.

I swallow back my laughter, quirking an eyebrow instead. My chest tightens and I realize how much I miss her. More than I ever considered. But Jesus, I like getting a rise out of her, like riling her up.

"No, I didn't trip over the ball." She lifts her hand, jabbing a finger in my direction like she's about to tell me off. Her expression is pinched but in the next blink, it relaxes and she bites her bottom lip. "I got red carded," she admits, her nose wrinkling adorably.

Laughter shakes my shoulders and I can't hold it back anymore. I chuckle loudly, pinching the bridge of my nose. "Let me guess, you let your sassy fly?"

She shrugs, her mouth tipping up at the corners. "Something like that." Her eyes meet mine knowingly, heat ringing her irises. She's always been a little bit wild, spirited, just skirting the edge of reckless. According to Eli, Bryce was always trying to curb her passion.

But Jesus, I crave her intensity. It makes me feel alive the same way fighting does. Her ferocity, her wit, her courage is restorative, not demanding.

The space between us flickers with energy. Except for Maddie's voice in the background, the rest of the world melts away.

Harlow is beautiful. I want to reach out and palm her hip,

pull her into me, drop my mouth to hers and…take. Instead, I curl my fingers into my palm and clear my throat.

"I'm ready, Auntie Harlow!" Maddie calls out.

Harlow nods, turning away from me and assuming her position.

I watch her and Maddie play for a few minutes. She lets Maddie score each time and then chases her around the yard. Harlow laughs loudly, caught up in the moment and Maddie's enthusiasm, like her heart wasn't broken on the internet a few days ago. Whenever her eyes meet mine, they're filled with mirth and a joy so deep, it renders me speechless.

This is the Harlow I know.

Not the coiffed and perfected lady who knew the gossip of inner Hollywood circles, but this woman, wearing short shorts and a crop top, her hair piled messily on top of her head and a grin stretching across her face. A woman with an unbreakable spirit.

When they take a break for Maddie to drink some water, I step closer. "You're really moving here?"

"I really am."

"You sure you want to work for Eli again?" I ask, only half joking.

Her eyes glimmer. "I'll let you know after I complete my first week."

I smirk and she smiles, her expression so sincere it sucker punches me. My throat dries as I work a swallow, wanting to ask her a million questions but not knowing where to start. Or how.

Maddie calls for her again and she runs off, copying Maddie's movements as they dance zig-zag patterns across the lawn.

Leaning back against my truck, I continue to watch them. It's beautiful outside. The heat of the day is receding as the breeze of dusk kicks up. The sky is cotton candy swirls dotted with massive clouds and the first fireflies are flickering.

I drink in Harlow's happiness like I'll never be able to quench my thirst, never be able to get enough of her. It's a dangerous realization because I know that we don't have a future together. We never did. If I was smart, I wouldn't be here right now.

Minutes pass but I don't move to get back into my truck.

I'm drawn to Harlow and I'm too damn exhausted to fight against it, especially after last night's nightmare coupled with Pop's rough morning.

"Madison Ann." Zoe steps down the front stairs, grinning at me. "Hey Connor."

I hold out an arm and Zoe steps into my embrace. Dropping her head to my shoulder, she watches Maddie and Harlow with the same quiet amusement as me.

"She doing okay?" I jut my chin toward Harlow.

"Yeah, she's okay. The hurt comes in waves. Sometimes, like right now, Maddie's enough of a distraction to have Harlow laughing and present in the moment. But there are little reminders or thoughts throughout the day that make her go quiet until her face crumples. I hate seeing her hurt like this. I wish I could do more for her."

I remain silent, my attention focused on Harlow. The thought of her hurting hurts me. The realization that there's nothing I can do to ease her pain cuts even deeper. Shame fills my stomach, churning with the helplessness I constantly carry for Pop.

Next to me, Zoe sighs and I peek over at her.

"You good, Zo?" A ball of nerves wells in my throat even though I know I'm being paranoid. Three years ago, Zoe had a lot of health scares that pushed Eli into a constant state of concern. He hides it well, but it's always lurking just under the surface.

With the hole my life is currently tumbling down, I've become paranoid as well.

"Yeah, just tired," she murmurs, her eyelids heavy.

"Hey," I jostle her shoulder until she opens her eyes. "You sure that's it?"

A small smile flits across her lips as she shakes her head and my heart sinks.

"It's good news, actually," Zoe adds.

I frown at her, confused.

Then, her hand rests over her stomach and I narrow my eyes at the smallest swell there.

It finally clicks and I chuckle, a mixture of happiness and relief floating upward. "You're fucking pregnant?"

Zoe nods, her smile growing. "We're telling Maddie tonight."

"Jesus, Zo," I squeeze her close and drop a kiss to the crown of her head. "I'm so happy for you."

She tips her head toward Harlow. "Thanks, Connor. I'm happy for you too."

I shake my head. My jaw hardens and a muscle ticks under my eye.

"All part of the fun, my friend," Zoe jokes, rolling her eyes. "You guys will figure it out." She pushes off my truck and claps her hands, signaling for Maddie.

After Zoe wrangles Maddie into the house, Harlow slips on her flip flops and approaches me. Strands of her hair have escaped her bun and fall around her face, sticking to her neck. She looks a million times more beautiful than she did the morning of Maddie's birthday party. This version of her, the effortless one, is my favorite.

I kick off my truck and stuff my hands into my pockets, rocking back on my heels.

"What are you doing here?" Harlow asks coyly, stopping just shy of reaching distance.

"Came to see you," I answer.

A ripple of worry passes over Harlow's face, the green spark in her eyes dimming. "Connor, I —"

"I wanted to see if you were hungry. Pancakes?" I cut her off before she says something to turn our easygoing vibe into something uncomfortable. For both of us.

She brightens. "Breakfast for dinner? You know that's my favorite."

"I do," I tip my head toward my truck.

"Let me just grab my wallet." She starts for Eli's house.

"Harlow Reid. Get your ass in the truck." I hate it when she plays this stupid I'll-pay-for-my-meal shit.

She smirks and rolls her eyes but she rounds the truck and slides into the passenger seat.

I climb back behind the wheel, flip the ignition, and back out of the driveway. "I know a spot."

"I'd hope so; this is your hometown."

"Smartass. I meant, I know a really good place. Best pancakes you'll ever have."

"Connor, I'm from L.A."

"You're from Georgia." I hang a left toward the tiny diner with the best breakfast.

"True," Harlow chuckles, kicking off her flip flops and crossing her legs on the passenger seat. "I am from Georgia." She thickens her Southern drawl, which is so slight these days it's barely discernible.

"You ever miss it?"

She glances thoughtfully at me before turning back to the window. "Sometimes. It's strange, you know? If I were to go back now, I don't think I'd fit in. It's hard to go back to what was once you've been away so long."

"Do you ever visit?"

"No. Not since my grandparents passed. When I was a kid, I spent the entire summer at their farm. Eating peaches right from the trees and riding horses all day."

I reach a hand over and squeeze Harlow's knee. I picture her, horseback riding at sunset, her hair wild, her laughter loud. "True Southern girl, huh?"

"Hell yeah," she says with a giggle. "But now, I guess Chicago is home."

I glance at her, the right side of my mouth lifting. "Welcome to the Windy City."

"You're so lame."

I tip my head toward her, giving her side-eye. Hanging with her like this is nice, familiar. I clear my throat, knowing I'm about to veer into uncharted territory. "How you holding up?"

My words hang suspended between us as I wait for her response. Christ, I hope she's not pining for limp dick Golden Boy. I hate that he hurt her, but I hate that she was going to fucking marry him more.

She sighs, kicking her feet up on the dashboard and leaning back. "My head is imploding. My phone has been blowing up like crazy. My mom is furious with me for ending things with Bryce. Jack—"

"Your stepbrother?"

"Yeah, my brother. He's making a ton of memes of Bryce and sending them to me, just to make me laugh, you know?"

"Did your brother like Bryce?"

"Couldn't stand him."

Her words are a salve to the tightness in my chest. Even though I never met Jack, I decide he's all right.

"I'm just trying to figure it all out," Harlow continues, facing me. "I know I'm lucky I have a safe place to land. Zoe pretty much moved me into her home and Eli cancelled my reservation at the W. Plus, I love getting to spend all this time with Maddie. It's just…"

"What?" I meet her gaze, curious.

"I don't know where to go from here. I really, truly believed I was building the life I wanted."

"And now you don't?"

"And now that it's crumbled, I feel like if it was really the life I wanted, I'd be devastated. Don't get me wrong, I'm hurt. I feel stupid and embarrassed. My ego is bruised and my heart is broken. But, if I was creating the life I truly craved, I shouldn't feel even a little bit relieved, right?" She stares at me, her expression so trusting that my heart rate ticks up and my mouth grows dry.

"No, babe," I clear my throat. "Relief means something about it, your life, your relationship, was causing you stress."

"Yeah."

I want to ask her if things weren't as perfect as they seemed with Golden Boy.

Before I can utter the question, she turns her intelligent gaze on me. "Why didn't you tell me about your dad?"

I run my hand down the length of my face. "Seemed like a strange thing to call and tell you when we weren't even talking."

"That was stupid."

"Not calling you?"

She points and flexes her toes on the dashboard. "No, our not talking. Even when we were hooking up, we were friends. I ruined that when I asked—"

"It's cool. We were both dumb about it," I cut her off, not

wanting to recall her crestfallen expression when I ended things.

"You were dumber than me," she shoots back.

I swat at her and she giggles again.

"How's he doing?" she asks and I'm relieved that I don't detect pity in her tone.

"Not well," I admit. My throat constricts and I grip the steering wheel tighter. "About three months ago, I moved him into a full-time care facility. He needs around-the-clock care and each week, it's like there's less and less of the man I love."

Harlow exhales out a shaky breath but I can't look at her. If I do, she'll see how much Pop's diagnosis is killing me.

"Is that why you stopped fighting?" she whispers.

I freeze, her question knocking the air from my lungs.

"You're going all in, huh?" I shift my weight, sliding my palm over the top of the steering wheel.

She doesn't apologize or change the subject, something I've always admired about her. She doesn't shy away from the uncomfortable.

"No, Pop's not why I stopped fighting. I got knocked out in the last round of my last fight. The concussion was pretty brutal."

"I saw the fight."

Humiliation blazes through me that Harlow watched me lose. The end of the fight was pitiful and the one time I watched the re-run, I was mortified that I went down the way I did.

"Didn't think to reach out?" I clear my throat but out of the corner of my eye, I see her body stiffen. Guess she caught the accusation lacing my words.

She grimaces, her expression streaked with apology. "I didn't know what to say."

"I know. It was fucking awful."

"But now you're running the gym."

I shrug, pulling into the parking lot of the diner. I cut the engine and drop my head back against the head rest. Seeing Harlow brightened my mood after a shit day, but right now, recounting my failures and admitting how much of my life is out of my control is causing my bitterness to swell. "Gym's on its last leg. I got fighters jumping ship left and right. If I'm lucky, I'll keep it going 'til the end of the year. But I need to figure something else out. My construction jobs barely keep my lights on. I got nothing left to channel into the gym."

Harlow pulls her feet down and sits up straighter, her expression stricken. "Connor."

"Don't feel bad. I spent too many months pissed at the whole fucking world. Instead of counting my blessings, I wasted time agonizing over what I lost."

Her hand settles on my forearm. Her touch soothes as much as it aches. "If you want to visit your pop now, we don't have to—"

"He's having a bad day," I interject, looking out the window and biting the corner of my mouth to keep my emotions under control. "He had a really rough time today. The nurses think it's better if I … visit tomorrow."

"I'm sorry, Connor."

I shake my head, casting off her concern. "You know, the night I lost the fight, he sat me down, passed me a glass of Johnnie Walker and told me to find something new. Something that consumes me, the way fighting did. Does. He told me to write a new chapter and discover something that give me purpose, that lights me up. Something that sets my soul on fire."

Harlow tilts her head, waiting for me to continue.

"For the longest time, I thought he was feeding me B.S.

Something to cheer me up, like when people say it's good luck if a bird shits on you."

Harlow snorts.

"But today..."

"What?"

"Today, at the site, I was hauling toilet bowls for a new build and I realized that I don't want this to be my life. Construction, manual labor. I want something more. Something that consumes me and sets my soul on fire."

"And..."

"I miss training. I love my gym. I'm not ready to let it go. But I don't know how to hold onto it and work construction and spend time with Pop the way I want to." I chew the corner of my mouth, turning toward Harlow. It's the most forthcoming I've ever been her, the realest glimpse into my life I've ever offered. Part of me doesn't want to meet her gaze, but the other part...

I look up.

When my gaze connects with hers, I bite down harder. Because she's not looking at me with pity. She's staring at me with her whole heart bleeding from her eyes and compassion etched into the angles of her face. The ways she gives herself so damn freely causes the emotions I keep tamped down to swell. My chest feels funny, my heart beating too fast.

"You're a fighter, Connor. You always have been," she murmurs. "This is just the toughest challenge you've ever faced." Her hold tightens on my arm and I lean closer to her, like a moth to a flame.

"I'm tired, Low," I whisper, admitting the truth when I would much rather swallow it down.

Her expression softens. "You're going to figure it all out, Connor."

"How do you know that?"

Her eyes are hypnotizing, her touch so damn soothing.

"Because you're a warrior. You may have lost one battle, but you're not going to lose the whole war."

Her response is so...*her.* I breathe out a chuckle. The pull between us is undeniable and the space flickers with energy and heat.

"I missed you, Connor," she says, patting my arm once before letting go.

I nod, tipping my head toward the diner, "Pancakes?"

"Pancakes," she agrees, sliding from the passenger seat.

5

HARLOW

"Blueberry or banana pancakes?" Connor's eyes gleam with playfulness. After the serious moment we shared in his truck, I can tell he's desperate to change the direction of our conversation to something lighter. But this side of him, joking and playful, is still dangerous. I could fall for him again if I'm not careful.

"Banana," I answer.

"*Really*?" he draws out the word, leaning back in the booth. "Okay, what about —"

"It's my turn," I cut him off, resting my elbows on the table. "Coke or Pepsi."

His face twists in disgust, as if I've offended him. "Dr. Pepper."

"What?" I smack my palms on the table. "You're kidding, right?"

"I can't believe you're not. Coke or Pepsi? That's the most generic question you could ask."

Grinning, I stick my tongue out at Connor.

"Book or movie?"

"Book," I point at him accusingly. "You're going to say movie, aren't you?"

He nods, a smirk rippling over his mouth. He grabs his coffee mug and shakes his head at me. "So far, Reid, we've got nothing in common."

"Haven't you ever heard that opposites attract?" I quirk an eyebrow.

Connor actually laughs. That surly, serious, always silent behemoth of a man who I've rarely gotten a smile out of outside of the bedroom laughs. In public.

He takes a sip of his coffee. "Why are you staring at me like that?"

I wave a hand at him. "Just processing this monumental moment."

"That we have nothing in common?"

"No, that you laughed. In public. Where people can see you."

He scowls. "I laugh."

"What? You are the most serious man I've ever met. Sure, you're not growly and grumbly like Eli, but you've always been so…severe. I like this version of you."

His eyes flash, a ripple of amusement. "I aim to please." He tips his head toward me before his chocolate eyes meet mine. "But I do laugh more when I'm with you, Low."

Unable to stop the goofy smile from splitting my face, I cross my elbows and lean forward on the table. "Keep talking."

Connor tosses a wadded paper straw wrapper at my face and we both chuckle.

"What's Eli got in store for you?" he asks, taking another sip.

"*Well*," I draw out the word, shifting back in the booth. "He's asked me to rejoin his team as his manager. So, a bit like being his P.A. but on steroids. Since his life is split between here and L.A. and his career is moving in new directions with directing, it will mean more balls to juggle."

"That awesome, Low."

I fiddle with the handle of my mug. "Yeah, it is."

"Hey? Where's the sassy girl I know?"

"Ahh, it's just…it's a lot."

"Yeah, but you're up for it. Right?"

I nod, chewing my lower lip.

"What?" Connor prods. "When you were Eli's P.A., you were a million percent on top of everything. You knew who was who for everything, what was happening on set, and even when Eli last took a freaking vitamin."

I chuckle.

"You got this. Why are you questioning it?" he asks.

Thanking the waitress as she drops off several plates of stacked pancakes, I pick up my fork. "I'm just, I don't know, nervous. It's been awhile since I've been so…on."

"What? Chaperoning wannabe actors at high altitudes wasn't as difficult as babysitting Eli?"

I throw a paper straw wrapper back. "It's just been awhile since I've been in a position that was so… real. You know?"

"Is this what you want?"

"Absolutely," I answer immediately. "This move with Eli is what I need to get back on track."

"On track?"

I scrunch up my nose, debating how much to share with Connor. I haven't told many, not counting Eli a very long time ago, about my goal to work in PR. I knew if I shared my intentions, my stepdad would have me placed with an agency, working a position I don't necessarily have the experience for. My friends in L.A. don't understand me at all. In a city where connections are life and networking is more natural than breathing, no one understands why I don't lean on Kent to hook me up.

But I've always wanted to prove to myself that I could achieve the life I want, the career I was working toward until I quit Eli's team, on my own.

"I really want to work in public relations."

Connor's eyebrows rise. "Really?"

"Yeah, it's what I've always imagined doing. One of the reasons I loved being Eli's P.A. is because I was always on. Twenty-four-seven, I was reachable, in the know, putting out fires in this crazy vortex of disasters and to-do lists. It was a wild ride and I thrived in the chaos. Plus, I learned so much working for him, especially because he encouraged me to network and connect with other people in the industry. To be behind someone's image, to be pushing their brand out into the world and shaping it, growing it, doing damage control when necessary..." I shake my head, leaning back in the booth. "It's the career I've always wanted."

"Wow," Connor says, peering at me closely. A strange expression ripples across his features but in the next instant, his face is smooth. "I had no idea, Low."

"I don't really tell people."

"Why not?"

"Because my stepdad could get me a job in two seconds and I really, I just —"

"Want to prove you can do it on your own. On your merit, not your stepdad's last name." Connor finishes my thought.

"Exactly."

"Do you, Low. You got this gig with Eli. You're going to rock it, and then you're going to grow and expand just like the brands you want to build."

"I hope so." My chest warms at how easily he under-stands, accepts my desire to work for the career I want from the ground up. His perspective is refreshing after having to always rationalize my motives to my friends in L.A.

I smile at him from behind my water glass. His support means more than he knows. This conversation is the most real we've ever been with each other. In the past, we always had fun together but rarely delved into our feelings, our dreams. Sharing my goals with him now is equal parts thrilling and liberating.

"You'll be great. You always are." He pours a heaping puddle of syrup next to his pancakes.

His words strike me harder than he probably intended. It's the weight of them, the severity with which they hang in the air. It's like he really believes that I'll be an asset to Eli's career. That he believes in me.

His words echo in my eardrums as something shifts in my mind. Thoughts collide, memories snap into focus. My past and present overlap and I realize two important facts.

First, Connor cares about me for *me*. My happiness, my ambitions, the pieces that comprise my life matter to him because I matter to him.

Second, Bryce never did. With Bryce, the events in my life circled back to him. My opportunities were considered in light of his career.

The realization sours my stomach and my fork clatters to the table.

"You okay?" Connor asks, his brow furrowing.

"Yeah," I say, grappling with my thoughts.

Connor's eyes darken in concern as he pauses, his fork hovering between his plate and his mouth, his eyes locked on mine.

My heart stutters and I smile at him. A genuine Harlow smile. "This is nice." I gesture between us. "With the exception of Zoe and Eli, I forgot what it's like to be honest with someone. To let my guard down, even a little."

"Not ever Bryce?" Connor asks, his tone gruff.

I shrug, not wanting to talk about Bryce. Especially not now. "What about you? Any serious relationships?"

Connor snorts, his fork clattering to his plate. "You really went there?"

"Hell yeah. I'm...curious."

His expression sobers. He runs a hand over his face. "No one serious. I'm not going to pretend I've been a saint the past few years, but no one ever came close to you, Low. What we had was... good. Real."

My heart explodes at his words, my insides turning to goo. I feel like seventeen-year-old Harlow and I fight the urge to show how happy his words make me by beaming sunshine at him.

But his next words halt my runaway feelings. "Besides, I don't have time to date even if I wanted to."

"What do you mean?" I ask, disappointment already sinking in my stomach. Jesus, I need to steer the conversation in a different direction. I just got out of a life-altering relationship. The future I envisioned for myself ten days ago looks nothing like the reality I'm currently living.

The last thing I need right now it to try for real with a guy who already shot me down once.

So why does Connor's brush-off scrape at the scabs of old wounds?

Why is the back of my throat stinging and my stomach knotted too tight to properly inhale?

Connor sighs, shadows shifting in the depths of his eyes. I wish I could read his thoughts; I wish I could understand him as easily as he seems to understand me.

"At the end of the day, I don't have a lot more to give," he admits. "Most days, I'm up before dawn. If I'm not early on a site, I train with the guys at my gym before heading to my construction job. My days are grueling. Manual labor, the heat, the monotony of it all. I'm drained before I even get to Pop's. If he's having a good day and in good spirits, I like to have dinner with him and hang out until visiting hours are over. By the time I get home at night, I'm ready to conk out. Come on, what woman would want to be with me? And if there was, would she really want to stick around? Be an afterthought to everything else I'm juggling?" His words clang between us, charging the air with the discomfort of their truths. An edge of bitterness lines his face and he rakes his napkin across his mouth.

My pulse quickens, my stomach twisting at the acidity in his tone. Doesn't he realize how amazing he is? Doesn't he see even a fraction of what I see when I look at him? "Connor, I'm sure —"

"Nah. This is going to be it for me. For a while at least. I'm so far into the grind, I can't climb out. It's impossible. My bills, Pop's medical bills, the gym bills keep stacking up. Then, there's Pop's care…" He trails off, blowing out a deep breath.

"His care?"

Connor runs a hand over his face, looking miserable. "The facility Pop is in is really great. It's the best managed-care place in the area. But around-the-clock care comes with a hefty price tag. Especially when your insurance is shit. I don't care about the money. I'd cut my right arm off to help Pop. But fuck, Low, the monthly payments are astronomical. If things were going better at the gym…" He trails off again. "I don't know how to keep things going and keep him there long-term." His voice tightens and grief slashes across his face.

I remember the statistic Eli shared with me. While the reality is that Cameron probably won't be there long-term, it's obvious Connor is wishing he'll be around forever.

"What about the gym?" I ask.

"What about it?"

"Could you re-finance?"

He blows out a breath that sounds like a strangled sob. "I wish." He scrubs a hand over his face like he wishes he could hide. When his eyes connect with mine again, they're so dark, they're bottomless. "I was a fucking idiot with money. Instead of investing my earnings when I was on the UFC circuit, I bought the gym. Instead of building it slowly, I kept expanding and expanding. I've already mortgaged the shit out of it. Now the whole venture is sinking."

A wave of helplessness washes over me as I stare at Connor. He looks so desperate, so afflicted, that I reach out a hand and squeeze his fingers, "What about…"

"What?"

I chew the corner of my mouth, knowing he's going to hate the next words out of my mouth. "What about Eli?"

"No." It explodes from his mouth like a bullet, sharp and straight. His eyes flash.

"Connor, I'm sure he would—"

"He doesn't know. About the gym, I mean."

"What?" I gasp. "How did you, why wouldn't you—"

"Because, I know he'd help. Hell, he'd fund the whole damn thing. But I…I will take care of my pop. No one else. Me." He pulls his hand away from mine and smacks the center of his chest.

"You need to prove to yourself that you can," I murmur, understanding the reasons driving his decision. They're the same reasons I don't drop my stepdad's name.

He scratches his cheek, glaring at me miserably. Then, he

nods. "Jesus, we're a fucking pair, huh?" His fingertips tap against the table, nervously, like he's not used to sharing any of the real pieces of himself which I know from experience, he's not.

So when he feeds me this morsel of truth, I lean forward until the table is cutting into my chest. I hold my breath, worried that the slightest shift in air will cause Connor to clamp down on his tongue and continue bearing the weight of his truth alone.

"Is there anything I can do to help?"

"Don't do that." His tone is sharp and I suck in an inhale.

"Don't do what?"

"Pity me."

"I'm not."

"Yes, you are. Everyone does, and they don't know the half of it. But I can't bear it from you, Harlow."

"Then tell me what you need from me?" I ask, the question bolder than I feel, especially when his sharpness cut through my chest like a knife.

"I need you to treat me the way you always have. Not like a charity case because my pop is dying and I'm about to have no goddamn family."

My throat burns at the realization that Connor is about to lose the only family he's ever really had. I nod, taking my time chewing my pancakes. "So..." I glance at Connor, hating the vulnerability that flares in his expression and clinging to it at the same time. "Not like the guy who lost in the last round?" I risk the dangerous joke at an attempt to lighten the mood.

Connor's eyes flash darker than midnight as I hold my breath.

Then, he bursts out laughing, the tension between us evaporating. I smile back, mostly in relief.

"Yes. Exactly like this, Low."

"You got it, Scott. As long as you don't treat me like the social pariah who was publicly cheated on in broad daylight."

Connor grins. "Deal."

"Has your mom reached out at all?" I ask, knowing Connor's mom left when he was a kid. But surely, she reached out now that Cameron is sick.

"No. I don't expect her to."

"Have you heard from her since…"

"Never." Connor sighs, his gaze heavy and hurting when it connects with mine. "I don't remember her much. She left when I was five. Ran off and remarried the guy she was having an affair with. Pretty much broke Pop's heart. It destroyed him. He worked his ass off, always trying to give her everything she desired, meet every damn need she had. And in the end, she chose someone else."

My stomach twists as dots in my head start to line up. Connor's dad worked hard to offer his mom material things, a plush lifestyle. Does Connor think all women want those things? Is that why he feels like he has nothing left to give?

Working a swallow, I say, "But he got you."

"Yeah," Connor chuckles humorlessly. "He got me. But really, I'm the lucky one. You know the worst part? She never looked back, never looked for me, never even fucking cared." He pauses, glancing up and thanking our waitress as she tops off his coffee mug. "Anyway, it was a long time ago."

My fingers dig into the edge of the table as I process everything Connor shared. My heart aches for him, for the boy he was and the man he's become, and the hurt he experienced as both. "Sometimes mothers have no idea the power they wield," I murmur, picking up my knife and fork.

Connor looks up, his sharp eyes swirling with questions.

"They act so powerless," I continue, "when they're in

these relationships, marriages, whatever, that don't bring them happiness. But to the kids, they're everything. Sometimes, they throw it all away and still, are too self-absorbed to realize the destruction they caused."

Connor clears his throat. "I'm better off without my mom. I hated when she left, cried about her for months. But Pop, there are none better than him. I'm glad my mother left me because she left me with the best."

"You're lucky," I admit, running the bite of pancake on my fork though a river of syrup before popping it in my mouth. "My dad left me too, but he passed, so I can't even be angry with him. It wasn't his fault. But he didn't leave me with the best."

"Things still tense with your mom?" Connor asks, curiosity thick in his tone.

"I love my mom. I really believe she tried her best, but it was too hard for her— single parenting, managing her grief after Dad passed, worrying about finances. Marrying Kent was the easy way out, and she took it. But when she did, she stopped being my mother and started being his wife."

"You were jealous?" Connor questions, clearly trying to get a pulse on my relationship with my mother.

But that's pointless. Freud couldn't get a pulse on my relationship with Debra Reid-Kinsley.

"I was hurt. The woman she became after," I pause, forcing the emotion welling in my stomach back down by shoveling a mouthful of pancakes into my mouth, "was nothing like the woman who baked chocolate chip cookies on snow days and read me bedtime stories. I didn't recognize her anymore. With each year, she drinks more, cares less, and our disconnect becomes more pronounced. It's ridiculous.

"I always swore I wouldn't become some stupid, Hollywood socialite who cares more about my waist size and touching up my highlights than I do about real issues, like equal pay for women and sexual harassment in the workplace. And then, boom, I fall in with Bryce and suddenly, I'm everything I never wanted to become. I'm my mother. And I was okay with it. Even now, I crave her approval.

"I know how I sound, but one of the reasons why I was so happy things with Bryce were good, were progressing toward marriage, was because my mom was finally proud of me. And I didn't want to disappoint her."

Ugh. Now that I said it out loud, I realize how stupid it… my mom sucks. But admitting that does nothing for me. It doesn't ease the pain from her rejection or soothe the hurt from her anger over *my* losing Bryce.

Connor's hand reaches across the table and settles over mine. His touch causes some of the knots in my chest to loosen. "I'm sorry you don't have the relationship you want."

I nod, grateful he didn't criticize or defend my actions. Instead, he let me confide in him and knowing I can trust him, after not being able to trust more of the people in my L.A. circle, is more than enough. "I'm sorry your mom left."

"Don't be. I made out okay. Maybe even better than if she had stayed." Connor offers me a small smile and it warms me from the inside out.

I smile back. "If there's anything you need, with your pop, with your new ideas for the gym, with anything, I'm your girl."

He snickers, quirking an eyebrow. "Oh, you're my girl now?"

I blush, averting my gaze.

Connor stares at me for a long moment. "Want to hear a ridiculous confession?"

"Hell yes." I rub my hands together for the juicy info and hunch closer.

"I can't believe I'm admitting this, but I bought a copy of a magazine that had you on the cover."

"Oh God."

Connor bites his bottom lip. "I bought it because you looked so damn beautiful in the picture. You looked so much like you, like you do right now."

His words flow through me, causing a confusing mixture of emotions to sweep my body in their wake. Shame. Relief. Hurt. Pride. "Did I really change that much?"

He nods slowly. "Yeah. For a long time, you just seemed...empty. Standoff-ish. Even from afar. Even from the cover of a magazine."

The word "empty" slaps me in the face, causing the shame to flare, stamping out the other emotions. Empty. Here I thought I was a master at hiding behind designer clothes and perfect makeup, but even Connor could see the cracks from the cover of a tabloid.

I avert my gaze, processing his words, their meaning. Silence hovers between us for a long stretch.

When I look back up, I gasp at the expression on Connor's face. His eyes are dark, his expression severe. Intense.

He licks his bottom lip, the corners curling upward. "I see you, Harlow Reid. The real you. The sassy, independent, fierce woman. In the past, I've done a shit job at acknowledging it. But I see you."

IT's LATE when Connor pulls into Eli's driveway. He shifts the car into park and we sit for a long beat.

Connor turns toward me. "Got an early morning?"

"Yes. I'm waking Eli's ass up by 9AM. He really shouldn't have invited me to live in his home."

"Yeah, well, I'm sure Zoe's happiness at having you here more than makes up for it."

Chuckling, I nod. "It's so good to spend time with her again. I forgot what it's like to have a real girlfriend. I missed her more than I realized."

"Didn't you guys talk all the time when you were in L.A.?"

"Not all the time. But, it's just different being in the same place with someone. You know?"

Connor shrugs, his hand running over the steering wheel before he drops it to the center console. "I'm glad you're here, Low."

"Me too. I'm going to start looking for a place tomorrow."

"For real?"

"Yeah. I can't stay with Eli and Zoe for forever."

"I know. But it's only been a minute. What's the rush?"

I bite the corner of my mouth, not wanting to spill Zoe's secret. Deciding to play it safe, I manage, "They're a young family and—"

"Zoe told you."

"Wait, she told you?" I exclaim, pointing at him.

We both burst out laughing.

"Guess we're going to be an aunt and uncle again," Connor grins, leaning back in his seat.

"I'm really happy for them."

"Me too." He rubs his lips together. A thoughtful expression crosses his face and we sit in silence again.

The longer the silence stretches, the more aware I become of it. Is Connor thinking the same things as me? Is he wondering if he'll ever have what Eli found with Zoe? Is he thinking about what it would be like to welcome a child into the world? Reaching over, I squeeze his hand and a shiver dances up my spine when he flips his hand, palm up, and clasps my fingers in his.

"Do you need help apartment hunting?" he asks, his voice low.

"I'm not going to turn down local insight, if that's what you're offering."

"I'm offering. I'm going to visit Pop for breakfast tomorrow since I missed him tonight. Does tomorrow night work?"

"That would be great. I'm free any time after four."

"Four?"

"Come on, you know Eli doesn't put in full days anymore," I snicker.

Connor leans his head against the head rest and rocks it back and forth. "True. I'll still be at the gym then. Want to swing by and then I can introduce you to a few people who may have some spaces up for rent?"

"Yeah, yes, thank you." I bounce in my seat. This is all coming together much faster than I anticipated. It should scare me, the way my life derailed and bounced back all in a week's time. But instead, I'm excited for the new start.

"Cool. See you tomorrow?"

"Absolutely. I'll come to the gym at…"

"Six?"

"Done. Thank you for dinner, Connor."

"Anytime, Low. And hey, since you're a local now, if you ever want to get a workout in, any time, come to the gym."

I tip my head at him. "You want to train me, don't you?"

He chuckles. "I'd be lying if I said the thought hadn't crossed my mind. But for real, don't pay membership at some fancy downtown spot when you've got a local joint that's free nearby."

Warmed by his offer, I thank him before remembering the financial stress he's crumbling under. "Connor, you can't keep trying to help people at the expense of yourself."

"This isn't that."

"Yeah, it is. You're always trying to do right by everyone, you forget to take care of you."

"I'm fine, Harlow. Really. I just, I want you to be happy here."

I stare at him. His expression is solemn, his dark eyes ringed with emotion in the moonlight.

This is the part where I leave his car but for some ridiculous reason, I don't budge. Connor and I have spoken more truths in the past few hours than in the entire two years we hooked up, and I don't want the moment to end. Instead, I want more. More truth, more realness, more him.

Tonight, he showed me more emotion than he ever has before. He shared more of his past, his life, himself. What does that mean? Are we embarking on a real friendship? Or is this the start of the relationship I've yearned for?

"What are you thinking about?" he asks after a moment.

Biting my lip, I glance at him. "Why are you being so real with me now? So open? Why not two years ago?"

He sighs, regret flashing in his eyes. "Because I was an idiot."

"And now?"

He reaches out slowly, his large hand cupping the side of my cheek.

It's impossible not to lean into his touch. His palm is warm and soothing against my face.

"Most days, I'm still an idiot. But I'm trying hard not to be."

"I don't know how to do this with you," I admit.

"Be friends?"

"Is that what we are?" I ask, hating the hurt that laces my words.

Connor sighs, his thumb brushing along my cheekbone. His hand is calloused and capable, the type of hand that fixes things when they're broken and holds things together when they can't be repaired. I lean into his touch because I can never not lean into his touch. "We're us, Low. I don't what it all means, but I know that when I'm with you, I don't want to be anywhere else."

His honesty centers me. It's not the answer I want because deep down, some part of me wants him to declare his undying love for me. But it's the answer I want because truthfully, I'm not ready for anything more. I think he knows that too.

The truck suddenly feels too small, the space confining. Connor's frame seems to expand, until I feel his touch everywhere, breathe in his scent, and hold onto his heat.

"Harlow," he whispers and his breath fans across my lips.

I have no idea when we both shifted closer but we did. My eyes pop open. Our mouths hover a few inches apart, inhaling each other's exhales.

He hesitates, his eyes shuddering closed. "I don't want to take advantage of—"

"You're not. See me, Connor. I need you to."

The words are barely out of my mouth before his mouth meets mine. His lips mold to mine in an instant, and a jolt of electricity followed by a surge of peace settles throughout my limbs.

It's a homecoming I didn't realize I needed.

And this time, we're both sober.

Connor kisses me slowly. His hands frame my face, cupping my cheeks. His lips shadow mine sweetly, delicately.

My lips part and his tongue sweeps in, meeting mine with a spark of passion and a gleam of intimacy.

I fall into his kiss as effortlessly as I did the first time he kissed me. Without thought or consideration or question. Connor Scott causes my mind to calm and my humiliation to fade. He fills up the empty parts of Bryce's betrayal and makes me feel like me again.

My hands reach up and wrap around his, fusing us together as he continues to kiss me like I'm the most prized possession in all the land.

For the moment, I believe him.

6

CONNOR

The sound of my fist connecting with the bag centers me.

I jab again, trying like hell to block out the noise in my head and let my instincts take over.

Jab, cross, hook.

The bag swings back and I swear, clenching it between my hands and dropping my forehead to the leather. Sweat drips down my face, pools in the center of my back. My shirt is sticking to me.

I've been at it for over an hour. Working out my emotions in the gym is nothing new. To be honest, it's the only way I know how to work out my emotions at all.

Running. Conditioning. Sparring. I've done it all today, and still my thoughts blare like a foghorn in my head.

Pop's rough night, followed by an even more tumultuous morning. Bills piling up I can't afford to pay. A meeting with my partner that ended with him squeezing my shoulder sympathetically but forcing me to swallow the hard truth. Cyanide MMA will be done come the new year if I don't come up with a big idea. A fresh vision. And really fucking fast.

Harlow.

Her face last night, the moonlight rippling over her expression, giving me a peek at the woman behind the perfect persona.

Her lips pressed against mine. Sweet. Sensual. Soulful.

"Connor?" Her voice breaks through my thoughts and I jump away from the bag, my gaze swinging to hers.

"Hey." I drop my hands to my sides and step toward her. "Sorry, I lost track of time."

"No worries, I'm early." She slips her hands into the back pockets of her tiny, too goddamn short cut-offs and rocks back on her heels. "You okay?"

"Yeah." Her ability to read me unsettles me. For years, I've been a master at concealing my thoughts. My poker face has been impenetrable for so long, I sometimes wonder if people assume I'm not thinking anything at all. But Harlow has always been able to see below the surface. In the past, she hesitated to call me out on anything, from even asking what I'm thinking, because she didn't want to rock the boat. She knew, as well as I did, that things between us were fragile, temporary, moments to be seized and enjoyed, not wasted away with complications.

But it's different now. She's here. I'm here. And we're... us.

"Just had a shit day," I answer honestly.

"I'm sorry, babe." The words come out of her mouth easily and she winces on the term of endearment, her cheeks reddening. "I brought you dinner."

"Dinner?"

"Yeah, have you eaten?"

I shake my head, an unfamiliar feeling expanding in my chest. It's been a long time since anyone besides Pop looked out for me. Since anyone's thoughtfulness surprised me.

"Okay, well, I got Thai."

"I love Thai." I brighten, hoping she got Pad Thai.

"I know." She shuffles toward the front entrance. "It's at the front desk. I thought we could eat before we start the hunt."

"Sure." I catch up to her, reaching out to touch her wrist. "Thank you, Harlow. You didn't have to bring me food."

"Shut up," she laughs. "Besides, how do you know it's not a ploy to spend time with you?"

"Is that what you're doing?"

She shrugs, tossing me a playful wink. "You have to eat, Connor. Don't make me Mother Hen you."

Chuckling, I hook my arm around her neck and pull her into my side. "You, Mother Hen? I remember a certain dinner party that —"

"Oh, shut it." Harlow giggles, pinching my ribs. "The oven timer was faulty!"

"Oh yeah. It had nothing to do with setting it for an hour longer than necessary."

She laughs, her fingers catching on my shirt. "Be grateful I didn't try and cook you anything."

"Trust me, I am."

Checking me with her hip, she points to the brown paper takeout bags on the front desk.

I flip my chin at Jay, the guy manning the desk. "You hungry?"

He shakes his head, smirking at me. "I'm good, man. Enjoy your...dinner."

Brushing off his innuendo, I gesture to Harlow to follow me. "We'll eat in my office."

"You have an office? So fancy."

"It's more like a closet, but thanks for the compliment."

I hear her walking behind me and can't stop the smile from splitting my face. My day has been shit, but in only moments in Harlow's company, the list of problems has quieted. She's blocked out the noise more effectively than boxing.

The realization stops me in my tracks.

For as long as I can remember, fighting has been my go-to. The one constant in my life that never left me, never even faltered, when everything else was falling apart.

Is that what it's like when you find the right person? Do they heal your soul enough for everything else to seem inconsequential?

Harlow slams into my back. "Oof," she wheezes, her fingers gripping the back of my shirt.

Spinning around, I wrap an arm around her waist to keep her from falling. "Sorry."

"A head's up would have been nice," she teases, her eyes glittering when they meet mine.

"You keep throwing me off balance." I joke, jostling her in front of me until we reach my office door.

When we enter the small room, I drop the takeout bags on the desk and clear off a chair for Harlow to sit on. She takes the containers out of the bag and lays them neatly on my desk before taking a seat.

She passes me a fork. "I got you pad Thai."

With every word she utters, the darkness of the day lifts, letting more light in. "Thanks." I pick up the container, lean back on my desk, cross my ankles and dig in. "This is really good," I say between bites.

"I'm glad you approve. I had to ask Zoe for a recommendation since I don't know any places yet."

"You will. Have you made a list of what type of apartment you want? What area you want to be in? Anything about your preferences?"

Harlow tucks her legs beneath her on the chair so she's sitting cross-legged. She sits up straighter, her fork paused between the takeout container and her mouth. "Yes. I'd like to be near an L stop. I know it's summer, but I'm enjoying not having to drive everywhere."

"You'll want a car come winter."

"That's what Eli said. I'm going to bring my car out here before then, but I'd still like the convenience of public transportation. Walkability is super important to me. I'd love to be more in the action, less in the suburbs. I'm not hung up on space since it's just me."

"Okay." I chew my bite. "So you want to be downtown? On the Blue or Red line?"

"Basically."

I pull my cell out of my desk drawer and scroll through the contacts I hit up earlier to see about renting Harlow a place. One of the perks of owning a gym is that I connect with people from all walks of life. That means when I need something, I generally have an idea of where to start or who to contact for more information. This is one of those times.

"My boy Troy will have a pulse on the area, what's available, and get you a fair price."

Harlow leans forward. "Perfect."

"Hey, Troy," I say as soon as he picks up. After a three-minute conversation, I hang up.

"So?"

"He's got three places to show you. We'll meet him in about forty minutes."

"Yay!" Harlow pumps her fist in the air. "I'm so excited."

I toss my phone on the desk and cut her a glance. "You sure about this?"

Her eyes connect with mine. "I really am. I need a change. A lot of changes if I'm being honest. This seems like a step in the right direction."

"Have you heard from Golden Boy?" I blurt out, not caring if I'm shifting the conversation or being too forward. Harlow's been in town for almost two weeks and the fuckface hasn't even shown up to win her back. While I'm relieved that he's backed down, I'm also enraged that he played Harlow like this.

"Uh," she groans, closing up the container and placing it on the corner of my desk. "He's been blowing up my phone like crazy, but the two times I was dumb enough to answer, he didn't offer anything. Just empty apologies and stupid questions."

"Questions?"

"Yeah. He wants to know when I'm coming home. What color dress I'm wearing to his premiere. If my stepdad wants us to work things out. He doesn't seem to care that we're not a couple anymore, he's just worried what he should tell people about our breakup. He even asked me if I'd do him a solid and come to his premiere just so he doesn't have to go through the trouble of coordinating with someone else." She rolls her eyes but I see the color blotching her checks. She's hurt. This punk just keeps injuring her. The worst thing is, he doesn't care.

I place down my takeout. "Look, I know this is hard for you. I know having your life dragged through the media is shitty."

"I've been staying offline. The tweets and comments have been too hurtful to read."

"What do you mean?"

She scoffs. "There are a few that call Bryce out for cheating. But most of them just say how he's too good for me, too talented, hotter. That I was out of my league, that I was weighing him down, that I'm a talentless hang-around who got what I deserved for thinking I could be on his level. That type of thing."

"That's bullshit," I spit out, fury rushing through my veins before Harlow finishes speaking. I'm practically vibrating with anger even though I know it's stupid. Futile. People are always going to talk. There will always be haters. But when that misguided judgement is directed toward Harlow, it affects me a hell of a lot more than when it's directed at someone else. "You know that's all lies, right?"

Harlow shrugs, "I'm just staying off social media."

"You're too good for him, Harlow. You're better off without him." I tap my sneaker against her sandal until she looks at me. "You know that, right?"

"All I know is that I'm ready for a fresh start. I'm ready to put some roots down and right now, I'm grateful it's Chicago."

"Okay."

I know whatever I say to try to make her understand her value, her worth, will fall on deaf ears. Not because she doesn't believe me, but because her heart is still too raw, the wounds Bryce inflicted too fresh.

Turning away, I pack up our leftovers and pass her the paper bag. "Give me ten minutes? I need to shower and change and then we'll go meet Troy."

"Take your time. And thank you, Connor. I don't know how I'd be managing all of this without you."

At the break in her voice I know she means more than just finding a place. In some way, my presence is bringing her comfort during one of the darkest times of her life. Her admission squeezes my chest with hurt for her but also sparks a ripple of satisfaction.

I like being here for Harlow. A hell of a lot more than I should.

7

HARLOW

"This place is perfect!" Zoe twirls in a circle, clapping her hands as Maddie runs around the empty space.

"It's barely a thousand square feet," I point out.

"Pssh. You should have seen the studio I used to live in. It could fit in your closet."

"Mama lived in a closet!" Maddie shrieks, racing to check out the closet in my bedroom.

"I need to buy furniture." I take in the space. "But then, I really think I can make this home."

"Are you shipping anything out from L.A.?"

"My brother just mailed me some boxes of clothing that I'm waiting on. I'll pack up some stuff, personal touches and whatnot, when I'm home for the premiere. But no furniture."

Zoe wraps an arm around my shoulder. "I'm so excited you're moving here. I missed having a girlfriend."

"You think Charlie will stay in New York?" I ask, remembering that Zoe's bestie Charlie is interning in New York until December.

"Ah, I don't know. The experience is good for her. She

needed to spread her wings a bit and have something that was all hers. She's really happy there."

"That's good."

"Yeah. I hope she decides to come back to Chicago. I wouldn't blame her if she stayed. New York is definitely the place to be for design but I just... miss her." She glances around my space again before smiling at me. "But I'm really happy you're here!"

"Me too." I drop my head to Zoe's shoulder. "How are you feeling?"

"Pretty good." She places a hand on her belly. "Much calmer than my last pregnancy. More tired trying to keep up with the Energizer bunny," she adds as Maddie swoops back in the room.

"Auntie Harlow! I can sleep in your closet when I come for slumber parties."

Laughing, I pick Maddie up and twirl her around. "You can sleep in my bed when you come for slumber parties. As soon as I have a bed, you want to sleep over?"

Her eyes widen and she nods seriously. "Oh yes, I'd love that. We can do nails and play with make-up."

I glance over my shoulder at Zoe who shrugs, helpless to the charms and energy of her daughter.

"I'm in, Maddie. We'll have a spa date."

"Yay!" Maddie cheers as I place her back on her feet and she continues to zoom around.

"Home sweet home," I murmur, walking to the large windows in the living room that overlook downtown Chicago.

Fighting down the swell of uncertainty that balloons in my belly, I remind myself that this move is what I need.

L.A. was draining my spirit.

Bryce broke my heart.

My "career" was almost as empty as the air the Boeing 747 flew through with random guys and insecure women having sex in tiny bathrooms, drunk out of their minds.

Yeah, this is the change I need.

But knowing I'm starting over again, at nearly thirty, when I should be settling down with my own sweet baby swelling in my stomach, aches.

I yearn for a time when I won't need another change. A new move. A different career path. I'm tired of searching for the consistency, the balance, the stability I've never had and always wished for.

One day, I hope for the calm that Zoe embraces, the certainty that Eli exudes, the contentment of their growing family.

"You should order a bed." Zoe cuts through my thoughts.

I face her. "And a couch."

"Plates would be good."

"Alright. Let's get going." I slide my purse higher on my shoulder. "I need you to drive me since I'm car-less."

"Yeah, what's that about? Why don't you get a car?"

Shrugging, I admit, "Trying something new. I want to be out in the world, among people. Not shuffling around in a car."

"Remember those words when winter hits."

"That's what Connor said."

"Because he knows."

"Yeah, well, I'll bring my car out before then."

"Okay. You better soak up your people watching and bustling around now. Where to?" she asks, pulling her keys out of her purse.

"Target," I say like it's obvious.

Zoe winces. "With Maddie, this is going to be an all afternoon thing."

"Got someplace else to be?" I quirk an eyebrow, knowing she cut her personal training hours at Connor's gym and is taking a leave from teaching her self-defense class since learning of her pregnancy.

"Nope," she admits, her voice popping on the "p."

"Let's go. Maddie girl, we're going to Target!"

My little munchkin comes running back into the room. "I love Target!"

"I know." I pick her up and follow Zoe out of my apartment.

Locking up behind me, some of the weight I've been carrying around releases as I take one more step into my new life.

I'VE BEEN SETTLING into my new life for nearly ten days when it happens.

The breakdown. The awareness. The staring into the abyss of the great unknown, unsure if I'm petrified of taking a leap of faith or staying right where I am.

Over the past two weeks, Eli, my brother Jack, acquaintances from L.A. have all commented on how well I'm handling everything. As if my catastrophic life collapse could be "handled" the way one takes out the trash. Dumped and forgotten about.

But the truth is, my turbulent emotions have been bubbling just below the surface. Beneath every grin is a sob I'm swallowing, after every blasé quip is a truth I'm ignoring.

On my twenty-third day in Chicago, Bryce's handsome face smirks from magazine covers. He's been nominated for some award. But that's not what stops me in my tracks. It's the woman next to him.

Anna Keaton.

My fucking friend.

In the photos, which I devour like Skittles, Bryce and Anna are holding hands. Laughing. Embracing passionately. And then, there it is, kissing.

What. The. Fuck?

Tears well in my eyes as I purchase the magazine and jog two blocks home, the balmy breeze drying my tears as they fall. Once I'm back in my new apartment, I look at the vacant space. Save for a mattress on my bedroom floor, none of my new furniture has arrived yet.

And I feel it again. The sharp pang. The acute ache.

Loneliness. Hurt. The awareness that I'm never truly enough.

I wasn't enough for Connor two years ago. My love wasn't enough for Bryce not to stray. My friendship wasn't enough for Anna not to break girl-code.

Sliding down to my kitchen floor, my back resting against the refrigerator with it's reassuring hum, I hug my knees to my chest and let my tears fall freely.

A knock on my door interrupts my pity party. I'm not sure if five minutes or five hours have passed but I know that I need to get off the kitchen floor.

I drag myself up to standing and rub my hands over my face.

When I glance out the living room windows, night has fallen.

My stomach grumbles. "Jesus," I mutter to myself as the knock raps again.

I blow out a breath and try to smile for Zoe's sake. Of course she would come to check on me after Bryce's new hook-up caused a media frenzy.

Pulling open the front door, I say, "I'm really fine Zo—"

"No, you're not," Connor responds, blocking the entire doorframe. His hands are braced on either side of the door and he leans forward, his upper body half inside my apartment as he dismisses my claim. "But you will be."

I falter back in surprise. Connor dips to pick up several takeout bags on the floor and enters my apartment like he's a normal fixture in it. "I like what you've done with the place," he comments, dropping the bags on the kitchen island.

"My living room furniture arrives next week," I explain, my voice monotone, as my brain tries to catch up with the fact that Connor is here.

He boosts himself up onto the kitchen island, his legs dangling, his expression unreadable. Rocking heavy work boots, ripped jeans, and a simple grey T-shirt, he looks sexy in an understated way. Like a man who spent countless hours toiling under the hot sun, working with his hands, his muscles bunching and rippling. I bite my lower lip, forcing my gaze upward. When I meet his eyes, I also see he is exhausted and concerned.

Knowing how much he has on his plate, the fact that he came downtown to check on me causes my stomach to flip-flop in anticipation before shame stamps it out.

"You didn't have to come," I say. "You should be with your dad."

"I was. Visiting hours ended. It's late, Harlow. Almost 11pm."

I chew my bottom lip, trying to calculate how many hours I sat on the floor staring at the photo of Bryce and Anna.

"Harlow?"

I glance up. "I'm fine."

"Don't lie to me, Reid," he answers easily. He reaches into a bag, pulls out a six-pack of Diet Coke, and tosses me a can.

"What? No alcohol?"

"Nope. You got that one night to drink your sorrows already."

I fold my arms over my chest, and stomp toward him. "For someone who barely dates, why do you think you're so qualified to weigh in on how to get over a break-up?"

He bites the corner of his mouth. I can tell he's fighting a grin. "Not an expert on that. Just know how long it takes you to get over a hangover."

I roll my eyes but I already feel a little better. I can't believe Connor came all the way downtown to check up on me. That he sought me out with the intent to cheer me up.

"And, how long it takes to get over a loss. I don't want that for you," he adds.

"Want what?"

"You to waste any more of your time pining over fucking limp dick, Golden Boy."

"I'm not pining."

"You're not confronting it either. You're burying it."

My throat tightens at the truth behind his words. I avert my gaze.

I hear Connor's work boots hit the floor as he slides off the island. The next moment, his arm is wrapped around my waist and he's guiding me into his embrace.

As soon as my face collides with his chest, I breathe in his scent and hold in my lungs, letting it, *him*, soothe the hurts he can't see.

Connor hugs me close, his cheek resting against my head, his frame concealing mine.

"Let it go, Low. You need to move on with your life."

I bury my face in his chest. Breathing in the scent of his cologne, I snuggle deeper. His arms feel strong and solid around me, like he really could shield me from pain. "How did you know?" I ask, pulling back to look at him.

"I saw you in the gym this week."

I raise an eyebrow. I went to Cyanide three times, secretly hoping to run into Connor, but I didn't see him.

"You had this look in your eye. Like you were just going through the motions. You don't want to live your life that way, doing each day without living it," he continues, his eyes dark and brimming with compassion. "Trust me. I've wasted too many years existing like that."

Sighing, I drop my forehead back to his chest. Peering at our kissing toes, I tell him, "I need something more."

"I know."

"Something for myself. Something that makes me feel…"

"Whole." He supplies the word that flashes through my mind. "Something that sets your soul on fire."

I step out of his embrace and add some distance between us. When Connor is near, my thoughts scatter. All my hurt seems to dissipate and I'm more concerned if he's going to kiss me than I am thinking about Bryce's betrayal. But once Connor leaves, the hurt from Bryce floods back along with an additional layer of shame for being so twisted over Connor when I should be too broken over Bryce.

"Come eat, Harlow," Connor says from the kitchen.

Spinning around, I watch as he pulls out the takeout containers and lines them up on the island.

"What'd you bring?"

"Mexican."

I grin in spite of myself. "Nachos?"

"Of course. Eat up. You've lost too much weight." He nudges a container of nachos in my direction.

"I'm depressed," I lament, slipping onto a barstool that, luckily, Target had in stock.

"You're overwhelmed."

I pop a nacho into my mouth. "I'm being dumb."

"You're too smart to ever be dumb," he counters, biting into a taco.

"Why are you here?" I ask, wondering if he's just stopping by or if he somehow knew that today was the day. That today, I would need someone, him, to hold my hand and tell me I'm going to be whole again.

He sighs, putting down his taco. "Saw the magazines."

"You really seem to have a thing for celebrity gossip."

He chuckles and looks down at the countertop. "I remember seeing you on that magazine cover and feeling like I couldn't breathe. You looked so beautiful, so effortless, and I hated, *hated*, that Bryce was the guy who made you smile like that. Today, when I saw him on that cover with that other girl —"

"Anna."

"Whatever. I figured you must be hurting." He looks back up, meeting my gaze.

"So you thought you'd come check on me?"

"And feed you." He pops a tab on a Diet Coke and hands it to me. "A lot has changed in the past two years, Low."

I quirk an eyebrow. "Like what?"

His expression turns serious, almost severe. My stomach knots as I wait for him to continue.

"Like me. I'm done being stupid and not showing you that I care. I'm done being silent and avoiding things that need to be talked about. Right now, I'm here for you. So whatever you need, I got you. Even if you just want to eat tacos and chill in silence."

"Thanks, Connor."

"Always, Low."

8

CONNOR

"Use your body weight. Turn into it," I explain to one of my fighters early the next morning. I need to be at my construction job at 9AM so I scheduled Jay for a 6AM workout.

"Got it," he replies, returning to the center of the ring where he's sparring with another trainer.

"Don't drop your guard!" I call out.

"Assalamu alaikum."

Turning, I see my friend Moe as he walks toward the ring.

"Walaikum assalam," I greet him, grasping his hand and slapping his back. "What're you doing up so early?"

Moe chuckles, stepping back and flipping his chin to Jay. "He looks good. Getting faster."

"Yeah, we've been working on footwork."

"No doubt."

"Why aren't you at your own gym?" I ask. Moe owns Madness, a boxing gym about twenty minutes farther out of downtown than Cyanide.

Moe blows out a long exhale, shuffling his feet. When he

meets my eyes, I see the hesitancy in his as indecision flickers across his face.

I turn away from Jay and lower my voice. "What's going on?"

"Do you have a minute?" Moe asks and I know it's serious.

Moe and I have been in the circuit for about the same amount of time. He never fought as much as me, but he's a strong fighter, a dedicated competitor, and one hell of a coach. I respect and admire him, even traveling out to Madness from time to time just so we could spar and shoot the shit.

"Of course." I indicate to the trainer to keep sparring with Jay. "Want to step outside?"

"That'd be good," Moe agrees.

We exit Cyanide and round to the side of the building where we won't be overheard.

The early morning breeze is dying down as the heat of the day rises. The chirps of birds are loud, interrupted only by the occasional passing of a truck on the main street.

"What's going on?" I ask, kicking my foot up on the brick of the building behind me.

Moe raises an eyebrow. "This stays between us?"

I study my friend for a long beat and nod.

"You know my cousin Salma?"

"Yeah," I say, recalling the quick-witted girl in her early twenties who trains at Madness.

"Her best friend from school, Callie, got into it with her boyfriend two nights ago."

I kick off the wall, stuffing my hands into the pockets of my shorts where they curl into fists. If there's one thing I don't stand for, ever, it's violence against women. Assault is too fucking common, a hell of a lot more than it should be. Because it should be nonexistent.

"Is she okay?"

Moe grimaces. "Two broken ribs, a fractured jaw, split lip, black eyes. He messed her up, Connor. Real fucking bad. And she...she's like family to my family, man."

"Jesus, Moe, I'm sorry. How can I help?"

Moe taps the butt of his fist against the building, choosing his words carefully. "Callie's staying at my aunt and uncle's until things settle down. She's got a lawyer and is pressing charges, broke off all communication with Daryl."

"Good," I rasp out, knowing how often the opposite occurs. A woman stays because she feels like she has no other options, no out. The violence doesn't end, the man never changes, but the woman endures.

"Just got me to thinking, man. I gotta do something. I can't, I won't let this keep going unchecked if there's something I can do about it."

"What are you thinking?"

"It's not just Callie, although if you see her, her spirit is broken more than her body. But there's been other women too. Wives, girls in college, young kids with braids or pigtails in their hair, coming into the gym, wanting to learn to protect themselves."

"They want to feel empowered."

Moe snaps his fingers and points at me. "Exactly. They need to regain a little shred of something they lost."

"Zoe used to run a weekly self-defense class here." I tip my head to the building. "She's taking some time off, but—"

"It needs to be more than that," Moe cuts me off. "Zoe's class was dope. She knows her shit and I know how successful her YouTube Channel is. *The Fit Bitch Life* has a serious following. But her self-defense class focused on how to defend your-self if you were grabbed from behind while putting groceries in your trunk or found yourself in an alley with some drunk dude."

"Yeah, and?"

"These women, they're not trying to ward off an isolated incident. They're trying to survive with their husbands, the father of their children, a repeater of brutality against them. Some of them break ties and walk away after the first time their man comes at them. But other women…"

"They stay," I whisper, my eardrums roaring, my anger spiking the longer Moe talks.

"Yeah. They stay. Sometimes until they feel strong enough to leave. Sometimes forever. Sometimes until it's too late."

"What are you thinking?"

"I want to do something more. I want to build a program that offers these women skills to rely on in situations when they need to protect themselves."

I finally put two and two together. "Okay. You want to build something that's geared more toward empowerment."

"Something that's non-combat though."

"Something for survivors and victims."

"Exactly."

"A support group, a circle where they feel safe," I continue, ideas popping into my mind.

"A place that offers consistency and hope. Two mornings a week, before the gym opens to regular members."

"You could bring in speakers. Therapists, professionals who know how to provide other types of support and resources."

Moe nods, excitement rippling across his expression. "Yes. Man, I love that idea."

"Okay. So you want to do this at Madness two days—"

"I want to do this at Cyanide. That's why I'm here. I want to do this with you, Connor. Your gym is so much closer to the city. The blue line is two blocks away." He points in the direction of the L station. "I don't know how to go about doing all of this. I want a partner. I need you to do this with me."

I stare at him, trying to absorb everything he's telling me.

Partner up. A new venture. A chance to support women, to help them feel empowered after being the victim of violence. A fresh start. Something with a larger purpose…

"Man, really? You sure?" I finally ask.

"I'm positive. You already have the self-defense participants. I'm sure some of them would be interested in a more dedicated program."

"Yeah," I nod, recalling at least three of the women from Zoe's class having pressed charges against their spouses or been in altercations in their own homes.

"You have a wider reach than me. More notoriety."

I raise an eyebrow.

Moe chuckles. "Dude, anyone would have lost to the Bulldog. He had been preparing for that fight for eight months, with no distractions, no other obligations."

"My name is currently worthless," I sigh, gesturing toward the gym. "I don't know how much longer I'm going to be able to keep the lights on here. I want to help you; I want to do this. But I also need to keep the gym running."

Moe nods, biting his lip as he thinks. "I got you. Of course, it has to make financial sense. What about if we hold a fundraiser? A launch? I don't know, something to really spread the word. It's got to drum up interest. See if we can get some of the fighters behind it? I don't know about this publicity stuff, but there has to be a way to—"

"I know the perfect person to reach out to," I say

suddenly. "She might not have the answers, but she definitely knows people who will." Knowing Harlow's network is wide and her personal connections are strong, she is the perfect person to connect with before launching this new program. Plus, isn't this the type of work she wants to get into? Albeit in a different way...but still.

"Okay," Moe grins, feeding off the energy I'm giving off. "Give him a call and let me know."

"Her."

"Huh?"

"It's a she. And she's going to be all over this idea."

Moe claps his hands, relief evident in the way his shoulders relax. "Okay then." He slaps my back as we walk back toward the entrance. "Let's do this, Connor."

"Let's do it. I'll hit you up later."

"Yeah, sounds good. Thank you, man, really."

"No, thank you." I punch his shoulder lightly. "Take care of Callie. Let me know if you guys need anything."

"Thanks."

As Moe walks across the parking lot to his car, I pull out my phone and send Harlow a message.

Me: I have an idea I want to run by you.

I'm surprised when she answers moments later.

Harlow: What idea? Why are you awake?

Me: It's 6:30AM. I've been awake for hours. Why are you awake?

Harlow: My dumb brother drunk dialed me.

Chuckling, I shake my head.

Me: At least he misses you.

Harlow: (5 x sleeping emoji) Tell me about this idea.

Me: I will. You free for dinner tonight?

Harlow: Is this your lame game way of asking me on a date?

I snort, laughter bubbling in my chest. Leaning back against the building, I re-read her message, a strange lightness filling me up at the truth behind her playful words.

Me: No. You're not ready. When I ask you out, Harlow, it won't be concealed as anything but a real date. I've got mad game, baby.

Harlow: (3 x laughing emojis) Okay, hot shot. We'll see about that.

Me: Dinner tonight?

Harlow: Persistent. I like it. Tonight works.

Me: Going to visit Pop. Pick you up at 9PM?

Harlow: Sounds good.

Me: See you then.

Harlow: XO

Grinning at her hug and kiss, I slip my phone back into my pocket and re-enter the gym. A newfound purpose begins to take shape in my mind as I run Jay through the rest of his training. It follows me to the construction site where new thoughts form. By the time I pick Harlow up for dinner, I'm bursting with ideas, purpose, and a new mission for Cyanide. I'm also excited that she's the first person I'm sharing my new vision with.

9

HARLOW

"You clean up nice," I look Connor up and down after I pull open the door to my apartment.

He stands in the hallway, biting the corner of his lip to keep from smiling. I think he's still wary of how much he wants to smile or laugh when I tease him.

"You look beautiful," he replies, running his hand over the back of his hair.

I beam. Is it lame that I like to keep him on his toes a bit? Or that a kaleidoscope of butterflies ascends through my stomach and chest when he compliments me? If it is, I'm fine being lame.

"Thank you." I smooth my hands over the simple summer dress I paired with strappy, silver sandals and oversized hoop earrings.

"You ready?"

I swipe my purse off the console table. My furniture finally arrived! Settling my purse on my shoulder, I lock up my apartment and turn to Connor. He takes my hand and a zing of awareness travels up my spine.

It's strange. When Connor and I were hooking up for real

— all the passion, all the smoldering looks, all the orgasms (I really miss those) — he would never hold my hand. He would never treat me like anything more than a friend in public. But now that we've shared PG-rated kisses and pancakes, he's holding my hand like I'm his girl.

It makes me feel giddy. I tamp down my excitement knowing I'm getting my hopes way up.

Once we're settled in Connor's truck, he breaks the comfortable silence that always seems to stretch between us now. Not like before, when his pauses made me desperate for his words, when his hesitations caused anxiety to swell in my throat. Now, it's different. Better.

"How was your day?" Connor asks. .

"Good. Really good. I finalized everything for Eli's premiere next month and I started interviewing local candidates in L.A. to be the point person for some day-to-day tasks there. I'm going to discuss a more detailed schedule with Eli this week so I can better plan my time between Chicago and L.A."

"The premiere for the movie Golden Boy starred in?" Connor's voice is rougher than it was a moment ago. This time, when he peers at me, his eyes are narrowed, a glint of steel in his irises.

"Yes," I say. "Eli was an assistant director on the film so he'll be there."

"And the coward?"

"Bryce will be there. He was the lead actor."

Connor shakes his head, his jaw tight, as he stares out the windshield.

I wait for him to ask the question and he doesn't disappoint.

"Are you going?"

"To the premiere?"

"Yeah."

"Of course. I mean, I have to go. I'm on Eli's team."

Connor clamps down on the corner of his mouth again, this time in frustration. "I know," he blows out. "I'm sure it's going to be great. Plus, it's a special night for Eli." He says finally, his voice controlled.

"It is. He's been angling to get a foothold in directing since *Dangerous Devils*."

"I know." Connor taps out a staccato rhythm against the steering wheel with the heel of his hand. "I know. Just don't let Golden Boy get in your head, Reid." He fixes me with a solemn expression.

"Pssh." I flick my wrist, injecting lightness into my tone to brighten the mood in the truck. "This has nothing to do with Bryce. This is about my career. And trying to do a good job in my new position."

Connor nods.

"What's your news, anyway?" I ask as we pull into the parking lot of a steakhouse in downtown Chicago. "Fancy."

"Uh…" Connor snickers.

"What?"

"We're hitting up the little Italian place." He points to a tiny restaurant that looks more like an extension of the steak-house than its own restaurant.

"Oh." I feel my cheeks blaze. "I love Italian."

Connor lifts an eyebrow. "I know. This place is one of Chicago's best kept secrets." He slips out of the truck as I climb out of the passenger seat.

Once I'm standing, my dress straightened and my purse hanging off my shoulder, Connor takes my hand again and tugs me toward the restaurant. "Once we sit down, I'll tell you everything. But you have to promise to be straight with me. I feel strongly about this new idea, but it may also be my last chance to save Cyanide. I need to go about it the right way and be smart, not just emotional. If it's not going to work, that's fine, but I can't sink the rest of what I have into it. You know?"

"I got you. You'll get my brutally honest thoughts."

"Don't be too brutal, Reid," he quips, holding the door open for me.

We're seated at a back table with a red-and-white checkered tablecloth. The restaurant is small but bursting with warmth. It feels like I stepped into a nonna's kitchen somewhere. Familiar and comfortable, sitting at the table, listening to soft Italian music and breathing in the scent of all that Italian deliciousness, it feels like being enveloped in a hug. I'm immediately at ease and order a glass of Sangiovese wine. Connor asks for a beer and a variety of appetizers to start off.

"Cheers!" I hold my wine up to his beer.

"Cheers, Low," he clinks his glass against mine and takes a sip.

Once I've tasted the delicious wine, I place my glass down and raise my eyebrows at Connor. "Tell me," I gesture my fingers in a "gimme" way that causes his eyes to spark.

"Okay." He puts his beer down and hunches forward. Leaning closer to me, he whispers, "I want the truth, though."

"Swear it," I cross my heart.

"Today, my friend Moe, who owns a gym farther outside of the city, came to visit me. His cousin's best friend was messed up pretty badly by her boyfriend."

"What?" My mouth drops open in horror. This definitely was not what I expected Connor to say.

Connor reaches out and clasps my wrist. "Moe's been thinking about the women who come into his gym, and there have definitely been women at Cyanide looking for an outlet, a place to find something that will help them heal. Something more than the self-defense class that Zoe teaches. These women are looking for confidence, empowerment, a shred of the woman they were from before."

"Dignity."

"Exactly." Connor squeezes my wrist. "Moe and I got to talking. We're considering starting a non-contact program at Cyanide that would meet, I don't know, two or three mornings a week and focus primarily on women who are victims of violence and trauma."

"Wow," I breathe out, my mind darting off in a million different directions.

The merits of the idea. The help it can provide. The community of women. The benefits for the gym. Recognition of the issue. Financial influx for Cyanide.

A new vision and purpose for Connor.

"Low?"

"Yeah." I look back up, feeling a blush work over my cheeks.

"I don't know what to do now. I mean, we need a name for the program. We need to figure out the actual mission. Do we get speakers to come? Do we try to build a community for these women? How do we advertise? Is it better to publicize it or do things quietly? What if they're too scared to come? How do I pay for it right now?"

"Hey." I flip my palm and slide my fingers through his. "One thing at a time, okay?"

He nods.

"I think this is the best fucking idea I've heard in a really long time."

A slow smile spreads across Connor's face, his eyes gleaming as my words register. "Seriously?"

"Seriously! I love the concept. It's so important to recognize the issue. So many women are victims of violence, even in their own homes, by the men they pledge themselves to. But God, honestly, harassment against women is everywhere. I know a lot of attention was brought to sexual harassment with the #MeToo movement and in some industries, things have improved, especially in terms of the stigma associated with highlighting sexual harassment and assault. But it's still really bad."

Connor slips his hand out of mine as it clenches into a fist. He takes another sip of his beer and clears his throat. "Have you ever, I mean, did anyone ever —"

"Oh God, yeah," I chuckle, partly from nerves and partly because I don't want Connor to freak out. But that's dumb, because the truth is that I've been sexually harassed more times than I can count, and it's nothing anyone should ever laugh about. Sure, I managed to get myself out of the situations with a little humor and a brush-off, but certain men that I've worked with on Eli's films over the years make my skin crawl even when I spot them now at a L.A. brunch. "It's kind of impossible not to experience if you work in the entertainment industry."

"What do you mean? What happened?" Connor presses. His jaw is tight again, even tighter than in the truck. Anger blazes from his eyes and his shoulders bunch with the emotions he's trying to control.

"I'm not trying to compare myself to the women you are talking about with regard to your program. It's not the same thing."

"No, I get that. But it's still important. It's still not something to blow off," Connor points out, his tone harsh.

"True. To be honest, I saw it all the time growing up. My stepdad is a famous producer. The number of dinners and soirees he hosted always had some douchebag guy — usually famous, wealthy, and egotistical — getting handsy or mouthy with a girl. Kent, my stepdad, would always tell me that if anyone does anything to make me uncomfortable, I shouldn't brush it off, but look them straight in the eye and tell them, in a firm voice, to knock it off and that I would report them to my stepdad. So, I kind of had an out, because of who Kent is. But still, I've had men corner me. Ask me who I had to blow to get my job or demand to know if I was fucking Eli. I've been roofied, twice." My tone sours as I stack all of the instances up in my head. "For sure, I've been lucky that nothing really bad ever happened to me but there have been a lot of encounters. On *Dangerous Devils*, Eli fired his acting coach one week in for grabbing my ass at the refreshments table. And, you know, there's always..." I trail off as I get a good look at Connor's expression.

He's seething. Hot rage rolls off his shoulders and the hatred flaring in his eyes could melt steel. "There's always what?"

"Nothing. Forget it. Just suffice it to say that harassment against women is commonplace, and there are more women who endure violence than you, or anyone, probably realizes. I like your idea, Connor. I like it a lot and I'm really proud of you for wanting to pursue something that will provide women with a safe space and a chance to confront their fears and build up their confidence again."

He sighs, pinching the bridge of his nose. "Did anyone ever hurt you, Harlow?"

"No."

His eyes snap to mine. "I'm serious."

"So am I."

"Did anyone ever threaten you?"

"No."

He blows out a long exhale, some of his anger abating.

Our waitress drops off an insane amount of appetizers. I glance up, thanking her as Connor continues to compose himself.

Adding some bruschetta and arancini to my plate, I tilt my head toward Connor. "I wasn't trying to make you think all of these awful things. I just wanted you to know that your idea is a good one. It's worthy and it's important."

He nods, adding some appetizers to his plate. "I fucking hate that you were put in compromising situations."

"I know. But I was lucky. I got out of them."

"I never thought about everything you would experience working in L.A. For Eli. On that fucking plane."

I chuckle, pointing the tines of my fork at him. "That whole experience was a shitshow."

"Do you regret it?" he asks, his tone more curious than judging.

"No. I think I needed to do something on my own, to prove to myself that I could. Plus, I learned a lot. Mostly about myself. I think that's always a good thing. You know?"

"Yeah," Connor replies, adding some Caprese salad to my plate. "You really think I can do this?" He peers at me, his expression so vulnerable that my heart leaps into my throat.

"Yes, Connor. I know you can do this."

"I know this isn't your area of expertise. But I also know you want to move toward public relations. So, given your network, and your passion, any idea on how I get it all rolling?"

I grin at him, leaning forward and dropping my voice. "I've got ideas."

He snorts. "Like what?"

"Well, I work for one of Hollywood's most celebrated celebrities. He's a client of one of the best PR agencies in the country. Plus, his wife is a badass trainer with a crazy YouTube and Instagram following."

Connor's face falls. "I don't want to ride on the coattails of—"

"You're not." I hold up my palm, cutting him off. "You're not riding on anyone's merits except your own. What we're going to do is use the platforms of really famous people to raise awareness of this really important issue. Then, we can slip in the action you and Moe are providing — with the non-contact program and safe space, we'll have to refine all of that more. But Eli and Zoe, with their unique platforms, are going to highlight the issue more than the solution. This will generate interest and buzz about your program and gym without it seeming like we're selling it."

"Oh. Okay. I never thought about it like that."

"The issue is the most important thing, Connor. But it's still necessary that you're able to earn some type of income from the program and then funnel that into gym memberships and other ways to expand your business."

"Isn't that," he pauses, his shoulders dipping, "I don't know, fucked up?"

"Which part?"

"It's like benefitting from someone else's pain."

My expression softens. "This is why I like you so much."

"Why?"

"Because of how much you care. Your heart." I reach my hand across the table to wrap around his forearm. "It's not selfish. You're not going to get rich from this, trust me. You're going to launch a program that allows you to draw attention to the gym and keep your doors open while raising awareness about an important issue. The media surrounding the launch is what you'll need to capitalize on for other aspects of your business. You're just doing good while trying to do well. And it's okay. It's really hard to do anything meaningful and important without any capital, right?"

"I guess so."

He sounds unsure and I secretly admire that he seems more invested in the program than in the future of his gym.

"I got you, Connor. I'll draw up a list of contacts for you to connect with about the launch. You're going to kick off this program and you're going to save your gym at the same time."

10

CONNOR

"Soul Sanctuary," Harlow says before draining the last of her wine. Her cheeks are flushed, the golden in her eyes dimming as the green flashes. She looks beautiful.

"Soul Sanctuary?"

"As a name. For the program. What do you think?" She leans forward, her excitement evident in her demeanor.

We discussed the program for most of dinner and the more we talked, the more the thought formed into a possibility. Now, wrapping up dessert, it's bursting with promise.

"Soul Sanctuary," I test it out. "I like it, Low."

"Really?"

"Really. It's pretty perfect. I like Sanctuary because it's supposed to be more than just a safe space but a place where women can feel connected to each other."

"Exactly."

"And soul because…" *Find something that sets your soul on fire.* I shake my head, "Thank you, Harlow."

"Don't thank me yet. Wait until you see all of the prep work we're going to have to do."

"I'm up for it."

Harlow beams across the table and I stare at her, mesmerized. Why didn't I hold onto her with everything I had two years ago? Why didn't I fight to win her back a year ago? Before everything with my career and future went to shit? How the hell did I let someone so special, so real, slip away?

Why is she even giving me another chance?

"Want to get out of here?" I ask, wondering if she is giving me another chance or if I'm reading the situation wrong.

"Sure," Harlow dabs a napkin against the corners of her mouth.

I get the check and settle the bill before Harlow and I slip from the restaurant. My mind is buzzing with theories about why Harlow is spending time with me. My nerves, something I haven't felt in a really long time, are rattling in my veins.

"Penny for your thoughts," she asks, interrupting the downward spiral circling in my head.

I chuckle and Harlow grins up at me, her expression so open I want to fall into it. "I've missed this."

"Hanging with me?" she quirks an eyebrow, surprised.

"Being myself with someone. You."

"Ah," she shakes her head, her eyebrows swooping inward. "Were you ever yourself with me?"

"More than with any other woman."

The realization hits me hard. Shouldn't that have been a sign? The fact that I confided more to Harlow than any other woman should have been a slap in the face that I couldn't let her go. But I never gave her what she really wanted. I never gave her all of me; I couldn't. Not when her future was so big and bright and...there.

For nearly two years, our arrangement was easy, casual. Then she told me she wanted more.

Fuck, if her hopeful expression, the damn light in her

eyes, didn't make me burn for her, make me wish I could want the same things she does.

But my future wasn't a fairytale. I don't have a rich step-daddy and a plush life. I don't have a proper pedigree and lofty connections.

At the time, I had Pop, my fists, my gym, and my fighters. In that order. I still don't know what foie gras is or anything about skiing in Aspen. I only know sweat, determination, and how to throw a right hook.

Back then, the only right option seemed like ending it. So I did. I told Harlow we shouldn't keep hooking up because we were no longer on the same page. She tried to hide her tears from me, but the sight of them bothered me. The sight of her hurting hurt me. She left my place in a hurry and I did nothing to discourage her.

When she returned to L.A., I knew she wouldn't be coming back. I pushed her away. I made her Bryce's for the taking.

The thought of her ex fills my mouth with a sour taste and I grimace.

I made her Bryce's. But when she left, I never even tried to replace her. Not really. I made me alone.

"Really?" Harlow asks.

I squeeze her hand. "Really."

She sighs, glancing up at me, emotions flickering quickly across her expression. "Take me home with you, Connor."

"What?" I stop walking and turn toward her. The request knocks the breath out of my chest because, is she for real? There's nothing more on Earth that I want right now than Harlow. But, "Are you sure?"

"Yes. We have unfinished business, Connor."

"Are you wanting to explore that or put it to rest?" I ask,

needing to know her thoughts, needing to have a pulse on her feelings if we take this next step.

Needing to manage my own damn expectations. Hopes.

Harlow's quiet next to me, and my stomach sinks.

"The first," she finally whispers. "But I don't know how to do that with you and be casual."

"Why would you have to be casual?"

"Didn't I scare you off the last time?" She snorts, but the sound is derisive. "I definitely did something to push Bryce away."

At the mention of his name, anger rushes through my blood, the sound roaring in my ears and a litany of swears swelling in my throat. But at the forlorn expression on Harlow's face, I swallow the swears back down and gentle my tone. "You didn't scare me off. I mean, you did, but not because of anything you did. I got scared off because of the way I felt about you." I say the words I know she needs to hear but more than that, they are the words I need to say.

After my loss to The Bulldog, admitting defeat and being honest somehow became easier. Maybe because I didn't feel like I had so much to lose. Maybe because I started recognizing just how important the other aspects of my life are. Whatever the reason, I finally say the words to Harlow that I should have shouted out over a year ago.

She stills beside me, her pace slowing. "How do you feel now?"

I stop again, causing her to halt beside me. When she looks up, I place my hand on her cheek, brushing her hair back from her face. We're nearly to my truck but this time, I want to see her expression. Read her eyes. She looks so innocent, so damn expectant and hopeful, with moonlight casting her face in the softest glow.

"I feel like I don't deserve this second chance. But if we

do this, tonight, take the next step, I'm not wasting it, Harlow. So this time, you need to be all in because I'm not going anywhere."

She gasps, her eyes widening. Slowly, a smile spreads across her face. Pure joy rocks through me.

"I'm sure," she says.

"Me too." I tell her before I dip my head and kiss her.

Sensual and deliberate, Harlow's mouth molds to mine. Her beautiful face rests between my palms as I tilt her head and deepen the kiss, spilling my want and need into her mouth like secrets, like all the words I should have said before but didn't.

She responds immediately, her body arching into mine until her breasts are pressed against my chest and her fingers are twisted in the back of my shirt.

"Take me home, Connor," she murmurs, breathless.

I rip my mouth away from hers, settle her into the passenger side of my truck, and drive straight home.

The porch light flickers when I pull up in front of my small townhouse. Flipping the ignition, we slide out of the truck.

Harlow trails me through the front door, dropping her purse just inside and kicking off her sandals. "It's been ages since I've been here," she comments.

I head right for the kitchen. "Too long. Want a drink?" I lean into the fridge and pull out a couple Dr. Peppers. I pop the tab on one and take a long drink. When I turn back toward Harlow, she's staring at me demurely, biting her lower lip.

Keeping my gaze glued to hers, my mouth dries as she reaches up and undoes the tiny row of buttons down the center of her dress. When the slinky material slides off her shoulders and pools at her feet, she steps out of it and walks past me toward my bedroom, the globes of her ass causing my adrenaline to kick up.

My pulse quickens as my anticipation and desperation for her spike. I follow her, yanking my shirt over my head and discarding it on the floor.

When I enter my room, she's already in the center of my bed, leaning back on her elbows, a confident expression on her face. But her eyes, bright green now, flare with vulnerability. I know how hard this is for her. I know that right now, she's proving something to herself that is equally as important as showing me she wants this.

This time, we understand each other's feelings better. We have a pulse on each other's mental state. We're more mature, having grown due to the hurts we both experienced.

"I want you, Harlow. More than this moment, I want you." I step closer to the bed as she shifts to the edge of the mattress, her fingers finding the waist of my jeans and settling there.

"I want you too," she whispers, popping the button on my pants. I lose them real fast.

Hovering over her, I guide her down until her back settles on the mattress and I can crawl over her body, shielding it with mine, allowing her heat to meld with the inferno blazing through my limbs.

The moment my mouth claims hers, a homecoming I wasn't expecting washes over me.

The chemistry between us flares. The understanding between us soothes. The heat between us envelops until we're lost in our own world.

We fit. Harlow and me.

I kiss her fiercely, my mouth trailing a path down the side of her neck that causes her to shiver in my arms. I spend time kissing the sensitive spot at the base of her throat before she guides my mouth back to hers, her tongue swiping across my bottom lip.

I brush her hair back, my eyes finding hers. Desire heats her gaze as she runs her hand up my length, already hard and craving her touch.

"Please, Connor," she murmurs, her fingers working a gentle rhythm over my boxer briefs that has me desperate for her touch, skin on skin.

"Tell me what you want, Harlow." I bite down on her earlobe, my hand gripping her hip.

She trails open-mouthed kisses over my shoulder, up the side of my neck until her breath fans across my jawline. A soft moan fills the air as I lick a path down the column of her neck, pressing kisses and gentle nips into her skin, waiting for her response.

"I want you to make me feel everything at once. Fill me up so I'm not so empty." She breathes out and I hesitate at her words, coupled with the hurt behind them.

I start to pull away but her legs hook around my back, grinding my dick against her center. I feel her heat even through my boxer briefs and the scrap of lace between her legs and I falter.

"Harlow." It comes out as growl mixed with a groan.

Her hands run up the length of my back, pulling me into her.

"Please Connor. I need you to see all of me."

11

CONNOR

His eyes bleed into mine, dark and swirling. Reverent and hungry. Under my touch, his shoulder blades bunch, his back muscles rippling. Strong, resilient, and complicated, Connor Scott undoes with me with his gaze alone.

The air around us sparks to life, a million feelings I lean into rolling through me like a summer storm.

His hands, rough and callused, caress my skin with a gentleness that causes me to shiver under his touch. His mouth lifts the tiniest bit in the corner at my response and he dips his head again, capturing my lips with his.

I sigh into his mouth, slipping my tongue in between the seam of his lips to dance with his. His grip on me tightens and I moan, letting the sensations he elicits flow through me.

The void that has captured my heart, growing larger in the past two years, begins to crack under Connor's heady attention.

The hurt from Connor's first rejection, the ache from Bryce's betrayal, the sting of my own feelings, flare inside of me. Slowly, Connor's touch, his care, erases my pain, replacing it with yearnings that I've tried to lock away.

I'm so grateful I could cry. Emotion swells in my throat as I lose myself to his kiss. Hot, needy, and desperate, our teeth clash as the kiss grows hungrier. He pulls away awkwardly to remove his boxers and we both laugh. But in the next instant, my laughter dies in my throat. My hands track his back as his slips between my legs and tugs my panties down until he parts my core.

Throwing my neck back, I arch into his touch. He chuckles under his breath, the sound vibrating over my skin.

"Greedy girl," he whispers.

"More."

Connor growls, pushing two fingers inside of me, the pad of his thumb finding my clit and pressing until I gasp.

I shift my weight, climbing over him until he flips on his back. His eyes never leave mine as I stare down at him. Positioning myself over him, I slide onto his dick. He inhales sharply, his eyes widening.

His hands settle on my hips. "We've got all night, baby."

"Need you," I murmur, starting to move up and down.

Connor's eyes close and I throw my head back, one hand splayed wide in the center of his chest, the other gripping the top of his headboard.

"Fuck, I missed you," he whispers.

"Me too." I move faster, needing this moment where Connor's truth, his desire, his vulnerability fills me up with so many things, I overflow.

I need right now. I need this moment to catch up to the woman I used to be. Before L.A. Before Bryce. Before the last year filled me with doubt and distrust and just existing without living.

I set the pace of our rhythm, the sound of my ass

smacking against his upper thighs turning me on until I move faster.

"Fuck, Harlow," Connor breathes out, his hands gripping my hips savagely as he guides my body until our pace is frantic.

He rolls us again, settling on top of me and plunging deeper inside until I cry out. Our sweetness obliterated, our union turns savage, with each of us working out our hurts and betrayals, showing our vulnerabilities and the scars we keep hidden.

Our panted breathing colors the air as our truths spill out. Raw and honest and so fucking real with everything we couldn't admit two years ago. Our past hurts explode in between us, forcing us to acknowledge our mistakes, to come to terms with the people we've become instead of the people we should be.

"I'm going to come." My back bows off the mattress as my chest meets the hard wall of Connor's chest.

"Come for me, baby. Now," he commands, as I pulse around him.

I cry out, gripping his shoulders as he swears. On my next inhale, Connor lets out a strangled cry as he finishes inside me. Connor drops his forehead to mine, sweat slicking our skin. I feel his mouth smile against my lips as he kisses me sweetly. Then he rolls off me and takes my hand in his.

He squeezes once, air leaving his lungs in a long *whoosh*. My heart gallops, my thoughts obliterated as I float down from the high of being with Connor.

I turn toward him and he drops my hand. He shifts his weight, his hand sliding up my thigh before resting in the dip of my waist.

"That was amazing. You're fucking amazing," he

breathes out, his fingertips drawing lazy circles along my hip, up to my ribs, and back again.

"I missed you, Connor. So much more than I knew."

"Me too. I know I should have asked you this sooner but, are you still on the pill?"

"Yeah," I snuggle into him. Our breaths mingle as my mind begins to fill with thoughts. Thoughts I know I shouldn't run with but hell, if it isn't hard to quiet my mind. "Now what?" I whisper, wrestling with my runaway thoughts as my heart craves his with more intensity than I thought possible. Still wounded, bruised, from Bryce, I never antici- pated I could feel so much, so deeply, again for Connor.

But there it is. The truth. The want. The homecoming.

Connor grins, a small laugh erupting in the air as he shakes his head at me. "Now, it's whatever you want. I'm not going anywhere, Low. But I know you've had a rough time lately and I'm not trying to rush you."

His words, honest, are meant to soothe, but all they do it cause my self-doubt to flare. "So, you don't want to be together?"

He frowns, his fingers stop their circles as his hand grips my entire hip. "What do you mean?"

I sigh, screwing my eyes shut for a breath. "Is this just because we both need something right now? I mean, did you mean the words you said or were they just—"

He swoops forward, his kiss catching the words I didn't say. He kisses me fiercely, as if trying to talk some sense into my hard head. When he pulls back, his expression is severe. "I meant every single thing I told you. I'm here. I'm here and I'm not going anywhere. But you just got out of a relationship with an asshole. Don't jump into my bed unless you're plan- ning to stay a minute. I thought I made myself clear, I'm not letting you go this time. Not without one hell of a damn fight.

So this is whatever you want it to be until you can commit. Because when you do, I won't have the strength to walk away again. This time, you're the one who has to be sure."

Anger rolls off his shoulders, crashing into mine. His eyes are so dark I can't discern his pupils from his irises.

Holy shit.

Relief snakes through my body, filling me with so much hope, I smile.

"What are you smiling about?" he asks, his tone still laced with frustration.

I dip my head forward and press a sweet, chaste kiss against his lips. "I've been waiting a long time for you to be that passionate toward me."

"Jesus," Connor groans, closing his eyes and pulling me even closer, until his hand is splayed wide in the center of my back. "I know I fucked things up between us, but I never realized how much I hurt you. How much doubt I caused."

"Bryce didn't help."

"Don't say his name. Not now, not when we're in bed, together, like this."

I nod, understanding his irritation immediately. If he so much as muttered the name of a woman he's been with right now, jealousy and hurt would rip me wide open. "Sorry," I whisper.

"Don't be sorry, either. You're being real with me. Honest. That's the most important thing. That we're straight with each other. Before, I messed up by not telling you the truth about how I felt. I thought you were better off without me. I didn't think I was deserving of a woman like you. Hell, I'll never be good enough. I'm never going to be the guy who buys you a three-carat ring or takes you on exotic trips, but I swear I'll always be honest with you."

My palm finds his cheek and rests there, my eyes boring

into his. I can read the truth and sincerity in the blackness of his gaze and I accept it wholeheartedly.

"I don't need anything but you, Connor. You're what I've always wanted. I'm yours."

The corner of his mouth tugs upward, some of the hardness leaving his expression. Pulling me closer, he cradles me in his arms. I snuggle deeper, loving the feel of his arms around me. His presence blocks out my doubts while his caress makes me feel whole. Safe. Content. Loved.

We stay coupled together until we drift to sleep, my fingertips pressed against his heart, his breath whispering sweet nothings in my ear.

12

CONNOR

Zoe waggles her eyebrows at me. "Give me the deets."

Eli snickers and I groan, turning away from my friends to grab the pitcher of lemon water Zoe set out. I fill a glass and take a long drink.

"What? You're going to pretend the thing we've all been agonizing over for years, isn't finally happening?" Zoe throws her hands in the air, appearing in my line of sight again as she steps in front of my face.

"Zoe," I warn.

She grins, her eyes dancing with delight. "It's about time, Connor. That's all I'm saying." She holds up her hands in surrender. "Well, that and Harlow looks exhausted. Nice work."

Eli guffaws and I flip him off, only encouraging his laughter.

"Is she here?" I ask, ignoring their delight even though it eases some of my concern over this thing Harlow and I just dove into. Talk about a giant leap of faith.

"She is. Just stepped out for a minute. Something about her mom." Zoe tips her head toward the front door. "But she should be back any second. Here." She moves around me to grab a dish with pastries and plops it down in front of Eli and me.

"When did you start eating sweets?" I ask, breaking off a piece of chocolate croissant and popping it in my mouth. One of the small perks of no longer being in training. However, it's not a perk I've ever seen Zoe the trainer indulge in.

"Since this guy knocked me up." She hooks her thumb toward Eli before swiping the rest of my croissant. "I just want carbs and sweets."

"You're having a girl," I declare.

Her and Eli stare at me, dumbfounded.

"What?" I shrug.

"How the hell do you know that?" Eli asks.

"I know a lot of things. What's going on with Low's mom?"

Eli sighs, tapping his fingers against the kitchen island. "She's been blowing up her phone all morning. Probably trying to force her to agree to be some blowhard's date to the premiere."

"Yeah, but isn't she working?"

Eli nods. "She's working a lot. Even assisting my publicist Helen with some things for the premiere. Plus, managing my whole life."

"She's so good at it," Zoe adds.

I turn this new development over in my mind. If Harlow goes to the premiere with a date, will she be off the clock as soon as her work commitments are over? Will she return to Chicago straightaway or spend additional time in L.A.? Will she party with her old friends, making headlines on celebrity blogs around the planet? Will she see Bryce? Will she care?

"Hey guys!" Her sunny voice echoes as she enters the kitchen. "Ahh, no more sweet treats." She throws her head back, walking slowly to the kitchen counter where she grabs a blueberry muffin while staring at the ceiling.

"They're low fat," Zoe says.

Harlow glares at her as she bites into the muffin. She bumps her arm against mine and smiles up at me, her mouth full and crumbs sticking to her lips and chin.

I smile back, dusting some of the crumbs off her mouth.

Zoe clasps her hands and bounces on her toes. "Aren't they the cutest?" She asks Eli.

"Like a puppy meme," he agrees.

"Oh, shut it," Harlow laughs at our friends. Rounding the island, she slides onto the barstool next to Eli. "We have some serious things to discuss with you guys."

"Like what?" Eli lifts an eyebrow, already looking bored.

"Like this amazing idea for a new program Connor is launching at Cyanide."

This piques both Eli and Zoe's interest, and they swing their gazes toward me.

"You guys know Moe from Madness?" My hands grasp at each other, a bundle of nerves skating low in my stomach. For some reason, this moment seems important. Of course, I know Eli and Zoe will support me no matter what, but given their own professional success — hotshot Hollywood A-lister and boss trainer killing the YouTube game – their support seems more significant.

"Yeah. He's awesome," Zoe says.

"Right. So he came to me last week with this idea..." I explain the concept behind Soul Sanctuary. Harlow watches me proudly as I fill Zoe and Eli in.

"Wow," Eli blows out a deep breath when I'm finished.

"I love this idea!" Zoe exclaims, throwing her arms around me. "This is so important, Connor." She leans back and her expression wobbles.

"Are you going to cry?" Eli asks, horrified.

Zoe sniffles and shakes her head. "Ignore me. It's the hormones. I just, I love that you're switching gears and bringing attention and action to an important issue."

"Thanks, Zo." I pat her back, a little troubled by the tears welling in her eyes.

Eli shakes his head at me, letting me know she really is okay.

"How can we help?" Zoe asks.

Harlow claps her hands together, directing the attention of the kitchen to her. "Excellent question, Zo. Here's what we're thinking." She reaches into her bag and pulls out a folder. From that, she takes out several bound proposals that we spent the last few nights working on and passes them around.

"Our approach is two-prong…" As Harlow launches into the pitch, I flip through the pages which covers the details of similar programs, a range of statistics of sexual violence and physical assault in Chicago, and a fundraising initiative and launch strategy for Soul Sanctuary.

Slowly, excitement begins to buzz through my veins. Harlow has taken my thoughts, my vision, and turned it into something tangible that other people can understand and want to take part in.

Flickering my gaze to my girl, who is animatedly explaining the speaker series to Zoe and Eli, my heart thuds so loudly I can hear it.

This woman, she undoes me. She supports me. She cares about the same things I care about.

And I'm falling in love with her.

"THEY'RE IN!" Harlow whoops, throwing her fist in the air.

"Yeah, well after that presentation, how could they not be?" I hold out my fist and Harlow pounds it.

"I'm so excited Zoe wants to help with the launch. It'll be fun to work with her, hang out, just do something together again."

"Me too. But you were really incredible, Low."

"Thank you," she curtsies, before sitting down across from me at my kitchen table.

I reach over and grab her hand. "No, Low. Thank you. I don't even know what the hell I'm doing. If it wasn't for you, I doubt I'd be able to get this off the ground."

"You would. You don't give yourself enough credit, Scott."

"You don't either, Reid."

She wrinkles her nose. "I need to ask you something."

"What's up?" Trepidation fills my body at those six words. Did something happen? Is something wrong?

"Don't look so scared. It's not a bad thing. Well, depending on who you ask…"

"Low?"

"Would you go with me to the premiere in two weeks?"

"Eli's premiere?"

She nods, worrying her bottom lip between her teeth.

"Bryce's premiere," I add, putting two and two together.

Harlow sighs, hugging her hands to her chest. "You don't have to come. I just thought, well, it could be fun. I mean, I'll have to work but not for that long. Mostly at the beginning and end to make sure Eli is in the right places for photos and interviews. It might be a little boring for you, but I'm sure Zoe would love the company and —"

"Does this have something to do with your mom?"

Harlow's mouth drops open before she closes it, working a swallow. "How did —"

"Zoe mentioned she was blowing up your phone."

Harlow sighs again, rubbing the space between her eyebrows. "She wants me to bring Chris McCallister."

"The actor?"

Harlow gives me a look. "No, the dental hygienist. Of course the actor! You know what my mom is like."

She says the comment off-handedly, because in many ways, having known Harlow for as long as I have, I do know what her mother is like. Social climbing, meddling, infuriating. But still, I've never met Mrs. Reid-Kinsley and I was stupidly hoping she might like me when I did. My stomach sinks as I realize that in Harlow's mother's eyes, I will never be good enough for her daughter. I mean, she's right. But it sucks to know I have no chance of impressing her.

"You don't want to go with McCallister?"

"Connor!" Harlow smacks her palm against the table. "Of course I don't want to go with Chris. I thought, I thought we were —"

"We are," I cut her off, standing from the table and pulling her up until I can wrap my arms around her. She sighs into my chest, the heat of her breath trapped between us. Pulling back, I clasp her hands in mine. "We are. I just... it's stupid, but I hate that you have this entire life I know nothing about. Well, maybe I know about it, but I don't understand it. Or like it. L.A., parties with famous people, featured in celebrity gossip." I pause, choosing my words carefully. A flicker of panic flares in my throat but I swallow it back down. "It's like you have this whole other identity that I don't know. That's nothing like...*you*."

The flecks of sage in Harlow's eyes burn as she stares at me. "I know it may seem like that but trust me, Connor, you know the real me."

I lick my lips, my stomach twisting and my chest tight. "I

just…I feel all these things for you, Low. And I fucking hate the thought of you going to some fancy premiere, getting all dressed up and looking sexy, for a fucker like Bryce or a wannabe like McCallister."

"You're jealous?"

I groan, hating the truth of it. I'm so fucking jealous my skin should glow green. I nod once, embarrassed but honest. "I don't want to lose you, Harlow. Not again to that damn city and it's pull." I tug her closer until her hands are splayed against my chest once more. The feel of her in my arms only heightens my frustration of her going to this premiere on the arm of another man. I run my hands down her back, my fingertips teasing the sliver of skin above the waistband of her shorts. Jesus, I want her. "I'm more jealous than I've any right to be, I know that. But, I don't want our chance to crash and burn before we even take it."

"Then come with me. Be my date." She leans back. Her eyes hold mine, beseeching.

My fingers continue to stroke her skin and she melts back into my frame. "Okay," I agree, the corner of my mouth lifting into a smile as Harlow's face blossoms into a sunflower.

She cheers, leaping into my arms and wrapping her legs around my torso. "Really?"

"Really." I start walking toward my bedroom, some of my panic easing now that I know she'll be on *my* arm.

"Ah! God, I can't wait to see you in a sharp suit."

"Hold up." I halt.

"And I'm going to wear an incredible gown. It's emerald, with a plunging neckline and a slit that goes all the way up my right thigh."

I start walking again. "Keep talking."

"I'll wear my hair up."

I toss Harlow onto my bed.

"And these gorgeous shoes I just purchased. Strappy, high, so damn sexy," she groans as I kiss under her jawline, my tongue flicking out to taste her sweet skin.

"Your dress sounds hot, babe."

"It is."

I pull her shorts and underwear down her legs in one sharp tug. "But I prefer you like this," I grin at her before lowering my head.

Harlow bucks off the bed when my mouth connects with her core. Her hands grasp at my hair. "Wait til you see the lingerie I'm wearing to the premiere."

I raise my head, glaring at her.

"You'll love it even more." She says saucily, before arching her back and collapsing into the mattress.

13

HARLOW

"Hey!" Eli calls as I slip out of Connor's truck. "You're late." He points to the Rolex on his wrist.

"But I'm ready to work!" I holler back, racing past him and into the house.

Of course, he's on my heels. "Low, I need —"

"I know. To run through your interviews for the premiere, discuss talking points for your appearance on the Night Show, and an update on the renovations in your L.A. condo." I pull a folder out of my bag and hand it to him.

Eli frowns. "You already did all that? It's only," he glances at said Rolex. "10AM."

"This is why you hired me, Eli." I remind him.

"Yeah, I know."

I walk into the kitchen and sit down at the island, rifling through the various folders in my bag. "Connor's coming with me to the premiere."

Eli chokes on the coffee he's sipping. "Connor? In a suit?"

"I know. He's going to look so fucking —"

"Stop talking." Eli holds up a hand and I snicker. "Want a coffee?"

"Iced?"

"Yeah. I'll just make your Nespresso over ice." He turns, filling up a mug with ice before popping a pod into the Nespresso machine. "You know, you used to make me coffee," he grumbles.

"Don't tell anyone I ever admitted this, but I really missed working for you. I'm glad we're back."

He turns to me in surprise. "Seriously?"

"Yeah. I mean, not the grunt work or dealing with your moody, hungover ass, but the other parts. The travel, the camaraderie with the team, the hustle. It's like I never slept and was on 24/7. Every day was this clean canvas. A million unknowns, endless variables, total chaos. It was fun!"

"Yeah," Eli agrees, drawing out the word. "I know what you mean. There was this... I don't know, an energy in those early days. I was the underdog, everyone bet against me, and with something to prove I felt almost unstoppable."

"Exactly. We *were* unstoppable."

Eli chuckles, setting my coffee in front of me. "It was a hell of a ride."

"It was. But it can't beat any of this." I gesture toward the expansive kitchen filled with every new gadget and top-of-the-line appliance known to man.

"No," Eli grins. "You're right. Nothing can top this. Being with Zoe, having Maddie, about to have another little nugget...this is the fucking best. I wouldn't trade it for anything."

"I'm happy for you, Eli."

Eli pauses, fixing me with a curious glance. "What's really going on with you and Connor?"

"We're...us. Figuring it out as we go."

"Look, I know you've been into him for a while and you guys have a twisted history…"

"But…"

"I just don't want you to get hurt, Low. Or Connor."

"I'd never hurt Connor."

Eli sighs, wrapping his hands around his mug. "I know. I didn't mean it like that. It's just, you guys live in two different worlds, two different realities."

"Like you and Zoe?" I quirk an eyebrow. Their relationship was even more unlikely if someone was taking dumb realities into consideration.

"I'm not saying it can't work. I'm just saying it's harder. There are curveballs and things that come up that you don't think are an issue because they're normal for you. But they're not normal for the other person. Look, I want you both to be happy. You guys are my best friends."

"Aww." I place a hand over my heart until Eli flips me off.

"I'm just saying," he continues, "be careful. Talk things through. Don't take anything for granted. It's a surefire way to waste time putting distance between you when you should be growing closer. Feel me?"

"Yeah. I never thought I'd take relationship advice from you."

He grins, lifting his chin at me. "I never thought I'd have anything to share. But marriage teaches you a thing or two. Just know that Connor will always have your best interests at heart. He will always put you first, even if it hurts him. Be aware of that, Low. He might not ever say it but he cares a hell of a lot more than he lets on."

"I know." I bite the corner of my mouth. Connor's jealousy over my potential dates to Eli's premiere flares in my mind. The truth is, premieres and events in Hollywood circles are part of my job. They've been part of my life since I was a kid because of my stepdad. They're nothing I think twice about. But of course, they would be a much bigger deal to anyone not in those circles. They would bother Connor and if our situations were flipped, they would bother me too. "You're right."

"Of course I'm right. Okay, before we talk about the premiere, let's talk about the other appearances I've got coming up…" Eli opens the calendar on his phone.

I open mine too, to sync his schedule.

Reaching over, I punch him in the arm. "You really missed me, huh?"

He snorts, flipping me the bird again.

I laugh.

Nodding at the dates Eli rattles off, I tamp down my happiness. Eli and I haven't always had the best working relationship, mainly because we're too damn close and care about each other too much to keep the professional just business when we're more like family, but, it works. Now, working for him again instead of going back to host reality TV, seems like a gift. I'm grateful that I'm not in L.A. I'm happy that I'm building the career I've always wanted.

I'm relieved that Bryce's ring isn't binding my finger.

CONNOR: *What are you wearing?*

I snort and re-read his message.

Me: Are you for real right now?

My phone rings. I answer immediately. "Didn't take you for a sext-er."

"I'm going to fucking kill Evan."

I laugh, "What are you up to?"

"Nothing, I was going to call you in a bit but then Evan sent that stupid message…"

"What's going on?"

Connor clears his throat, "What are you doing tonight?"

"Nothing really. Want to hang?"

"I want to take you to dinner."

"Like…out?"

Connor chuckles again and I grin. Who is this man who laughs so easily? "Yes, Harlow. Out. On a date. With me." He spells it out for me, but I hear the humor underlining his words and my smile widens until I'm sure my face is going to crack.

"Are you spitting your best game?" I joke.

"Baby, you can't handle my best game."

I laugh again.

"Go to dinner with me tonight, Low."

"Okay."

"I'll pick you up at eight. And even though I'm not a sexter, I'm not opposed to you wearing something sexy."

I giggle. Giggle! "I'll see you then."

"Okay." Connor says, then hangs up.

I stare at my phone in my hand, still smiling like a lunatic. Connor is taking me out on a date. A real date.

Excitement buzzes in my veins and I feel giddy. Standing from my couch, I tap out a message to Zoe.

Me: I have a date.

Zoe: Hallelujah! What are you wearing?

Me: That's what I was going to ask you…

Zoe: Come over. Bring the stuff for Soul Sanctuary. We'll do some work, you'll drink some wine, and we'll sort out your outfit.

Me: Done!

I pack up my Soul Sanctuary folder and notes and head

straight to Zoe's. My body feels lighter, like it's floating through air. I realize it's been too long since I've felt this kind of excitement. It's innocent and sincere, the way I used to feel about first dates a thousand moons ago. The building anticipation, the girl-time gossip, the getting ready for a big night out with a boy who makes my head spin.

It feels so good to lose myself in all of it.

When I reach Zoe's house, she's sitting on the front porch, watching Maddie play in the yard.

"Yay!" she exclaims when she sees me, standing to her feet.

"I feel like a teenager," I admit. "I haven't had a date like this, one where I'm giddy and breathless, in years."

"That's how it's supposed to be." Zoe hugs me hello. "Maddie's babysitter should be here any second. I thought we could do some work on Soul Sanctuary before we raid my closet."

"Sounds good," I agree.

Maddie's babysitter Kaylee arrives five minutes later and stays outside playing with Maddie as Zoe and I slip indoors.

I pull out my folder and spread the papers out on the kitchen table.

"Okay," Zoe says, sitting down. "Tell me all the things."

"I really want to see how we can use your platform to build buzz about both the program's mission and Cyanide MMA."

"Right." Zoe picks up a pen and starts jotting down some notes. "I can do an episode, or at least an introductory video, for *That Fit Bitch Life* that raises awareness about the issue and then plugs Cyanide as a gym that's launching a program to address it?"

"That sounds like a great start."

"Okay, let's come up with talking points for that first."

Zoe and I dive into the work, settling on the statistics to flag, the scope of the program to share, and Cyanide's vision.

"Drop your pen!" Zoe exclaims out of nowhere, her expression alarmed.

"What?" My pen clatters to the table as I lean toward her. "Are you okay? Is it the baby?"

She rolls her eyes. "The baby is fine. It's your date!"

"Oh my God," I glance at my phone, blanching when I see it's already 6PM. I let out a slow breath, trying to calm the panic in my mind. "I totally lost track of time."

"Me too."

"I have two hours."

"Right," Zoe nods, exhaling slowly.

We look at each other and crack up. "We're ridiculous."

She rolls her eyes. "I know. I really thought you were late for a second."

"So did I! You looked so scared!"

She chuckles, pulling herself up from her seat. "Come on, let's go play in my closet. Grab a bottle of wine. At least one of us should drink."

I duck into the bar fridge, find an open bottle of Riesling, and pour myself a glass. "Yes, please. The clothes Jack shipped me arrived, but you know how guys pack."

"Nothing matches?" Zoe guesses as we start up the stairs.

"Not a damn thing! I'm going to bring over my clothes and personal items after the premiere. It will be a good time for me to pack up my L.A. life."

Zoe guides me into her bedroom and points to her closet. "Until then, what's mine is yours."

I place my wine glass on her bedside table and bounce into her to-die-for walk-in, lined with shelves of shoes and an absurd amount of clothes.

"I think you should wear a dress. Something flirty and

summery and a little bit sexy." Zoe explains, pulling six different hangers before I can even see what she chooses. She pushes the dresses in my arms. "Let's start with these." She grins, gesturing to a little changing area in her closet. "I'll pull some shoes."

"You're like a stylist!" I gush, dropping the dresses on a small bench she has set up and wiggling out of my shorts.

"If only. I just miss this part. The getting ready, the gossiping…it's so fun!"

"It is," I agree, beaming at my friend. I've missed this girl time more than I even realized. "Thank you, Zoe."

"Please," she flicks her wrist at me. "I'm so happy you're here. Your moving to Chicago has been my secret plan all along. Now, I just need to get Charlie back here."

I try on the first few dresses as Zoe hums, but on dress number four, her eyes light up. "That's the one!"

I turn slowly to check myself out in the mirror and I inhale sharply when I see my reflection.

The dress is beautiful. Sleeveless, with a ruffled neckline, fitted bodice, and full skirt, it's flirty yet elegant. A diamond cut out down the back shows some skin without being too much. The white pops against my summer tan while the floral pattern makes it a perfect fit for the season.

"I love this," I breathe out, toying with the skirt. My eyes are glowing, my hair is shining, and I look better than I have since landing in Chicago.

"You look beautiful, Harlow. Happy." Zoe hands me a pair of nude, strappy heels.

I grin at her, our gazes meeting in the mirror. "Happy is the best compliment you can give someone."

"I know." She smiles back before checking her watch. "We need to start on your makeup if you're going to be home and ready in time. You know what? Let's drive to your place now and I can help you and slip out before Connor arrives."

"Are you sure?" I ask, even though I love this idea.

"Absolutely." Zoe grabs some chandelier earrings from her jewelry box. "These will look perfect. Finish that wine and let's go!"

14

CONNOR

"Let me guess. You need my help planning the perfect date?" Eli says in greeting to my phone call.

I lean back in my office chair and grin at no one. "How do you know about my date?"

"Zoe and Harlow are giggling like two schoolgirls upstairs in her closet. I just came home from some meetings and I swear, my place feels like a sorority house," Eli jokes.

I chuckle and straighten in my chair. "I do need your help. I have no idea where to take Harlow. The place Evan suggested earlier is fully booked. Who the hell makes reservations weeks in advance?"

"People who want to eat at a good restaurant."

I scoff.

"I got you," Eli says. "What vibe are you going for? Gastro pub? Farm-to-table? Fancy? Any cuisine preference?"

"Who are you and what have you done with my broody bastard of a friend?"

"Hey! I'm trying to help you out here."

I snort, "Gastro pub or farm-to-table. Something nice but not crazy fancy."

"Okay. I'd suggest either Maurice's on Michigan Avenue. It's a gastro pub that's trendy and eclectic. Or, another place I haven't tried yet but have heard really great things about is Abigail's on Wells Street."

"Let's try Maurice's," I say, figuring it's best to stick with what Eli knows.

"What time?"

"I'm picking Low up at eight."

"Okay, give me a minute. I'll call you right back."

I place my phone on my desk and lean back in my chair. It's been a long, long time since I've had a real date. Usually, my interactions with women involve meeting at a bar, slightly drunk, and agreeing to spend a night together. No more, no less. Sure, I treat them with respect, make sure they have a good time, but when the sun rises, there's never even a need to exchange phone numbers.

But I'm looking forward to tonight. I'm looking forward to seeing Harlow, spending time with her, enjoying the moment.

My phone buzzes on my desk.

"Hey," I pick up.

"You have reservations at Maurice's at 8:30PM." Eli says and I can hear the irritating grin in his voice.

"Thanks, man."

"Anytime. Have fun tonight." He hesitates, clearing his throat as if he isn't sure to say what's on his mind.

"And?"

"And...look, I told Low the same thing. I'm not trying to be preachy but you guys have both been through a lot. Just, make sure you're being honest with each other."

"I'd never lie to Low."

"I know, not intentionally. It's not lying..." Eli sighs. "I just mean you guys are starting something back up and it's going really well. Make sure you stick to the same page. That's all."

I scrub a hand over my face and blow out an exhale. I know Eli is just looking out for me and Low. He's had both of our backs for a really long time and right now, he's trying to be a friend. Despite the fact that his words irritate me, because I've always been straight with Harlow, I try to take them from the place they're coming from. A good place.

"Yeah, man. I get it." .

"Cool. Don't forget to send a picture. Evan and I are taking bets on if you're going to wear sneakers or work boots," Eli jokes, chuckling.

"I own shoes, asshole."

"Really? I've yet to see 'em!"

"Fuck off." I wrack my brain to make sure I do have real shoes. A pair I wore to one of Eli's charity galas flickers in my mind and relief fills my chest. "I do." I confirm.

Eli's laughter booms through the line. "Have a great night, man."

"Yep. Thanks for the hook-up."

"Anytime."

Once I hang up with Eli, I glance back at my schedule. I have one more training session before I can go home and shower. I know it's only a couple of hours, but I really can't wait for 8PM.

I'M nervous when I knock on Harlow's door.

It's ridiculous because it's Low. I've seen her naked in more compromising positions than I can count. I've held her against my chest on several occasions as her emotions spiraled. I've fallen asleep on her shoulder.

But I've never taken her on a proper date. In many ways, tonight holds a gravity I wasn't anticipating, causing my stomach to tighten as I knock again.

Her apartment door swings open and my breath lodges in my chest.

Jesus Christ, she's gorgeous.

Her honey-blonde hair falls in waves around her shoulders and her green eyes sparkle. A flowy dress hugs her curves before flaring out from her hips. She's also several inches taller than normal. When I glance down, I note the sexy heels she's rocking as an image of her long, lean legs wrapped around my hips flickers through my mind.

I swallow and snap my head back up.

Harlow grins, biting her lower lip.

"You look breathtaking, Harlow. Literally." I manage to say, holding out the bouquet of flowers I bought. I felt like an idiot in the flower shop, but when I saw the number of guys in there buying flowers for their sweethearts, I realized the joke had been on me for a long ass time.

"Thank you." She takes the flowers from my hand and dips her nose into the bouquet. "I love peonies."

I clear my throat. Thank God for the woman working at the flower shop. I had no idea what the hell a peony was.

"You clean up nice, Connor." Harlow meets my eyes again, a soft smile on her lips.

I run my hand over my clean-shaven jawline. Clad in navy pants and a crisp, white button down, rolled up on the forearms, I'm more dressed than I've been all year. The entire ride to Harlow's, I felt fidgety, the material of my shirt tight against my skin.

All my discomfort fades the second I see her eyes widen in appreciation.

"Thanks, Low." I tilt my head toward the elevator. "You want to head out?"

"Sure. Let me just put these in some water. Here, come in for a second." She opens her door wider and I step inside.

I can't tear my gaze away from her as she rushes to the kitchen, drops the bouquet in a bowl of water, and glances at me sheepishly over her shoulder. "I don't have a vase yet!"

I chuckle and she laughs. My nerves dissipate and I grin at Harlow, just happy to spend time with her.

"I'm ready," she declares, smoothing the skirt of her dress as she sidles up next to me.

Not overthinking it, I take her hand in mine. My thumb swipes against her smooth skin, running over her knuckles. "Let's do this, babe."

We step outside into the breezy night air and I glance at Low. "We can walk if you'd prefer? It's only a few blocks from here." My gaze drops to her high heels. "Or drive…"

"Worried about these?" she lifts her foot, showing off her shoe. "Please, I can wear heels all day, every day. Let's walk!"

"Okay." I grip her hand tighter as we set off toward Maurice's.

Summer wraps around us, bursting with anticipation, filled with promise. I glance down at Harlow, wondering how the hell I got so lucky.

15

HARLOW

Connor is the hottest man I've ever laid eyes on.

I mean that. And I've seen a lot of hot guys in my line of work.

But Jesus, can Connor rock a button-down as easily as a T-shirt. No matter what the man wears, his biceps stretch the material, his shoulders and back bunching and rippling in waves of muscle I want to run my hands over. Of course, I've seen Connor dressed up before, at a handful of Eli's events. But those were always necessary. Tonight, he shaved and wore dress shoes for *me*. He bought flowers for *me*.

He showed up for *me*.

The realization sends a shiver up my spine. My skin feels too sensitive, even to the night air, and my heart rate ticks up.

With his large hand covering mine and his eyes drinking me in like he'll never have his fill, I feel like a damn movie star. Desired and alluring. This is already the best date I've ever been on.

"We're here," he says easily, tipping his head toward a trendy restaurant on the corner of the street. He holds the door open for me and I slip inside.

As Connor tells the hostess his name, I glance around the stylish space. Contemporary and open, with wood accents and a wall filled with quotes in bright, neon signs, I can tell this is a current hotspot.

"How'd you get a reservation so last minute?" I question as our hostess leads us through a fully packed dining room toward the only empty table set for two.

Connor glances at me and quirks an eyebrow.

"Eli," I guess.

He nods and pulls out my chair for me.

The gesture is simple, but something swells inside me as I slide onto the chair. I've known Connor for a long time, but tonight, it's like I'm getting to see a different side of him for the first time.

A romantic side. A vulnerable side he very rarely shows.

He sits down across from me and I smile at him, gesturing around the space. "Thanks for this."

His eyes meet mine. Dark and deep, they blaze with an intensity that surprises me. "Thank you, Low."

My smile widens and he grins. In this moment, a peace settles over me that I've been searching for for way too long. Being with Connor feels right. He feels like home.

"What are you in the mood for?" He glances at the menu, his question bringing me back to the now.

I look over the menu and settle on the sea scallops while Connor decides on some fancy kind of schnitzel.

When our waitress comes, we order a bottle of wine, a few appetizers, and our mains. As soon as she's gone, Connor leans back in his chair and glances around the space.

"I've never been here," he says.

"No?" I ask in mock-shock.

"Quit it. I haven't been to most of the restaurants downtown. If it wasn't for Eli or Evan, I'd probably never go out to eat. Takeout is more my jam."

"Do you brunch?"

He blanches and I giggle.

"I love brunch," I say, wrinkling my nose. "To be honest, I love eating out. In L.A., I'm out for dinner two or three times a week."

"Seriously?" Connor leans closer, the scent of his cologne perfuming the space between us.

I breathe it in as I nod.

"You must have a ton of friends," he comments.

"I have a lot of acquaintances. My true friends are all here."

Our server drops off our wine and pours two glasses.

Connor lifts his glass toward me, his eyes soft, like melted dark chocolate. Tenderness sweeps his expression and a wave of exhilaration rushes through me. "To you, Low. May you always be happy."

I lift my glass and clink it against his. "Thank you for tonight, Connor."

"Thank you for everything, Harlow." His eyes never leave mine as he takes a sip of his wine.

I shiver from the intensity rolling off of him, his eyes dark with desire. Already, my body is desperate for the delicious finale tonight promises. But right now, my heart is fluttering from Connor's heady gaze and truthful words.

It's a combination that pulls me under his spell. And I don't ever want it to break.

———

CONNOR DOES NOT DISAPPOINT.

After a date that ends with a delicious tiramisu, we walk

back to my apartment hand in hand. The city streets are lit up and the summer wraps around us, sultry and brimming with possibility. Even the stars seem brighter with Connor by my side. A certainty that everything happens for a reason, that I'm finally right where I'm supposed to be, settles over me.

I grin up at the sexiest man I've ever known. "Tonight was fun."

He squeezes my hand. "As far as dates go, that's the best I've ever been on."

I laugh. "You mean the only one you've ever been on, right?"

He snickers and I smile and our eyes catch and hold.

Desire darkens his already midnight eyes as he slows his gait. When I stop walking beside him, his hand reaches up to cup my cheek, keeping my eyes locked on his. His thumb sweeps along my cheekbone, sending a rush of shivers down my spine.

Connor holds my gaze for a long beat, his eyes swirling with emotions. The tension between us thickens as the city falls away. When his mouth arcs over mine, I tip my chin up and meet his lips. He kisses me sweetly, reverently and I melt into him. But when his hands drop to my hips and pull me flush against his body, our kiss turns spicy, offering glimpses of what's waiting the second we get to my place.

His tongue slips into my mouth and connects with mine. I moan, not caring who hears. My arms wrap around his broad shoulders, my nails taking purchase in his strong back. He hisses and I grin.

"Take me home, Scott."

Connor bends and sweeps me into his arms, like a fairy-tale princess. "It'd be a goddamn pleasure, Reid," he murmurs into my ear as he carries me the last half block home. I'm giggling again and Connor's smirking down at me, but the hunger in his eyes is insatiable and my body is tight with anticipation.

The moment the door to my apartment closes behind us, he settles me on my feet.

My hands slide up the corded muscles of his arms as he pulls me into his frame. His face is flushed with lust, his eyes flickering with desire that fills me with satisfaction and want.

So gently I shudder, his fingers slide the straps of Zoe's dress off my shoulders. His hands wrap around my back, keeping my chest flushed with his, as he slowly unzips the back of my dress.

I gaze up at him, falling headfirst into the longing etched in his expression. When my zipper is completely down, I shuffle back a half step and let the dress fall to the floor. Stepping out of it, I kick it to the side as Connor's gaze drops the length of my body and he swears.

"Jesus Christ, Harlow," he mutters, his hands gliding up my hips, skating over the thin lace of my panties, and clutching at my waist. "You're so goddamn sexy."

I bend to unclasp my shoes but he shakes his head.

"No, babe. Keep those on." His voice is rough, strained. The sound of it turns me on just as much as the wild look in his eyes.

I step closer. My hands skate over his shirt as I undo the buttons. He watches me, his gaze heavy on my face but I don't look up. Not yet.

Once I've cleared the last button, I push his shirt off his shoulders and drink in the ripple of his abdomen, the strength of his upper body.

Connor growls and lifts me easily. My legs wrap around his waist as he strides to my bedroom.

"Bet your glad my headboard arrived," I joke as he tosses me in the center of my mattress.

"Not if we break it."

I laugh, "So cocky."

He smirks, shaking his head as he scans my body again. "Just truthful. You have no goddamn idea what you do to me, Harlow." His frame shadows mine and I lay back into the soft bedding as he covers me. His eyes pierce me to my core, causing me to freeze as he brushes a kiss across my lips. "Not a fucking clue," he murmurs.

Then, his mouth drops to mine and my legs hook around his back, the heels of my shoes digging into his flesh. I pull him closer until there's no space between us and our bodies meld together until I don't know where I end and he begins. Connor kisses me with such reckless abandon that my thoughts cease to exist.

The only thing that matters is this moment.

This man.

Us.

"NOTHING FITS!" Zoe wails from inside her closet.

"I find that hard to believe given the number of dresses you've got hanging in there," I call back.

"I didn't go anywhere the last time I was pregnant." She flutters back into the room, her face streaked with panic. "Harlow, I don't have anything to wear."

"Okay." I know she's serious by the panic in her eyes. "Relax. Just, take a breath and give me a minute. Here," I pass over her phone, "call Charlie."

Zoe blows out a deep breath and calls her best friend in New York. Charlie, with her quick wit and unrivaled humor, will have Zoe laughing in no time.

In the meantime, I make a few calls to the teams of

designers I know will help Zoe – okay, fine, Eli – out in a pinch.

Fifteen minutes later, Zoe's flushed skin has settled and she's resting, her feet up, her eyes closed.

The moment I end my call, her eyes snap open and find mine.

"How's Charlie?" I ask.

"She's doing really great. I know she misses her mom and, obviously, me —"

"Obviously."

"But New York has been a dream come true for her. She needed a change of scenery after everything sort of blew up between her and Evan."

I wince, remembering just how fast the whirlwind between Charlie and Eli's brother Evan began. And how quickly it burned out.

"Didn't they break up a year ago?"

"Two," Zoe confirms, holding up two fingers. "The year after was so awkward with them trying to avoid each other. Charlie was working on the renovations at Shooters and Evan was leaning on Eli and me a lot for childcare as he was so busy at work. Their paths constantly crisscrossed and they could barely make eye contact. It sucked big time. Kind of like when you and Connor fizzled out and you refused to set foot in Chicago."

"I didn't refuse to —"

"I had to beg you to come see us." Zoe cuts me off, lifting a brow.

I tip my head toward her, ceding the point. "At least I can now make it up to you. Four gowns will be here within two hours."

Zoe bolts upright, her hands flying to her baby bump, her

mouth dropping open. All chat of Charlie and Evan is forgotten. "Seriously?"

"Yes! You are going to have a fabulous gown for the premiere."

"Oh my God, Harlow, thank you." Tears gather in Zoe's eyes and I chuckle, knowing it's partly relief and partly the raging hormones. "I seriously don't know what I would do if you weren't here."

"You're all good, Zo."

Zoe sighs, settling back in the chair once more. Her gaze floats over me and she bites the corner of her mouth.

"Yes?" I inquire, knowing she's desperate for the deets of my date with Connor.

"Are you seriously not going to tell me? After I lent you said closet?"

"Of course I'm going to tell you. I just thought we should put out this fire first." I gesture toward her closet and lack of suitable premiere gowns.

"The fire is out." She leans forward. "Tell me everything."

"It was perfect."

"Oh my God!" Zoe exclaims, clasping her hands to her chest. At the hopeful expression on her face, I smile and let myself revel into the swoony happiness of knowing that I am falling. Hard.

"I'm falling for him, Zo. For real." I admit, cheesing like a cartoon character. "The date was so... it was everything."

Zoe's mouth falls open as she peers at me. "You're blushing."

"I know."

She laughs, "I love it."

"He brought me flowers."

She gasps.

"And used Eli to make a reservation at a trendy little gastro-pub."

"I had no idea Connor could be so...romantic. And on top of things."

"I know," I sigh. "It was really great. By the way, I may need to keep those shoes."

She snickers, waving a hand at me. "They're all yours."

"You're a true friend."

"Don't I know it." She continues to watch me, her curiosity turning to concern.

"Now what?"

She wrings her hands once before dropping them to her lap. "He really cares about you, Harlow. I wouldn't be surprised if he's already fallen completely in love with you."

The thought, coupled with memories of our date, fills me up with so many butterflies, so much *hope*, that I'm ready to burst at the seams. "I care about him too."

"I know. You've cared for a really long time. Jesus, I remember talking about Connor when we were in the Seychelles for *Dangerous Devils*."

I nod, picking at the threads of the carpet. Memories from several years ago flicker through my mind. I was so hung up on Connor that I couldn't imagine ever finding love with someone who wasn't him. Several months after the movie wrapped, I met Bryce. I fell hard, fast, and never looked back.

"It's different now." I shift my weight until my arms are behind me, supporting my seated position. The way I'm falling for Connor, everything about Connor... it's nothing like it was with Bryce.

"Because of him or you?"

"Both." I turn the ring in my nose, thinking of all the ways Connor and I have changed, grown, since I lamented our hook-ups with no commitment to Zoe in the Seychelles.

"He suffered a big loss when he stopped fighting. My heart, well, my pride, was crushed by Bryce's cheating. We're more realistic now."

"That makes sense. The past year has been really rough for Connor. Everything with his dad hit him really hard, and working at the gym has been both a salvation and a curse."

I nod. Connor's financial burdens flicker in my mind but of course, I don't share that information with Zoe.

"Just, don't let him pull away from you, Harlow," Zoe cautions after a moment. "If things are as great as they seem, don't give him the chance to second-guess any of it."

I pinch my piercing before forcing my hand back to the floor. "Why would he do that?"

"Honestly, I think Connor is uncomfortable with all of this." She throws her arm up and I frown. "The glitz and glamor. The Hollywood circle. Him and Eli have been friends for a long time so it's different. But anytime he's come to one of Eli's events, he's quieter than usual. Withdrawn, severe. It's like he doesn't know how to act so he doesn't try to engage. But this world is a big part of you. Your family is very involved in L.A. Your job is Hollywood-centric. You flourish in the middle of a group of strangers. You're confident and poised, graceful. If Connor feels like he doesn't belong, he'll bolt before he makes you feel like you need to change. Does that make sense?"

"Yeah." I consider her words. "I never thought about it before because the majority of my and Connor's interactions have been just the two of us. The only times I've seen him in social settings were when we would go out with you and Eli or Charlie and Evan. I've never noticed his behavior at any of Eli's events because I've always been working them. But what you're saying definitely makes sense."

I chew my bottom lip, recalling how uncomfortable

Connor seemed when I first opened my door last night for our first real day. I wonder how Connor will handle the premiere. Will he relax and have a good time, get to know my friends? Or will he hate all the questions they throw his way? Will the constant buzz of people and camera flashes enthrall or irritate him?

"What's wrong?" Zoe asks, reading my melancholy correctly.

"We're just starting to click. For real. In the past, the sex has always been off the charts but the emotional bit, the knowing we were in things together, was never there. For the first time, it is. And I don't want him to pull away. I don't want to lose him."

"Then don't."

"But I also don't want to feel like I'm the only one holding us together either. These past few weeks, especially on our date, he's started showing me more of himself. He's really opening up and letting me in. But we're on his turf, in his city. I can't always be in Chicago, supporting his dreams and the gym. Sometimes he needs to put himself out there in my world, in L.A., right? Things are really amazing, and I don't want to rock the boat. But the last time things didn't work out between us, it was because I put myself out there and he didn't. What if it's more one-sided than I realize? Do you think I'm still chasing him or this time, is he going to catch me?" I hate the flicker of doubt that flares in my chest when moments ago, I was nearly euphoric. But Zoe's concern holds weight. The truth is, Connor and I are still getting to know each other. Just because we have a history doesn't mean we fully understand the people we've each grown into.

A swell of emotion flickers across Zoe's features as she pulls herself out of the chair and reaches a hand down to me. Once I'm standing beside her, she wraps an arm around my shoulders and agrees. "I understand your concern, Harlow. I didn't mean to worry you. Honestly, I think Connor is in this just as much as you are. I think he *will* catch you. But you still have to make sure you guys are being truthful with each other, sharing your concerns and worries. Relationships take work, and you both have a lot going on right now."

I mull over her words. Everything she's saying makes sense. I know she only has my and Connor's best interests at heart. Still, the seriousness of her tone kills some of my happy relationship buzz. Recalling Eli's warning from earlier this week, I stare at her from the corner of my eye. "Did you and Eli rehearse this?"

Confusion causes her eyebrows to pull together. "What do you mean?"

"He said something similar to me earlier, that's all."

Zoe laughs, bumping her hip against mine. "See, same page."

I manage a smile.

"Come on, let's record that video for Connor's launch. Then, we can talk about him more before Eli gets home and ruins girl time."

This time, I laugh for real and follow Zoe out of her bedroom.

16

CONNOR

"Morning sunshine," I greet Harlow as she pulls open the passenger door to my truck.

She's wearing a pair of cut-off shorts with tears through the thighs. A crop top shows off a sliver of her tanned, smooth stomach. Her hair is piled on top of her head in a messy bun and flip-flops dangle off her feet.

I work a swallow, my throat drying at how effortless she is.

"Oh, thank God," she announces, her hand curling around the iced coffee in the cup holder as she slams the passenger door closed.

I chuckle, reaching across her to pull her seatbelt over her chest and fasten it by her hip. My fingers graze the smooth skin of her thigh and she shoots me a cheeky grin.

"Sleep well?" I ask, ignoring her body's reaction to me in order to keep my own desire in check. Instead, I pull out of the parking lot.

"Like the dead. I feel like I'm catching up on years of missed sleep."

"Your life always seems full of events and meetings and commitments."

Harlow snorts. "And yours isn't?"

I shrug, running my palm over the steering wheel. "Mine is all work shit. Nothing fancy or fun. Just sweating on a construction site or sweating at the gym. The best is when I'm sweating under you."

"*That* is the best."

"Yeah. We should try to do it more often…" I swallow, hoping she doesn't catch the desperation in my tone.

I feel Harlow's gaze pierce the side of my face, but I don't turn to look at her. The truth is, Harlow is crazy busy. So am I. But our professional commitments and packed calendars couldn't look more different. Harlow has "drinks" for meetings. She has "Zoom calls." I have manual labor that leaves me exhausted and irritable without any of the mental stimulation or social connection she enjoys. At the end of the day, I just want to lose myself in her, and the past few nights, I've missed having her in my bed.

After a long beat, she turns her head to look straight out the windshield. "So, where are we going?"

"I want you to meet Moe."

She slurps down her caffeine. "From Madness?"

"Yeah, babe." My hand finds her thigh. The feel of her skin settles me, smoothing over my barely concealed concern from moments earlier.

She doesn't shake off my touch. I relax slightly, my fingertips grazing her skin.

"Does Moe know I'm coming?"

"Of course."

"Okay, good."

"Why? You nervous about meeting him?"

Harlow shakes her head. "Nah. I just want us to dive in. I've got ideas! Zoe and I have a whole list prepared."

"I'm sure you do. Share them all with Moe. He's a great guy and has been considering this program for a while. I know what happened to Callie really pushed him to take action, but…"

"What?"

"We should have done it sooner." My left hand clenches the steering wheel, my knuckles popping white. "I want this to work, Low." I turn toward her so she can see how serious I am. "More than I want Cyanide to grow, I want this to work."

Harlow places her hand on top of mine and squeezes. "It will, Connor. Trust yourself, you and Moe can get this off the ground."

"And you," I say quietly but I want her to confirm it. I want to know that she's planning on sticking around. That she's not going anywhere and after the launch of this program, she'll still play an active role in my life.

"And me," she smiles. "What are you thinking timeline-wise?"

"As soon as possible."

Harlow considers this. "Okay. I think you should launch in about a month then. Two weeks after Eli's premiere since we're going to miss out on some time when we fly to L.A."

My hand clenches reflexively against her thigh at the mention of L.A. and her palm flattens along mine, holding my fingers steady.

Shit. I hate that damn city. I hate its allure, it's fraud, it's wannabes and social climbers. But more than that, I hate the hold it has on the woman sitting next to me. Obviously, a place like L.A. has a hell of a lot more to offer a woman like Harlow, with her work experience and hustle, than Chicago. And I don't want to fuck things up between us again, the way

I did last time, resulting in her running straight for the Hollywood Hills.

"Okay," I murmur as we hang a left into the parking lot for Madness. I'm relieved we're here. "You ready?"

Harlow nods, unclicking her seatbelt. "I'm proud of you, Connor."

Her words are like a salve to wounds I don't realize I bear. They're reassuring and comforting and... generous. "I didn't do anything."

"You always do a lot more than you realize. I've always admired that about you." She hops out of the truck and closes the door.

Her praise causes my throat to clog with emotion. Is that how she sees me? It's funny, really, because I'm always so damn proud of her that I can't imagine what the hell she sees in me.

I climb out of the truck and trail Harlow.

"Pick up the pace, slow poke," she calls over her shoulder.

Jogging over to her side, I throw an arm around her shoulders and pull her into me. How did I get so lucky after messing everything up the first time around? How long will it be 'til I screw it up this time too?

———

"Assalamu alaikum," Moe grins when he spots us. He skirts the counter and tosses an arm around my shoulders in welcome.

"Walaikum assalam," I slap his back as he pulls away. "This is Harlow."

Moe turns his attention toward Harlow, his eyes warm. "How's it going, Harlow? I'm Moe. Welcome to Madness."

She shakes his hand. "Thanks Moe. Good to meet you."

"Great to meet you. Thank you so much for helping us out with this."

Harlow waves a hand, grinning. "I'm so excited about this program. I think it's a fantastic idea and an important option for women to have in Chicago. Connor told me a little bit about what spurred you to reach out to him. I'm so sorry about what happened to Callie."

Moe swallows, pain streaking across his face. "She wants to support the launch of the program."

"And she can do that in whatever capacity she is most comfortable with," Harlow says. "Is there somewhere we can sit and talk? I'd love to have a better understanding of your goals for this program. I also have some ideas I'd like to get your input on."

Moe nods, giving me a look over the top of Harlow's head.

I shrug, slipping my hands into the back pockets of my jeans. Harlow is a damn firecracker. Never shy, always landing on her feet, she can take control of any situation and own it. Her confidence is one of the sexiest — and most intimidating — things about her.

Moe tilts his head toward the hallway where his office is located. "This way."

Once the three of us are seated around a table, Harlow asks Moe a slew of questions. While they chat, I can't tear my eyes, or thoughts, away from her. She's so damn good at what she does, so talented. Managing Eli's life is no joke, especially when his career is moving in new directions. But Harlow's always been a quick study. She's organized, efficient, and disciplined. Helping me with the launch of Soul Sanctuary hasn't overwhelmed her in the least.

Will this be enough for her? Life in Chicago? Traveling to

L.A. when she's accustomed to living there? The L.A. scene, with its trendy restaurants and hot nightclubs, with its glamorous, glossy people, is a far cry from Chi-town. Will she be able to pursue her dream, work in public relations, without being in the center of all the action?

"You've got a woman's kickboxing class starting now?" Harlow asks, her voice cutting through my depressing thoughts.

"Yep. In about ten minutes."

"Mind if I watch?"

"Not at all. You can participate if you want."

Harlow wrinkles her nose. "I didn't bring workout clothes."

"Ah, I can help you out with that." Moe moves to his desk and reaches into a box to pull out a pair of women's shorts and a tank top. "What size do you wear?"

"Small or medium."

"Here you go." He passes her some clothes.

"Awesome! Thank you, Moe." Harlow's gaze swings to mine.

I grin at her excitement. She's exudes pure joy while I'm always surly. But damn if her sunshine doesn't warm the coldest parts of my heart. "Do it," I encourage her.

"You can change in the women's locker room. You got a gym bag with you?" Moe asks me.

"In the truck."

"Want to spar?"

I snort and raise an eyebrow. "And beat your ass?"

"You can try, bro. I'm still young." Moe retorts.

Harlow chuckles at our exchange. "I'm going to go change. Thanks, Moe. This was really helpful." She gestures toward the table where I'm still the only one sitting.

"No, Harlow. Thank you. You have no idea how much I

appreciate your interest and support. Connor and I would have no idea what to do next if you weren't guiding us."

"It's my pleasure." She shakes Moe's hand. "I'll see you out there?"

I nod.

"Salma is at the front desk. She'll show you where the class is and where you can leave your stuff," Moe adds.

"I'll meet you after, babe." I palm the back of her thigh. Jesus, any excuse to touch her. To demonstrate how grateful I am that she's here, helping me out with this. After half a year of hell, turns out Pop was right. I do need a new chapter, to dive into something bigger than myself, to find a purpose. Soul Sanctuary seemed to drop into my lap when I needed it most. With Harlow's support, it all seems to be clicking into place.

"Okay." She slides out of my hold as she heads toward the women's locker room.

When Harlow's out of the office, Moe lifts an eyebrow. "So that's her?"

"That's her."

"You let *her* go?"

"It was more complicated than that."

Moe whistles. "No way. Dude, you're screwed."

I rub the heels of my palms into my eyes, not bothering to refute Moe's observation. He's right – I am screwed.

"I would have followed her to L.A.," he continues.

I groan, leaning back in my chair.

"How's it going now that she's back?"

"It's going," I say, not adding that it's going too damn good to be true. That date, her touch, everything is so... effortless. It has me on edge. You can't go this long barely speaking to someone and miraculously be friends, then lovers. Can you?

Moe smirks. "You don't want to talk, it's cool."

I glare at him.

Moe's smirk grows. "Let's spar. I'ma go easy on you."

I chuckle, leaning back in my chair.

"What? You clearly have a lot of unresolved feelings on the issue."

"What issue?" I bite out, not wanting to admit that he's right.

Moe holds my eye, quirking an eyebrow.

I sigh, "When I'm with her, everything is amazing. And when I'm not, I'm worrying that I'm messing up the amazing." I hate myself for sounding like a goddamn pussy. "My head is all over the damn place when it comes to Low."

"Clear it," he clasps my shoulder, pushing me toward the parking lot. "Grab your shit and suit up."

Hustling out to the car, I grab my gym bag and beeline for the locker room. Once there, I drop my bag on a bench. I was planning to get a quick workout in, but Moe's option is more appealing. It will give me the chance to work out all the complicated feelings bubbling inside now that Harlow is back in my life. For so long, I didn't dare hope for a second chance, knowing I'd never get one.

But now that she's here and things between us are so... right, I'm scared as hell that I'm going to fuck it all up again. I'll lose her for good and I won't have one damn ray of sunshine in my life to keep me from slipping into my dark thoughts and even darker moods.

I can't risk that. I need to learn how to be the man that Harlow needs me to be. Not the hotheaded fighter who claims what he wants with his fists, consequences be damned, but the man who can talk about things like the future and feelings. I need to learn how to communicate with her, how to trust that she's being honest with me, how to grow together.

But fuck if that isn't hard when my default mode is to keep to myself. Where she's outgoing and engaging, I'm introverted. I retreat into myself when the outside world become overwhelming. How can two people, amidst a slew of life-changing events, make it work if they can't talk about their fears?

I still don't want to tell her how much it scares me that I'll do something to push her away and be forced to watch as L.A. swallows her up, turning her back into California Barbie.

I hang my bag up in a locker and crack my neck. A hint of a smile shadows my lips. It's been too long since I've properly climbed into a ring.

The night I lost to O'Brien, my confidence shattered. I've done a shit job building it back up, too busy dealing with the emotional tidal wave of Pop's diagnosis and the financial fallout that is piling up like stones in my stomach.

The thought of Harlow leaving, fleeing back to the world she knows in L.A., heightens my anxiety and rocks the shaky ground my life is currently built on.

If I don't get my own shit together, how will I prove to Harlow that she's right where she's meant to be, in Chicago, with me?

"Hi Pop," I stride into Pop's room.

He's sitting in his recliner, a TV remote control on his lap even though the television isn't on. At the sound of my voice, he turns his head. His eyes, as light as mine are dark, swing to meet mine.

They cloud over and the dip between his brows deepens.

"Hi," he says slowly, like he doesn't know who I am even though part of him knows he should.

My stomach twists at the perplexed look on his face even as my heart breaks at the constant losses he's forced to face. Sometimes, I think it's better when he has no recollection of his life before the disease ripped it away from him. In moments like right now, when I can tell that he doesn't recognize me but understands something is amiss, his eyes widen with a flare of panic and distress coats his features.

I wonder what it's like, knowing there are all these things you don't know but should. Is it like a phantom pain like people get after losing a limb? Or is it a mental anguish you don't know how to share?

I work a swallow. "I'm Connor. I came to visit with you for a bit."

He nods, some of the fear receding from his eyes. "You can take a seat," he offers, polite rather than friendly. His hand rises slowly from the armrest of the recliner and he extends a finger toward the kitchen table, shuddering as if the small movement cost him.

I turn away, knowing it probably did. His doctor warned that movement would become harder for him as his limbs grow stiffer.

"Thanks." I collapse into one of the chairs at his tiny, round kitchen table.

"Do I know you?" he asks after a few beats of staring at me.

"Yes," I nod. "You've known me for a very long time."

He nods, dismissing the information, like now that I've confirmed our connection, it doesn't matter. "Are you married?"

"No, sir."

"Kids?"

"Nope."

"Hm," he clucks in the back of his throat, shifting his weight. "I had a wife once."

"Really?" I ask, leaning forward in my chair. I search his expression for signs of pain, for the hurt and betrayal that my mother inflicted when she left him, but any of the negative emotions I associate with my mom are absent.

Instead, a smile stretches across his mouth and he beams at me.

"Oh yes. A beautiful woman, my Linda. Dark eyes, dark hair, and a smile that could dazzle the damn devil." He laughs, his hand lifting jerkily, all five of his fingers outstretched before dropping back onto the arm rest.

I grin back even though my throat tightens and my stomach suddenly feels hallow and too slick.

Pop's quiet for a long stretch of time. I open my mouth to ask a question about his Linda, but before I can, his smile fades and a grimace appears.

I'm halfway out of my chair when he growls, "She dazzled the devil."

I clear my throat. "Are you hungry?"

"He took her from me." His eyes latch onto mine, so blue they glow. "Snatched her away." He shakes his head, the pain I was waiting for exploding in his features. "I gave her my goddamn soul, everything I had I gave to her. Everything she wanted I did." He frowns and blinks. "Do you have a wife?"

"No, sir." I sigh, my body so tense, my muscles ache.

"You're better off," Pop advises, not knowing how much his words rattle me.

They shouldn't. I know he doesn't realize what he's saying, the implications of his words. He doesn't even know who I am in this moment, or the relationship I'm developing with Harlow. But his words, coupled with his expression, cause dread to expand in my stomach until it's crashing over me like a monsoon.

"You'll give her the world and she'll steal all the light. All that's left is the goddamn dark," he mumbles, nodding along with his words.

"Are you hungry?" I ask again.

Pop looks up, staring at me with confusion. "Do I know you?"

I blink back the tears that collect in the corners of my eyes and say, "I'm Connor. I came to visit with you for a bit."

17

HARLOW

"Thank you so much, Ria. That sounds great." I twist my nose ring as I jot down the information Ria rattles off. "Eli will be there."

When I hang up the phone, I glance over Eli's calendar. His events and interviews are stacking up. Everyone wants a piece of him before the premiere. I know that if the premiere is a success, there will be even more calls to field afterwards. Leaning back on my couch, I stack my feet on the coffee table and call Eli's publicist, Helen.

"Hi Harlow," she answers warmly.

"Hey! How are you?"

"Pretty good. Let me guess, Eli's schedule is filling up?"

"Yes," I laugh. "I don't know why everyone is connecting with me. I keep telling them to contact you directly."

She chuckles. "Because they know you're too kind to blow them off. Plus, you've got that Southern charm going for you."

Rolling my eyes, I pick up the notebook with my notes. "Eli's had two more interview requests." I give her the information. "I'm scheduling his tailor for the morning after he lands in L.A. Do you want to discuss his look for the premiere?"

"Absolutely. I'm shooting you the talking points for his interview with John Stein from *Timeless Corner* magazine now."

"Great. They're meeting at the Four Seasons on Friday."

"Yes, perfect," Helen agrees. "Okay, for the premiere, I want to tone it down a little. Something a little trendier and edgier than the clean, classic look that Eli usually wears."

"Okay," I say, scribbling more notes.

"He definitely needs a jacket and suit pants, but more trendy than timeless. Since Eli's attending this premiere as co-director instead of an actor, I want his look to stand out too."

"No black on black?"

"No. I definitely want him to have a pop of color somewhere."

"Statement with his shoes?"

"Exactly! It's like you're reading my mind."

I chuckle. "How about I pull some things together and send you some photos and we can talk about them?"

"That's great. Consult with his stylist as well. We can have some pieces pulled by the end of the week."

"Sounds good. And for his meeting with Stein, any specific look?"

"No, he can pick out his own clothes that day."

We both laugh.

"Okay Helen, I'll touch base with you later this week." Once I click off, I send some emails to Eli before contacting his stylist, Sophia.

This is the fun part of my job. Sure, on the day-to-day, it's a lot of organizing and coordinating. But sometimes I offer input on looks and styles, on talking points and interview engagement, and for a few seconds, I pretend I'm a publicist instead of a glorified P.A. with a "manager" title.

Besides, talking with Helen and Sophia always invigorates me by offering glimpses of what the future holds if I work hard enough, if I want it badly enough.

By the time I hang up with Sophia, it's nearing dinnertime. I blow out a sigh, stand from the couch, and walk into the kitchen. Dipping into the refrigerator turns out to be disappointing as I have nothing to eat and I suck at cooking.

I pour a glass of water and consider messaging Zoe since I know she'll invite me over for dinner, but I don't want to take advantage of her and Eli's hospitality. Instead, I pick up my phone and text Connor.

Me: Hey! Dinner tonight?

Connor: Hi, sorry, I can't. Visiting Pop.

Me: Want to hang after?

Connor: Rain check? I have an early morning.

Me: Sure, no worries. See you tomorrow?

Connor: Tomorrow is nuts. See you at Eli's BBQ Saturday?

Disappointment settles in my stomach at his brush-off. I haven't seen Connor for two days and although I know we're both busy with work, I can't help but worry if things are good between us. Coming off a bad breakup where I was blindsided by Bryce's cheating has me on edge in the relationship department.

I can't place what happened with Bryce on Connor. The fastest way to ruin a budding relationship? Needing constant reassurance and acting like a stage-five clinger.

I stare at the door to my refrigerator. My stomach grumbles and I sigh. I really need to make new friends. But in the meantime...

I pick my phone back up and message Evan, Eli's brother.

We've known each other for years and haven't had the chance to properly catch up since I've moved to Chicago.

Me: Hey Evan. I know this is super short notice but any chance you want to grab a bite for dinner?

He replies moments later and relief skates through me that I won't have to eat another meal alone like I have for the past two nights.

Evan: Hi Low! Ollie and I are having a steak dinner in about thirty minutes. Can you make it here by then?

I grin at his invitation.

Me: I'll bring the wine.

Evan: See you soon.

Eager to get out of my apartment after working all day, I quickly change and run a comb through my hair. Grabbing a bottle of wine, pretty much the only thing I've stocked up on, I swipe my purse off the table and lock the door behind me.

Evan doesn't live near an L stop, so I grab an Uber to his house. The summer breeze blows through the back windows of my Uber ride as the bustle of Chicago gives way to quieter streets and larger homes. Pulling up to Evan's massive, contemporary home, the driver lets out a low whistle and I laugh. "He's a lawyer."

Before I even make it up the steps to the front door, it swings wide open and Ollie appears, waving. "Hi Harlow!"

"Hey man!" I grin at him, bending down to kiss the top of his head. Slugging an arm around his shoulder, I ask, "How are you?"

"Good."

"Having a fun summer?"

He nods enthusiastically. "My soccer team is playing in a big tournament this weekend."

"That's good. What position do you play again?"

Ollie leads me into the house. "Forward."

"Hey, that was my position too." I kick off my sandals and drop my purse on the bench inside the foyer.

"You played soccer?" Ollie asks with wide eyes.

"Sure did."

Ollie rattles off a bunch of questions as we move toward the back deck.

"Hey Low," Evan waves with a pair of tongs, manning the grill, as Ollie and I step outside.

"Hey!" I hold up the bottle of wine.

"Bad day?" he smirks.

I shrug. Today isn't a bad day…it's an off day. I have no idea what to make of it other than I don't want to wallow through it alone.

"Corkscrew and wine glasses are in the bar." He gestures toward the house and I lope back inside to grab them.

When I return with two glasses of vino, Ollie is kicking a soccer ball around the yard, running drills.

"He's really good," I comment, taking a sip of my wine as I watch Ollie dribble through cones.

"He's crazy committed. A hell of a lot more than I was at his age," Evan explains, taking the steaks off the grill.

The deck is the perfect backyard oasis. A large table with chairs sits on a carpet in the center of the deck, shaded by a large umbrella. Firefly lights wrap around the entire deck, casting a soft glow as dusk settles. The space overlooks an expansive, manicured lawn with a jungle gym and soccer goal for Ollie.

"You have the perfect set up back here." I take another sip of my wine. The bold flavor explodes in my mouth and I settle into my chair.

Evan nods slowly, squinting out over the yard. "Ollie, time to eat."

"Five minutes, Dad!" Ollie hollers back, restarting his drill.

Evan sighs, placing a plate down in front of me and sliding into the seat across from me.

"This looks amazing." I pick up my fork, glancing at the steak, double baked potato, and asparagus.

"*Bon appetit*." Evan lifts his wine glass and I clink mine against his. "Cheers."

"Cheers." I cut into my steak. "How've you been? I've barely seen you since I moved here."

He sighs again, scrubbing a hand over his face. "Good. Busy. Work's been insane."

"Isn't it always?"

He nods, one side of his mouth tipping up but the smile is for show, it doesn't reach his eyes at all. As one of Chicago's top criminal defense lawyers, Evan has been busy since I met him nearly six years ago. He's always on his grind, hustling to balance the pressures of work with the responsibilities of being a full-time, single dad.

"Seeing anyone?" I try again, hoping he's at least managed to secure a few dates in his hectic schedule.

He chuckles, the sound dark and humorless. Chewing a bit of steak, he shakes his head and swallows. "No time for it."

I quirk an eyebrow.

"I'm serious," he insists, piercing me with his bright green eyes. "My job, my life, all of it, lately, each day is like trying to survive. I get to the end of the day, collapse into my bed, and I'm just grateful I made it. I don't have the extra energy to put into a relationship with a woman that's going to be a dead end."

"How do you know it will be a dead end?" I whisper, unprepared for the bitterness in his tone.

"How could it not be?" he shoots back. "After Charlie…"

I wince, knowing the relationship between Evan and Charlie took off just as quickly as it burned out. Both my friends seem scarred by their whirlwind romance, but neither of them likes to admit it. "You still care about her?"

His eyes snap to mine, swirling with conflicting emotions. He nods once, curt-like. "Of course I care about her."

"So…?"

He gestures to the yard where Ollie is whooping and running around. "My life is here. She's got her entire future in front of her. When we were together, I couldn't give her what she wanted. Now that she's had a taste of freedom, life in Manhattan, she's definitely not going to want anything I could offer. Besides, I'm not cut out for a real relationship anymore." He fixes me with a solemn stare. "Whatever is going on between you and Connor —" he lifts a hand, pausing the interruption on the tip of my tongue, "whatever it is, Low, you need to decide if you're in it for the long haul or not. The sooner you decide, the better off you'll be. Because, like me, Connor's life is here. He's got his gym, his career, his pop…"

He shakes his head again, placing his fork down next to his plate. "I knew Chicago wasn't it for Charlie. You need to decide if this life here is going to be enough for you. If life with Connor is going to be enough." He says the last words softly, his eyes distant, as if he's not talking about Connor and me at all.

A lump of emotion, of complicated feelings and frustrations, swells in my throat. I pick up my wine glass and take a long drink, trying to wash it away.

18

CONNOR

"Here he is!" Eli announces as I step into his backyard. I grin, throwing an arm around my best friend and slapping his back. "Sorry I'm late, man."

"Nah, there's no time on these things. How's Cameron?"

"Okay," I say, not wanting to admit that Pop's health is deteriorating by the day. His arms and legs are failing him, his anxiety is spiking, and some mornings he doesn't have any recollections of his life. The onset of his symptoms was sudden, but now, the changes in his body and personality are occurring so rapidly, I can't keep up.

I don't tell Eli that. Not today, when he's hosting a BBQ for his friends, when he's created a good-time vibe that shouldn't be ruined by the depressing thoughts running through my head.

"Hey!" I greet Zoe instead, pulling her into a hug before I shake hands with Evan and toss Ollie into the air. It seems like the only way I managed to make it through this week was by keeping myself engaged, busy. There's no way I can stop now.

"Connor!" Harlow calls out, appearing before me like a mirage.

I swallow, placing Ollie back on his feet. He scurries off, yelling something about a soccer game. I grin at my girl, missing her even though she's standing in front of me. "Hi, Low." I reach forward to tuck a strand of hair behind her ear and pull her in for a quick kiss. "I missed you, baby. This week has been hell."

At my words, she relaxes in my arms and I feel like an ass for keeping her on edge all week. But being with Harlow means being honest, and I haven't wanted to be forthcoming with all the shit swirling in my mind. So I've kept busy, but busy without Harlow.

"I missed you too." She squeezes me tighter. "How's your dad?"

I shrug, keeping the smirk pasted on my face even though it's desperate to slip. "How was your week? Everything ready for Eli's premiere?"

Harlow's eyes narrow, a flash of green, but she lets me off the hook. "My week was busy, but awesome. I've been working closely with Helen for the premiere, and it's been so…" she pauses, a grin spreading across her face, "fulfilling, you know? I'm learning so much more and it's just exciting to have a larger role behind-the-scenes. But yeah, things are coming along and will be good to go in the next week. The big thing is finalizing interviews for Eli and prepping him for them."

As she talks, I lead her over to a large cooler I know Eli stocked with beer. I hold one out for Harlow. She shakes her head, so I pop the cap with a bottle opener and take a long swig.

The beer is cold and refreshing and centers me after such a crappy week.

"I'm glad you're enjoying the work, babe." I say, smacking my lips.

The brightness of her eyes dims a little, but she nods. "Yeah, it's —" her phone beeps and she pauses, pulling it from her pocket. Whatever she reads on the screen causes her to chuckle as her fingers fly over the keypad.

"What's going on?" I ask, curious and slightly irritated that this is the first time I've seen her all week and she's this distracted by a message.

Because you haven't been distracted at all...

I take another swig of my beer, knowing I'm being unfair.

"Nothing, sorry." She shakes her head, still smiling. "My friends are trying to get me to extend our visit to L.A."

"Extend?" My tone is harsher than I intend.

I wince as she glances up. Her expression is slightly bewildered as she frowns at me.

"Of course you should extend if you want to spend more time with your friends," I blurt out.

"You don't want to stay longer?"

I raise the bottle to my lips and take another long drink. "I can't, babe. I can't leave Pop any longer than the weekend."

Harlow cringes, embarrassed. "Right, I'm sorry. I didn't even—"

"It's cool," I cut her off to put her out of her misery. Of course she's excited about the premiere, seeing her friends, being back in L.A. Just because my life is circling the drain doesn't mean everyone else's has stopped moving forward.

An awkward silence stretches between us. It should worry me. In the past, silences like this put me on edge. But right now, after the week I've had, I'm too tired to read much into it.

"I don't have to stay," Harlow says after a beat.

I flash her a quick grin. "You do you, babe. Whatever you

want." I flip my chin toward one of Eli's friends I haven't seen in a while. "I'm going to go say hello. You want a drink?"

She clears her throat, staring at me. "No."

"You good?" I ask after another stretch of silence.

"Yeah."

"'Kay." I tug the end of her hair before I escape to where Eli and his friends are talking.

Extend my stay in L.A.? The thought is so ludicrous I almost laugh out loud.

"Hey man," I say in greeting to Eli's friend Karim.

"Hi, Connor, how's it going?" Karim grins, slapping me on the shoulder and gesturing at his friend. "This is my buddy, Carlo."

"Hey, man." Carlo extends a hand and I shake it.

"Carlo, wait a minute, you know Harlow, don't you?" Eli asks, his eyes swinging from Sam to Harlow and back again. "She used to be my P.A. but now she's managing my life." He chuckles as Carlo nods.

"Shit, yeah. I haven't seen Harlow in like, a year. She's here?" Carlo asks, peering around Eli. When his gaze lands on Low, his grin widens and his tongue darts out, swiping over his lower lip.

Everything about this guy, from his designer shirt to the ridiculous Rolex gleaming from his wrist, pisses me off. But the way he looks at Low, like she's a goddamn steak instead of my girl, causes fury to flood my bloodstream.

"She's here," Eli points her out, oblivious to how his friend is practically salivating over Harlow.

"Let me go say hey," he says, smacking the back of his hand against Karim's shoulders before he slides his sunglasses over his eyes and strides toward Harlow.

I narrow my gaze, hating the way Harlow's face lights up

when she sees Carlo. He wraps his arms around her and hugs her close, for several seconds longer than necessary. When Harlow steps out of his grasp, both of them speak at the same time. Harlow's laughter, light and breathy, meets my ears and darkens my mood.

"How're things at the gym, man? Still training?" Karim asks and I'm forced to look away from Harlow and refocus on Karim.

Silently cursing myself for leaving Harlow, I mutter, "Gym's okay. Nah, not anymore. I had a career-ending concussion a few months ago."

"Shit," Karim swears. "I'm sorry, dude. That blows."

"Yeah."

Across from me, Eli's brows furrow and I know he's asking me if I'm okay. I tip my chin at him, excusing myself to use the bathroom.

The heat of the day suddenly seems unbearable. Sweat drips between my shoulder blades. I swipe another beer, swigging half the contents. Harlow's still talking to Carlo. She looks so carefree, so happy, so in her goddamn element while I'm completely on edge.

Maddie and Ollie play with other kids in the yard. A guy Eli hired is at the grill, flipping chicken wings and steaks. The women mill about with wine glasses in their hands. Everyone is smiling and unwinding, chatting and laughing.

Everyone except me.

Watching Harlow effortlessly engage in conversation with this dick who keeps touching her unnecessarily, a tap to her forearm, a caress to her shoulder, has my stomach in knots. This guy is encroaching all over her and she's oblivious.

She's pure sunshine while I feel like a solar eclipse, a dark shadow who's going to stamp out her light.

I'm staring at her, grimacing, when her gaze collides with

mine. Her smile widens and she waves me over. "Carlo, have you met my boyfriend, Connor?"

Carlo's expression never slips as his eyes swing to mine, but there's a tightness to his jaw I don't care for. "Yeah, we just met. Didn't know you guys were together. I mean, I know things with Bryce…"

"Yeah," Harlow's smile slides straight off her face at the mention of Bryce.

"Look, Harlow, sorry I brought it up…" This fucking guy wraps his hand around her elbow again.

She drops her head to my shoulder for a minute. I know I should slip an arm around her waist, provide her some comfort as she works through her feelings about Bryce's betrayal in front of this loser. Instead, I fucking hate that she has any feelings toward Bryce at all.

I widen my stance, knowing I'm coming off like a dick too but too far past caring.

"Carlo's going to be at the premiere too. We were just talking about the after party," Harlow explains.

"Yeah." He slides his hand from her elbows to her wrist and I feel the muscles in my arms clench, some of my knuckles popping as my hands curl into fists. "Hey, if you guys are in town afterwards, I'm having a dinner at Shark on Tuesday. You should come." He extends the invitation to both of us, but his eyes are glued to Harlow's.

"Ooh, I love Shark! Haven't been there in ages. Thanks, Carlo. If we stick around, I'll let you know," Harlow answers breezily. I know she doesn't mean anything by it.

Carlo's smile widens, and he flicks me a knowing look I'd like to punch right off his face.

I clear my throat, relieved that Zoe steps into our little huddle and engages Harlow in conversation.

I need to get out of here. I shouldn't have come. I'm not

in the right headspace for this. Everyone is acting like things are fun and easy. Everyone is relaxing and enjoying the BBQ, the goddamn summer which is the worst of my entire life.

I feel like I'm about to snap, coiled too tightly from the stress of this week, from the realization that my time with Pop is even more limited than I realized. From having to admit that Harlow shines brighter than the damn Hollywood sign.

In the past, I always knew she was too big for my world. But right now, coming face to face with it, hearing the excitement in her voice when she speaks about the premiere, about working with Helen, about going to L.A., it's like a slap in the face. Witnessing her gab it up with Carlo is like a damn sucker punch. Her world is always going to be larger than the tiny corner I occupy.

Understanding explodes in my mind like a volcano.

I need her right now. I need her so badly, I ache for her. She centers me, comforts me, and gives me something to hope for.

But for her, my need is limiting and restrictive. It closes up her world and makes her future smaller. It's the perfect breeding ground for resentment. Hell, I'm already resenting the hell out of myself for not being the man she needs me to be. The man she fucking deserves.

For the second time in ten minutes, I clear my throat and excuse myself, heading back to the goddamn cooler.

19

HARLOW

Connor's been distant.

Not only do I feel like he's avoiding me, but when we're together, he's lost in his own head. I'm not sure if he's worried about Cyanide, the launch, his dad, or things between us. Whatever it is, I hate that he's pulling away from me.

Eli's words ring in my mind about not letting him put distance between us. And yet, it's already happening. We're flying to L.A. in six days for the premiere and I've been busy with my own crazy schedule.

Since Eli suggested I help out with some of the PR for the premiere, I've been working with Helen to finalize his interviews and photo ops. The opportunity has been a dream come true. Helen's included me in conversations about talking points and even let me have a go at drafting a press release. Handling all the logistics, throwing myself into any of the tasks Helen engages me in, and ensuring that Eli's personal brand is consistent with the event, has me working late into the night. There are so many working parts that need to perfectly come together in order to do my job well.

In addition to work, I've been fielding phone calls from

my family and friends in L.A. asking how long I'll be in town for after the premiere. The thought of extending my stay fills me with mixed emotions. On one hand, it's comforting to know I can spend a night kicked back, drinking beers with Jack, or blow off steam dancing at a nightclub with my friends. But the thought also fills me with nerves. How will Connor react? Will he be upset if I stay longer? Will he be comfortable around my family and friends? Can he handle Mom's subtle jabs at his career choices?

Burying my face in my hands, I blow out a sigh.

I'm good, I've got this.

I stand from the table and fill a glass of water from the kitchen faucet, my eyes narrowing as it continues to leak after I turn it off.

"Seriously?" I grumble at the faucet which drips in response.

I swear, smacking my palm against the edge of the countertop.

"This is not a big deal," I remind myself. Deep down, I know it isn't. But on top of all the things I need to do to get through today, the leaky faucet feels like an omen of difficult times ahead. Turning my back so I don't have to watch the incessant dripping, I block it out and run through today's to-do list.

Call the tailor about my dress. Work out. Prep Eli for his big interviews. Connect with three different people in L.A. about appearances Eli is making. Run through—

A knock on my door interrupts my thoughts and saves me from contemplating how I'm going to get everything done before my flight. Deep down, I always know everything will get done, yet I can't help but agonize over it until the last minute, when I'm wheels up and ready to crash from exhaustion.

I pull open my door, relieved to see Connor standing on the other side. "Hey."

He's wearing a T-shirt with the arms cut off and a pair of cargo shorts. His work boots are caked with mud, his shirt stained with sweat.

"Hey," he replies, stepping inside my place and toeing off his boots.

"What's going on?" I look up at him, tilting my head and crossing my arms across my chest. "I thought we were getting together later?" I wince when I realize how defensive I sound. Why? Things between Connor and I were going so great and now, since Eli's BBQ, it's like we're a little off-balance and neither one of us knows the right steps to take to keep from capsizing.

"We are," he says. "I just, I had some time and I wanted to see you."

"Oh," I brighten, snuffing out the flicker of panic in my mind about the time I'm about to lose on my to-do list. "I'm glad you came by." I step forward, wrapping my arms around him.

He grabs my upper arms and steps out of my embrace. "I'm disgusting, Low. Don't ruin whatever designer dress you're wearing."

I swallow, hurt by his brush-off. Dropping my gaze to the floor, I try to rein in my emotions.

"Look, I didn't mean…" Connor trails off. His fingers come under my chin and he lifts my face to his. "I'm in a piss-poor mood. I'm sorry."

"Did something happen?" I ask, noticing the purple half-moons stamped under his eyes. He looks more exhausted than usual.

Connor sighs, closing his eyes and cracking his knuckles. "Pop had a really rough night. They're getting more frequent, more intense. Just…worse. I was there as soon as they would let me in at four this morning and then I had to get to the gym to train Jay before going to my construction job. I'm just glad we finished early today. I gotta shower and head back to Pop. I know we said dinner, but can we get together late? I want to eat with Pop."

"Connor, why didn't you call me?" I ask, horrified that this is the first time I'm learning about his dad. "It's 4PM."

"I didn't want to bother you. I know you have a lot going on." He yawns, pinching the bridge of his nose as if to wake himself up.

"Come here," I open my arms, stepping forward again. "I don't give a shit about this dress. I just want to be with you."

This time, he melts into my embrace. I tighten my hold around his waist, laying my ear against his heart so I can listen to the soothing rhythm of his heartbeat. "Is your dad okay?"

"Yeah." His hand runs down the length of my hair. "Just a rough night," he murmurs the words but I'm not sure if he's trying to convince me, or himself, of their truth.

"I'm sorry."

"It is what it is."

Silence hangs between us and I focus on the sounds of our breathing.

"I hate that things have been awkward between us," I finally admit.

Connor sighs, his hand cupping the back of my head. "It's my fault."

"No." I shift to glance up at him. "It's been me too. I've felt you pulling away and I didn't do anything to pull you back to me. I didn't know what to do."

Connor nods, licking his lips. "I knew this was going to happen."

"What?"

He chews the corner of his mouth, his eyes darkening the way they do when he's frustrated. "We barely spoke for two years and then, in two weeks, we're back in each other's beds, talking about the future. It's just…it's a lot."

"What are you saying?" I ask, my stomaching tightening until I feel like I could double over.

"I'm saying, I'm fucking this up with you and I don't know how not to."

"Just, say what you mean. Be straight with me."

"I'm worried about L.A." he whispers, his voice breaking.

"The premiere? Why?"

"I've never left Pop before. Not since his diagnosis."

My heart sinks and I realize that while I've been hinting to Connor that I want to extend my stay in L.A. to be with my family, he's been agonizing over leaving his dad for even twenty-four hours. "Connor, I'm sorry."

"No, don't be. You should go spend time with your family and friends. Of course you should. It's just that I can't extend my stay. And the thought of you being there, partying with your friends, seeing Bryce, eating dinner with that slimy Carlo, it makes me uncomfortable. But that's my fucking issue, not yours. I don't want to make you feel badly about it. Or guilty. So, instead, I just…"

"Said nothing at all."

He shrugs.

"We need to be honest with each other," I remind him.

"I know."

"I don't know how you're feeling if you don't tell me."

"Yeah."

"I understand if you don't want to come to L.A., but I would love for you to be my date to the premiere if things settle down with your dad."

Connor lifts his mouth in a wry grin. "Me too."

I hold out my hand, which he takes. "Come on." I drag him toward the bathroom.

I flip on the shower, pulling my dress over my head as steam fills the small space.

"What are you doing?" Connor asks, his hands at the button of his shorts.

I unclasp my bra. "Showering with you. We need to make the most of the time we have. I know we've both been busy, but I don't want to let you just pull away."

"You're not. Sometimes, I don't know what to do with all the things I feel for you, Low. I'm so fucking scared I'm going to mess it up that I'm messing it up."

"Self-fulfilling prophecy?" I reach forward to unbutton Connor's shorts for him.

"Or self-sabotage."

I inhale sharply at his confession. Glancing up at him, I see the severity in his expression and it scrapes at me. "Don't do that. Don't give up on us before we have a chance."

"I won't. Just don't give up on me. Please. I swear, I'm trying to work through all the shit in my head. I need you, Low. I need you so much more than you need me."

"That's not true. I need you too, Connor."

"I don't know why L.A. is proving to be such a big hurdle, but it is."

"I'm not going anywhere. I'm here for you." I give him a hard look before stepping into the shower. Connor follows a moment later.

Steam and heat rise between us as the water streams over my hair, causing it to hang over my shoulders, stick to my upper back. Connor steps forward, pushing my hair out of my face. Droplets of water cling to his forearms, his hard chest, slide down the ridges of his abdomen.

My hands find his hips and pull him under the stream of water with me.

Cocooned together, the hesitation of earlier, the misgivings between us, evaporate. I focus on the present, on standing in the shower with this incredible man who owns my heart and inspires my soul.

"I'm sorry, baby," he whispers against my skin, his hands sliding up my back, his fingers latching in my hair.

"I'm sorry too."

He shifts, his nose brushing against mine, before he kisses me. His mouth is hard and unyielding. His kiss is desperate and hot. I wrap my arms around his neck, pulling myself up onto my tip toes, my breasts pressing into his chest. He growls, lifting me until my legs wind around his torso. With one hand, he holds me, while his other arm braces against the shower wall.

"This part was always easy for us," I murmur before his lips find mine once more.

He crushes his mouth against mine and I drop my head back, reveling in the onslaught of his possessiveness. His apology. His need.

When his mouth moves down my neck, my head collides with the shower wall. Still, Connor shifts me higher in his arms until he latches onto my breast and I buck against him.

My fingers grip his shoulder blades, pure muscle and coiled tension.

His mouth is desperate. There is nothing gentle in his touch. Instead, it's like he's trying to convince me of his fervor for me. I melt under his mouth, desperate for more. For everything.

"We just struggle with the emotional part," I mutter, my eyes closed as the hot water envelopes me.

Connor stops his delicious exploration of my body. My

eyes pop open and I find his gaze, my breath stuttering in my chest.

His eyes are black, his expression severe. For a moment, he looks like he was carved from marble instead of flesh and blood standing before me. His lip curls, his eyes bleed and I wait, my body craving his touch, my heart yearning for his truth.

"I never struggled with it, Harlow."

I swallow.

Drops of water sluice across Connor's face. He looks so sexy, so untouchable, so intense, like a warrior preparing for the ultimate battle. He works a swallow and his eyes pierce my soul.

"I love you, Harlow Reid. I love you so fucking much, I'm petrified."

His words rock through me and a joy I've never known, a relief larger than the Milky Way, explodes inside of me. I open my mouth to tell him my truth but Connor's mouth slams over mine. Our kissing turns frantic, our fingers gripping, our hands feeling, our mouths tasting.

Connor makes love to me in the shower. I It's savage and desperate and so fucking real it simultaneously hurts and soothes. He claims me as his and I make him mine and we declare each other until we're us.

Complicated. Determined. Reckless. Authentic. And so true that I know with certainty no man ever has or ever will own my soul like Connor Scott.

20

CONNOR

Toweling off in Harlow's bathroom, I already feel better than I did when I got the call at three-thirty this morning.

Pop's condition is worsening, and watching pieces of his memory and personality fade away is agonizing. It makes me shudder to think about what the future will be like without him. Several of the nurses at his care facility have encouraged me to speak to a therapist, but the thought alone makes my stomach feel funny. What the hell would I tell a therapist that isn't glaringly obvious? I'm scared my pop is going to forget me completely and disappear from my life the same way my mom did, albeit under entirely different circumstances. I'm petrified that when he takes his last breath, I won't know how to move on without him. Swallowing the bitter truth, I pull on the clean sweats and T-shirt I left at Harlow's last week.

"How you doing?" she asks as I enter the kitchen. Her hair is wrapped in a towel, her long legs on display since she's wearing the tiniest shorts known to humankind.

"Better," I smile at her, gratefully accepting the mug of tea she passes me.

"I don't keep Dr. Pepper around."

"You're a smart woman."

"I am that." She tilts her head toward her living room and I follow her, taking the seat next to her on the couch. "Can I bring you and your dad some dinner tonight?"

My neck swivels toward her. "Huh?"

"I understand if you don't want me to. And I don't want to encroach on your time with Cameron. But, I'd like to see him again. It's been a long time and he...well, I have a lot of memories of him."

My throat clogs with unexpected emotion and I swallow it back down. Jesus, what is wrong with me? Ever since Harlow showed back up in my life, my emotions have been running rampant, catching me off guard and pissing me off. I used to be a fearless fighter. I didn't take anyone's shit and I didn't spend hours of precious time thinking about other people's feelings. Now, I can't rip my thoughts away from Harlow. I can't tear myself away from the depressing, foreboding truth about Pop.

Harlow's hand slips into mine. I look down, surprised by how fragile and small her fingers are compared to mine. Still, she has so much more of a quiet strength than I possess and I hate that I keep drawing from it.

"I'd like that," I say finally, figuring that after last night, Harlow's presence can only serve to cheer Pop up.

"I love you too, you know."

My gaze snaps to hers.

Her expression is serene, her eyes glistening. "I've loved you for such a long time that it's hard for me to reconcile your words toward me now with your words from before. It makes me nervous about trusting your feelings for me. I hate feeling needy, like I constantly need reassurance from you that you really care about me, that you love me.

But I do. I don't just need the actions. I need the words too."

"Harlow." I reach up to cup her cheek. "I'm so fucking sorry I keep messing things up between us. I swear, I'm trying. But that doesn't seem like enough. Not when you're confused about how much I care for you. Not when you feel like you can't trust me."

Her hand wraps around my wrist, keeping me anchored to her cheek as she leans into my touch. "We need to do better, Connor."

"I know. I will."

"I want this weekend to be fun for us. Let's go to L.A. and dive into it. Just a weekend of good times without all of this stress and uncertainty and fear. Remember how much fun it was when we would just be together?"

"It still is."

"I know. But this weekend, let's lose ourselves in it."

Biting the corner of my mouth, I nod as I memorize the lines of her face. Beautiful and smart and so damn soulful, Harlow Reid keeps extending me chances. This time, I won't disappoint her.

"Okay."

I'M VISITING with Pop for about forty minutes when a soft knock comes from his door.

"Linda? That you?" Pop asks, calling out my mother's name.

I wince, my throat tightening. Even as his mind slips, he remembers her. Some things truly aren't fair. She isn't deserving of this honor, and he isn't deserving of the pain and disappointment that her absence continues to cause.

"Nope. It's me." Harlow pushes into the room, balancing take-out boxes on her open palm.

I bite back a grin when I see them. Harlow is many things. A cook isn't one of them.

"Oh, well, hello there," Pop greets her, his eyes clear although I can tell from his expression he doesn't remember her. However, after last night, the fact that he is calm and chatting is a miracle in itself.

I stand to take the boxes from Harlow, murmuring thanks, and place them down on a table.

"Pop, this is Harlow."

"Reid." He snaps his fingers. Surprise flickers across Harlow's expression as my breath gets stuck in my lungs.

He remembers her. Maybe just for this one second, but that is more than enough.

Right now, he knows her.

"Yes, I'm Harlow Reid," Harlow says, sticking out a hand.

But Pop opens his arms and she dips down to give him a hug.

"I remember you, darling. You were the first one to catch my boy's heart." He guffaws loudly, an entirely different person than twenty-four hours ago.

Harlow giggles, Pop's smile widens, and a strange mixture of relief and elation swell in my chest. He really remembers her. Me. Us.

"I like the sound of that, sir. How are you doing?" Harlow asks, taking a seat on the other side of Pop. She leans toward him and he turns more in her direction. Before I know it, the two of them are deep in conversation.

Flabbergasted, I plop back down in my chair as my head swivels between them like I'm watching a damn tennis match.

He doesn't just remember her – he likes her. He's always liked her.

Harlow's laughing at something Pop says, her eyes bright, her shoulders relaxed. "He didn't!" she gasps.

Pop nods seriously, "He did. Ruined Mrs. Hart's entire flower bed."

"Connor!" Harlow scolds me, mirth dancing in her expression.

I grin. Pop is recalling a story from when I was a kid and dug up our neighbor, Mrs. Hart's, flowers, convinced there was treasure buried beneath.

"What did you do?" Harlow turns back to Pop.

He shrugs, "What else could I do? We had to replant them. That's when I learned about my green thumb, you know?" He shows his thumb to Harlow as she nods along. "Started my own garden the following spring."

"That's fantastic. My mom never gardened, but my grand-mother had a green thumb too."

"Oh yeah? Where does she live?"

"In Georgia," Harlow says, not mentioning that her grandparents passed years ago.

"Hm," Pop comments, nodding as he stares at her.

Several moments pass. I see the shift as it happens. His hands inch closer toward the center of his body, his expression changes, growing harder. His eyes cloud over, as if he's trying to hold onto a thought but he can't quite grasp it.

Harlow opens her mouth to say something, but Pop cuts her off.

"I'm sorry, dear. What's your name?" he asks. My stomach sinks.

Harlow doesn't waver for an instant. She smiles and responds, "Harlow Reid, sir. It's lovely to see you today."

Pop nods slowly, murmuring to himself.

"Would you like some supper, Mr. Scott?" she asks gently, reverting to formalities. Every time she saw Pop, he insisted that she call him Cameron, the way all my friends did. But now, she knows Cameron will seem too familiar for him. Now, he's Mr. Scott.

Pop smiles and Harlow stands to fix him a plate.

Inside, my heart aches and my body feels cold.

He's slipping away and there isn't a goddamn thing I can do about it. The truth hurts. Almost as much as knowing that without Pop, I don't have anyone in the world to call mine. I'll be an orphan. Yeah, that's not a big deal at thirty-one, but it's still not a reality I considered until this moment.

It still hurts.

Harlow carries a plate over to Pop's recliner where he sits and eats his dinner, lost in his own mind.

"Come eat," she beckons to me, pointing to the plate she made me.

Her generosity, so unexpected and sincere, expands the feelings I'm grappling with. The back of my throat stings, my eyes burn, and I have no appetite.

"Thanks, Low," I manage to say, sitting down on the chair she pulled out for me. I push the salad and Italian sausage and peppers around my plate, unable to eat any of it.

"I like Fredo's sausage and peppers best," Pop comments after a moment.

Harlow's expression softens, her eyes so tender, I want to reach over and hug her. "I remember," she says quietly to Pop.

He makes a noncommittal sound and finishes his plate.

After dinner, I can tell he's growing tired. While Harlow cleans up our supper, I help Pop get ready for bed.

"Hey Pop," I say cautiously.

He fiddles with the cuff of his pajama shirt.

"I'm heading out of town. Just for the weekend," I remind him for the eighth time this week. "You going to be okay? I'll be here tomorrow but I just want to remind you that for two days, I won't see you."

He waves a hand dismissively, shuffling toward his bed. "Hand me the remote, will ya?" He asks, easing his body down until he's seated on the mattress.

I pass him the remote control.

He stares at the blank television screen for a long minute.

"Want to watch something specific?" I ask.

He looks at me, his eyebrows furrowed. "Have fun in California, Connor," he smirks, his old self suddenly appearing. I hold my breath, unsure how long he'll see me and remember. "Don't come back without your girl," he chuckles, flipping on the television.

Within a few minutes, he's engrossed with the program. Harlow and I slip out of his small apartment quarters.

After saying goodnight to reception, we step into the parking lot.

It suddenly dawns on me that Pop's facility is a ways from the nearest L stop. "You walked all the way here?"

"It was nice. The weather's beautiful."

"Carrying all those boxes?"

She smiles at me, wrapping her arms around my arm and squeezing. "It was nice to see your dad again."

"Thank you for tonight. For dinner. For coming," I murmur, guiding her to my truck.

The heat of the day has receded and a welcome breeze kicks up around us.

I pull open the passenger door and Harlow stills. She tugs on the front of my shirt until I dip. She presses a hard kiss against my lips. "It's okay to be emotional, you know?"

"I know." I clear my throat, knowing she caught how unsteady I was during our visit with Pop.

She leans closer, lowering her voice. "You can even cry."

I snort.

She offers me a knowing, gentle smile. "I love you, Connor Scott. I love the man you are now more than the guy I fell for years ago."

21

HARLOW

Connor's whistle cuts through the air. His eyes widen, his mouth tipped up in a smile. He's looking at me like I'm the most exquisite creature he's ever seen, and my heart feels like it's going to burst.

I beam at him. "Thank you, kind sir," I extend my hand to his as he helps me down the steps toward my mother and Kent's living room.

"You weren't kidding about this dress," Connor whispers, kissing my hair. His hands shadow my hips.

"Or these shoes. Don't let go, I may topple over," I joke, but not because my shoes are incredible. I am definitely teetering in them.

"I'll hold you the whole night, baby."

Even so, his hold on me relaxes when we reach the bottom of the stairs and my mother swoops in.

"Ah, Harlow, you look beautiful." Mom presses an air kiss to each of my cheeks as I fight the urge to roll my eyes.

"Thank you, Mom. You remember Connor?" I say, hoping she is polite.

Her gaze flicks to Connor. She stayed in her room when we arrived, not bothering to come down and welcome us to the house. Maybe it was for the best, as Connor's first interaction in the Reid-Kinsley household got to be with Jack. They clicked instantly and spent the afternoon drinking beer and goofing off in the pool while I ran around like a lunatic sorting out last-minute mishaps for Eli.

"Hello, Connor," Mom finally extends her hand but averts her gaze.

Connor takes her hand and hesitates. "Ma'am," he says finally. "It's a pleasure to meet you."

"Yes, dear," Mom pulls her hand from his hold and looks over our heads. "Kent, we really must be leaving."

Effectively dismissed, I lace my fingers with Connor's and pull him toward the front of the house where the cars are already waiting to take us to the premiere. Once we are seated and driving away from my mother's coldness, I glance at Connor.

His jaw is tight, his lips pressed in a thin line.

"I'm sorry," I whisper.

"Don't be, baby. Just be you." I hear the edge in his tone.

"We're going to have fun tonight," I say but it comes out more like a question. As if I'm already doubting that we're going to enjoy this premiere, this special night out, all dressed up in L.A.

"Of course we are," Connor says, his other hand encasing mine. He shoots me a grin. I can tell it's forced, but the fact that he's trying as hard as he is, especially after my mom's blatant repudiation, calms my nerves. "You look beautiful, Low."

"You're really rocking the shit out of that suit, Connor," I whisper back. He snickers.

The closer we get to the premiere, the more Connor's muscles lock down. I know he's nervous, feeling out of his comfort zone, and unsure of what to do or where to go when we arrive.

"Zoe's going to meet you when we get there," I remind him.

"I know."

"She'll show you where to sit and everything."

He squeezes my hand. "I got it. I know you have a job to do. Don't worry about me, I'm a big boy," he says, exasperation in his tone. My nagging is starting to irritate him.

"Okay." I silently vow to let the issue lie.

As soon as we pull up to the premiere, the swarm of bodies overwhelms the car. Photographers, journalists, paparazzi. Bright lights, video cameras, noise. Red carpet, celebrities, chaos.

I hear Connor's audible inhale but I don't comment on it. This scene is overwhelming, even for those of us seasoned in the industry. When the door opens, I slip out of the car, my gaze scanning the crowd. Relief fills my chest as soon as I spot Zoe. She makes her way to us, arriving just as the car door is closed behind Connor.

She shoots me a knowing glance, kissing my cheek in greeting.

"I'm so glad you're here," she says, clutching Connor's arm.

"You're not walking in with Eli?" Connor asks her. I hear the thread of frustration in his tone. He thinks we're all babying him because we know how much he dislikes events like these.

Zoe's hand passes over her stomach as she shakes her head. "No, he went in on his own. There are going to be enough rumors about my little baby swell without me posing for photos from every angle. I'm still in my first trimester."

"Oh, right. I'm sorry, Zoe." Connor shifts, angling his body to hide her stomach from view.

"I've got to go," I say, glancing at them.

"Go. We'll be fine." Zoe shoos me away.

"Rooting for you, beautiful," Connor kisses my lips.

While his words are sweet and the fact that he's here fills me up with a wild giddiness, the ease with which he reacts to Zoe's predicament, which I didn't realize until this moment is real and not just a ploy to put Connor at ease like I previously thought, nags at the back of my mind. In many ways, Connor and Zoe are outsiders to these events. They aren't in the industry and they don't hitch their identities to whatever is trending in the moment.

Leaving them to make their way inside, a part of me is grateful that they have either other. But I'm also frustrated that I can't soothe Connor's worries with the same ease that Zoe can.

I dislike knowing that I can't be enough for what he needs in this moment.

Sighing, I show a badge to security who lets me pass. As I work through throngs of people, I'm quickly snagged by Helen.

"Glad you're here," she says, glancing around. "We need to get Eli up front for interviews and photos."

I scan the crowd for him. "Where is he?"

Helen grimaces. "Signing autographs."

"Of course he is," I switch gears, diving headfirst into the work that needs to be done.

Bryce is phenomenal.

I hate to admit it, but there it is. Watching his performance in *Reckless Waters* tugs at something inside my chest, scraping over and over until my emotions are raw. The film is deep, ripe with all the feels, and Bryce executes perfectly.

On film, it's impossible not to fall a little bit in love with him. Or rather, the character he is playing.

My mind is captivated, my body on edge. I'm utterly transfixed.

Too late, I realize Connor is more focused on me than the film. His pinkie finger grazes along my forearm and I swallow, coming back to the moment.

I turn toward him. His eyes gleam in the darkened theater but it's impossible to read them.

"You okay?" he whispers. I know he's asking because of Bryce. The concern he shows me, even when I know how much he can't stand Bryce, causes shame to burn in my chest.

Here I am, at a film premiere, dressed up, ready for a wild night out, and at my side is the man I've always wanted. I used to dream for a moment like this and instead of reveling in it, I'm letting the guy who made me into a pathetic meme get inside my head.

Through a freaking film.

I smile at Connor gratefully and slip my hand in his.

We turn our attention back to the film. Slowly, Connor relaxes beside me.

When the final credits roll, applause breaks out in the theater and the lights flicker on. Up front, I spot Eli as he stands, grinning at the crowd and shaking hands with the head director. Pride for him, for his involvement in such a spectacular film, swells in my chest. Zoe's hair, styled in beach waves, is visible but she quickly ducks behind Eli. I realize how uncomfortable she is about fielding questions related to her pregnancy. My misplaced irritation from earlier fades away and I glance at Connor.

"We need to shield Zoe from all the cameras at the after party."

He nods, biting the corner of his mouth. "Got it. Eli did an incredible job."

"Yeah, he really did."

Neither one of us says anything about Bryce's performance, which is like ignoring the massive elephant in the room.

I scan the crowd, clapping along with the other viewers, and my eyes lock onto Bryce's. The laughing and praise filling the theater instantly fade away. It's as if I've been plunged underwater and I can hear the noise from a distance, but everything is muffled.

My heart sounds in my ears and my palms tingle.

A grin stretches across his irritatingly symmetrical face as he accepts congratulations from industry executives, but his eyes never leave mine and the flare of regret in them picks at my wounds.

Connor clears his throat next to me, and I feel the tension rolling off his shoulders, crashing over me. I can't move. I can't turn toward him to reassure him that I'm fine.

Instead, I watch everything as it unfolds, as if from above, as though it unravels in slow motion.

Bryce excuses himself and strides toward me.

Eli's concerned expression hovers over Bryce's shoulder.

An incessant chatter hums, like buzzing bees, through the crowd.

Connor stiffens behind me, his fingertips pressing into the small of my back.

By the time Bryce reaches me, the theater seems paused.

Like everyone huddled inside is collectively holding their breaths, waiting for whatever comes next.

A reunion.

A brawl.

I'm sure the crowd would prefer the latter, but no one will admit it. In my peripheral vision, I see several cell phones twitch in their owner's hands.

Thank God cameras and paparazzi aren't permitted inside the theater.

"Harlow," Bryce says, his voice washing over me like a thousand memories at once. "You look gorgeous, sweetheart."

"Hello Bryce," I manage to reply, relieved my voice comes out neutral. "Your performance was flawless. Congratulations."

He grins, his signature smile causing my heart to stutter even as anger flares to life low in my belly, fanning out to my fingers and toes. Is he seriously going to pretend like we're friends? Casual acquaintances? Like the last eighteen months didn't even happen? Like I didn't think we'd be engaged right now, celebrating his film premiere on the eve of wedding planning?

"I'm glad you decided to come."

"I came for Eli."

Bryce's smile slips as his eyes narrow but in the next breath, his face is smooth again and I wonder if I imagined his annoyance. "Of course. I hear you're his manager now."

"That's right." I lift my chin higher, knowing an insult is coming.

I'm too in tune to the inner workings of Bryce Hawke. Knowing he's going to try and tear me down right now, on his big night, flares in my mind like a warning. Why have I ignored it for so long? Why didn't I admit that his inner ugly doesn't match his outer beauty when I first suspected it?

Bryce turns his head, lowering his voice. He touches my hand. To anyone staring at us, it would look like a sweet gesture. His face dips toward mine, his lips just brushing my cheek as he murmurs, "Must be nice to always have that safety net. I doubt Holt would be so forgiving if you didn't stick with him from the start. I guess he feels bad watching you flounder, shaking your ass and trying to corral drunk frat boys, and calling it television."

Connor growls next to me but I place out a hand, letting him know I'm fine.

Bryce doesn't miss the movement. A flicker of surprise flares in his eyes before he shifts his weight back, his grin turning sinister. "Oh, you brought a date." He flips his gaze back to mine. "Where'd you hire this ex-convict?"

He glances back at Connor, his voice still quiet. Menacingly so. Still, his face never slips, which is credit to what a great actor he is. "I'm sure you need the money, man, but if you want some action tonight, I wouldn't try with her. She's less engaging than your right hand."

"You motherfucker," Connor steps closer, not bothering to lower his voice. Fury is etched in every line of his face. It's impossible to be conscious in the theater and not feel his wrath.

Several people standing near us gasp. One woman exclaims, "Oh my."

Eli appears, chuckling but I don't miss the anger in his eyes. He clasps a hand on Bryce's shoulder, harder than necessary. Bryce winces from the slap.

"You've got somewhere to be, Bryce. Better start moving."

Bryce nods, his smarmy smile still in place. But when his

eyes meet mine, they're cold. "Take care of yourself, Harlow. Someone should."

"Go fuck yourself, Bryce," I mutter back, proud of myself for saying the words and for keeping a straight face while I say them.

Bryce snorts, jerking his arm out of Eli's hold and striding toward a crowd of women. He holds out his arms as he nears and a cheer rings out.

Sickening.

"You okay, Low?" Eli asks.

Connor's hand is splayed across my hip now, holding me against his frame. His touch is comforting and I lean into him.

My finger twists my nose hoop for one full turn as a sense of calm washes over me, stamping out my anger and hurt from moments ago. "Yes," I say, and I mean it. "I'm okay. I'm better than I've been in a long time." A bubble of laughter bursts from my lips.

Eli exchanges a look over my head with Connor as my laughter tumbles out of me, drawing more curious gazes.

Connor's hold tightens around me as he pulls me into his side and drops a kiss to the crown of my head. "Okay, Rocky. Let's get you out of here."

"Rocky?" I snort, looking up at him. "Shouldn't I call you that?"

"I don't know, Low. You looked like you were going to sock him square in the jaw."

I giggle and Connor's expression softens.

"I'm proud of you, Harlow," he says, steering us to the exit.

"For what?"

"For standing up for yourself."

"Even though you wanted to do it for me?"

"I would have laid his ass out in two seconds," Connor says flatly.

"He'd deserve it."

"He deserves a hell of a lot more than a busted face."

"Ahh." I sigh, snuggling into Connor's side. "Let's forget Bryce. We've got an after party to attend."

"What happens at the after party?"

"You'll see."

22

CONNOR

The after party is nothing like I expected.

First off, it's themed. It's got this dark and twisted vibe with an ocean, water thing going on. Sure, it fits the depth of the film, but drinking a tiny blue shot with what looks like goldfish swimming in the bottom is fucking weird.

Second, after the first hour, the amount of drugs I see passing hands is mind-blowing.

Harlow is pulled away the moment we enter. Everything in this circle is always urgent. I don't know how urgent anything can be when people are snorting lines of coke and taking shooters with tiny, fourteen carat goldfish in them, but what do I know?

Zoe appears at my side. "Thank God you're here."

Some of my apprehension of being at this party, surrounded by people who look vaguely familiar but who I still can't place, eases with her presence. "Could say the same to you, Zo. Where's Eli?"

"Talking to someone." She gestures toward the little groups of people. "Are you having fun?"

I glance at her and she laughs.

"I know. I remember what my first few events were like. Terrifying." She shudders.

"Yeah. Want to eat?" I dip my head toward the elaborate spread. "There's no line."

"That's because no one ever eats at these things," Zoe explains, setting off toward the plates.

"Seriously?" I scoff, taking a plate from her hand.

"More for us to enjoy." She smiles at me, dumping a big spoonful of salad on her plate.

I trail her down the table. "How are you feeling?"

"Okay. The morning sickness is mostly gone. I just feel tired. I don't know how long I'll be able to stay out tonight."

"I hear you. If you need to go at any time, let me know."

Zoe glances back at me.

"What?" I ask, adding shrimp cocktail to my plate.

"Are you offering out of your good heart or because you're desperate to leave?"

"Both."

"Thought so."

A roar at the other end of the room draws our attention. I watch as Harlow is pulled into a group of girls. She's shaking her head, but she's also laughing. She looks radiant, and I can't tear my eyes away.

One of the girls presses a shot glass into her hand which Harlow tries to dodge, but moments later I watch as she drinks it, her face twisting.

"Are those Harlow's friends?" I ask Zoe.

Her eyes are dimmed when they meet mine again. "Sure," she says. I immediately understand that no one in this room save for us and Eli would put Harlow's interests above our own.

The music changes, a DJ jumping up to a raised platform. House music blares and the crowd starts hollering, dancing.

Suddenly, the space seems transformed, like we're suddenly in a nightclub. The energy is wild, raucous, pulsing through the room until it seems like even the floor and walls are vibrating.

In the distance, an entire wall of sliding doors over-looking the sea are pulled open, spilling out onto a deck.

I lose sight of Harlow.

She's working. I remind myself over and over, even though after twenty minutes of not being able to spot her, my frustration flares into concern.

I'm sitting along the periphery of the party, shielding Zoe from view, picking at my plate, when I catch sight of her green dress.

Strands of her hair have slipped from her updo. Her face is flushed, her eyes bright, and she looks like she's having the best time. Carefree in a way that I haven't seen in a long time. As if she's completely present in this moment and never wants it to end.

Her laughter rings out, mingling with other partygoers. Flashes snap from cameras. Bryce appears, his arrogance filling the space with a sour note. Carlo trails after him and a blaze of anger streaks through me. They're friends?

I shift in my chair, ready to spring into action if Harlow needs me.

Bryce steps to her. I watch as she shakes her head and tries to duck under his arm.

Someone yells something, and a group of people cheer and whistle.

Harlow twists away and I'm on my feet, striding toward her just in time to watch as Bryce grasps her face and kisses her hard on the mouth.

She shoves against his chest, her eyes wide.

Fury like I've never felt before overwhelms me until I'm

nearly vibrating with rage. I reach for Harlow but I'm still too far away.

Bryce's hold on her tightens, completely ignoring the fact that she's pushing him away.

Carlo's jeering and laughter cuts through the air.

"Get your fucking hands off her," I command, my voice eerily controlled when I reach them. Yanking Bryce's arm, he loses his hold on Harlow and her eyes collide with mine, wide and panicked.

Our corner of the party quiets, an uncomfortable, stuffy silence that claws at my throat.

"You okay?" I ask Harlow.

She nods, slipping past Bryce and coming to stand next to me.

"Calm the fuck down, man," Bryce laughs but one look at me has him backing down.

My hands are clenched in fists, my body naturally springing into a boxer's stance. It feels like I'm straining against my own skin, desperate to rip free and take this fucker down. Harlow's hand touches my arm and her presence, the worry flaring in her green eyes, centers me some. I glare at Bryce, hard and unyielding, until one of his friend's along with Carlo moves him out of my line of sight and a sick beat drops, filling the party with noise and laughter again.

"Hey, you good?" Eli mutters next to me.

"Fine," I bite out, my voice curt as I try to keep a handle on all the emotions bubbling under the surface, ready to burst forth. My fingers itch, desperate to knock Bryce's teeth down his throat.

The image of him touching Harlow, of him taking something from her she wasn't willing to give, sears my mind, causing me to see red.

"Time to go," Eli correctly reads my intentions and jostles me from the room.

When we step outside, the night air slams into me.

"Where's Harlow?" I ask.

Eli steers me toward a limo. "Right behind us with Zoe."

Once the four of us are seated in the back, Eli communicates with the driver and we pull away from the party.

I stare out the window, adrenaline still coursing through my body. I can't even look at Harlow. I can feel her stare on the side of my face and the fact that she hasn't reached out to me, touched me at all, pisses me off. Why the hell did he think he could put his mouth on hers? Why didn't he let go of her when she pushed against him?

The more streets we cross, the calmer I become. My anger begins to morph into reason and my fingers uncurl from the fists they've been locked in.

"I'm sorry," Harlow murmurs next to me.

I swing my face toward hers. "For what?"

"For Bryce kissing me."

"Why the hell are you apologizing for that?" My anger flares again, churning deep in the pit of my stomach. "You didn't ask for it."

"No, but I... I shouldn't have put myself in that position."

"What? Having some shots with your friends? You're right. You should have stayed attached to my side the entire night."

Harlow's eyes widen and Eli shoots me a warning look.

"What the hell, Harlow? You didn't do anything wrong! You were having fun with your friends. Golden Boy shouldn't have stepped to you, touched you, kissed you. And he sure as fuck shouldn't have been able to just walk away afterwards."

Harlow closes her eyes. I watch as a tear slips out, sliding down her cheek.

The sight of it causes my chest to ache and I slip an arm around her shoulders, pulling her into my side.

"Don't fucking apologize for him being an asshole." I say into her hair, breathing her in.

She curls into my side. "You're not mad at me?"

I could drown in her green eyes. "I could never be mad at you, Low. But I hate that I can't fucking protect you. And I hate that I don't understand your world at all. I don't get how any of that is okay." I gesture to the outside of the car, indicating the party and everything we left behind. "And Carlo's friends with Bryce?"

Across from us, Eli and Zoe are silent.

Harlow closes her eyes again.

We spend the remainder of the car ride lost in our own thoughts.

BY THE TIME we return to Harlow's family home, we're both irritable and drained from the events of the evening. I shrug out of my jacket and unbutton the top of my shirt, feeling like I can inhale for the first time all night.

While Harlow pulls pins from her hair and scrubs makeup from her eyelids, I walk out onto the balcony attached to her bedroom. Bracing my arms against the railing, I lean into the quiet of the night.

It really is beautiful. Dark sky, shimmering stars, the scent of summer and flowers and sea. Slowly, the adrenaline pulsing through my body slows, my heart rate returns to normal, and some of the anger I've been harboring since I came face-to-face with Golden Boy subsides.

Cracking my neck from side to side, I roll my dress shirt up my forearms and close my eyes.

Glitzy premieres and after parties. Sharp suits and fake laughter.

Could this ever be my life?

Who would want to live like this? It's like existing inside a lie where each move you make adds another layer. Nothing seems genuine, authentic, real.

"Hey." Her voice is soft when it reaches my ears.

Resting my back against the railing, I drink Harlow in. The woman who stands before me now is the one I fell in love with.

No makeup. No pretenses. No facade.

She looks more beautiful now, her hair cascading around her shoulders in big waves, no goo concealing her features, clad in cutoffs and a tank, than she did this evening, posing as a glossier version.

I doubt she would take my musings as a compliment.

"Hey," I reply, clearing my throat.

She steps closer. "Can we talk?"

My stomach sinks at the uncertainty in her expression. "Sure."

She looks as me before her eyes shift to a spot on the ground, about three feet from my shoes.

"What's going on, Low?" I prod, hating the tightness in my tone.

Her eyes flash up to mine. "I know tonight was…complicated."

"It was okay."

She chuckles, shaking her head. When she reaches the banister, she rests her elbows on top. Her fingertips skate over the hoop in her nose. I feel nerves scatter through my veins, like coins thrown in a fountain.

She stares out into the darkness of the night, and I feel the shift as she recedes into her own thoughts. Not meeting my gaze, she sighs heavily. The sound tugs at my chest, filling me with dread.

For the first time ever, Harlow is pulling away from me.

The realization is unsettling and it fills me with anxiety and frustration and guilt because fuck, how many times have I pulled this shit with her? Except one look at the doubt in her eyes makes me burn with shame. Of course she's not doing this purposefully, in some stupid tit-for-tat tally. She's seriously unsure about me. About this.

About us.

"Harlow."

At the sound of her name, she peers up at me, her green eyes swimming with tears. "I wanted tonight to be perfect. I wanted you to see my world and fall a little bit in love with it and understand why I'm so passionate about my career."

"I do understand." I rush to reassure her. "And I'm so unbelievably proud of you. When you P.A.'ed for Eli, I was fucking proud of you. But seeing all the things you're working toward now…baby, I think you're amazing."

She shakes her head. "The second we got out of the car tonight, you were relieved to find Zoe. With me, you felt unsure of yourself. By my side, you were on edge."

"I've never been in a setting like this before."

"That's crap, Connor. You've been to a ton of Eli's events over the years."

"Yeah. As his friend. Not as your boyfriend."

Her voice rises several octaves, exasperated. "How is it any different?"

I bite the corner of my mouth, trying to keep my annoyance at bay. "Because now I'm representing you. You don't think people saw you with me tonight and wondered why the hell you, beautiful, charismatic, alluring Harlow Reid, were slumming it with some nobody from Chicago?"

Her mouth drops open, her eyes widening. "Is that what you think?"

I laugh but it's humorless. "Come on, babe. Your own mom—"

"Don't take anything she says seriously."

"There were a lot of looks tonight. I mean, you were dating Bryce 'Golden Boy' Hawke."

"I thought you didn't like him."

"I can't fucking stand him. But doesn't a part of you wonder if I dislike him because I know he's the type of man you should be with?"

"What? A guy who—"

"No!" I cut her off, rocketing my fist behind me until it clangs off the bannister, the vibration running down my arm. "Not Bryce. Not a fucking douchebag who cheats on you. But a guy with his credentials. A famous actor who can buy you the three-carat-ring and the home like this one." I throw my arm out to encompass the mansion she grew up in. "A man who can help you grow your career and not be a social liability."

"You think you're a liability?" she practically shouts at me.

"I don't fit in here." I lower my voice, slapping my palm against my chest. "I don't fit in this world that you call home."

She sighs, her eyes closing. In that one breath, it's like the fight's gone out of her. Her shoulders round forward and suddenly, she looks crushed. Exhausted. Done. "I love you, Connor. I have for so damn long."

"I love you too, Harlow."

She nods, a tear spilling onto her cheek.

I stop it with the pad of my thumb and she hiccups.

"But it's not enough," she whispers.

"What?" I shift toward her, my hand encircling her wrist.

She shakes off my touch and backs away a full step, causing me to reach for her as warnings clang in my brain and confusion swirls in my stomach. "What are you talking about, Low?"

"I know you love me. At least, you think you do. But you don't love all the parts of me. Just the parts you like best. The parts you understand the most," she says, her voice breaking.

"What are you saying?"

"My career, L.A., this world, it's part of who I am. The Harlow I am with you, the one you used to like to hook up with when you visited L.A. or I was in Chicago, was just a sliver of the woman I am. Sure, we've gotten to learn more about each other over the past two months. But let's be real, Connor. We never really showed each other our lives until now. And tonight, the first time I try to share my world with you, you dismiss it. You almost got into a fight at an after party I helped plan."

"That doesn't mean that I don't want you."

She sobs openly now and my heart cracks. Reaching for her again, I growl when she takes another half-step back, the heels of her hands pressed into her eyes. "I'm tired of chasing you, Connor. This is who I am." She drops her hands and lets me see her. The woman I want more than my next breath.

"Harlow, please."

"Please what? Please change so you don't feel insecure? Please don't come back to L.A.? Please only show you the parts you like?"

"No, no. That's not what I meant."

"You know what, Connor? It's been a long night. I'm tired and emotional and right now. I just want to sleep. I agree, there are things we need to talk about. But I'm not up for hashing them out tonight. I think I should spend a few more days in L.A., visiting with my friends and family. I understand if you can't, though I'd love it if you wanted to. To try, to give this the shot it deserves. It's your choice." She throws the ultimatum at my feet. Then she turns on her heel and leaves me on the balcony.

Under the beautiful stars.

With the scent of summer lingering in the air.

For the first time since I met Harlow Reid, I fear I may actually lose her for good.

Not because I pushed her away.

But because I didn't run fast enough to catch her.

23

HARLOW

Crawling under the covers in my bed, my heart lunges into my throat and I fight the onslaught of tears.

Tonight was supposed to be perfect. Magical. Tonight, I was supposed to feel secure walking into that party with Connor by my side. Instead, it all went sideways. He was distant the entire night. On the outside he looked perfect, but his expression was stony, his eyes too dark to read, and his signature smirk gone.

Instead of having an adult conversation, I reverted to default mode – damage control.

I covered with my friends, creating excuses for his behavior and silence. I talked up his career to build him up, knowing deep down my embellishments only tore him down.

Exhausted and a little bit heartbroken, I close my eyes and yearn for sleep. I never thought I deserved Connor. For years, I chased and wished and tried to make something out of nothing. But tonight, a small part of me that flickers larger with my indignation, feels like Connor doesn't deserve me.

Fine, he doesn't fit in with the Hollywood scene.

Big fucking deal. He doesn't need to show up for those

people. He needs to show up for me. The same way I've showed up for him. The way I supported the new direction of his gym and threw myself into the launch of Soul Sanctuary regardless of everything else on my plate.

My anger crests and crashes as a sob I've been holding back breaks free. Tears stream freely down my face. I'm grateful Connor is still glowering outside, where he can't see my expression and try to make me make sense of everything I'm feeling right now.

The truth is, I'm feeling pretty worthless.

Why am I not enough?

Not for Bryce, not for Connor.

But I am for me. And that has to mean something, right?

The sliding door catches and I force my breathing to even out. Keeping my eyes closed, I ignore the sounds of Connor moving quietly around my bedroom, feigning sleep. When he slides under the covers next to me, his warmth spreading over me despite the inches that separate us, I finally drift to sleep.

———

WHEN I WAKE in the morning, my bed is empty.

Panic shoots through me and I bolt upright, my eyes swinging around the bedroom.

Connor's overnight bag, which he had stored on the chaise lounge in the corner, is gone.

"What the hell?" I mutter, throwing back my sheets and swinging my legs to the side of the bed.

The moment I stand, my head pounds, an emotional hangover. Sighing, I scan the space for clues.

Is he out for a run?

Did he need to work and took his laptop and entire bag downstairs?

A piece of ripped notebook paper under a photo frame on the bedside table catches my attention.

I stride toward it and rip the paper out from under the frame, my eyes bouncing all over the page, trying to make sense of the message.

Low,

Nurse Jeannie called early this morning. Pop's in bad shape. I took the first flight out. Didn't want to wake you after such a long night, especially with more sad news. Take your time in L.A. When you come home, I'll be waiting.

Connor

"Shit!" I dash for the clutch I carried last night. Rooting inside, I pull out my cell phone. It's freaking dead and I forgot to plug it in last night!

I jam a charger into the phone, bouncing from one foot to the next as I wait for it to turn on. When it does, a slew of voicemails and messages from Eli and Zoe appear on the screen.

I quickly redial Zoe. "What happened? Is he okay?" I ask as soon as she answers.

"Hey. Are *you* okay? We've been trying to reach you for hours."

Glancing at the clock in my room, I swear again. How did I sleep past noon? "My phone died. How's Connor?"

Zoe draws in a shaky breath and a fog of apprehension creeps over my senses, numbing them. "Harlow, his dad passed."

"What? What are you talking about? I just, I just saw him." I rationalize, pointlessly.

"Low." Eli takes the phone. His voice is strong and solid. Unshakeable, like the man. "We're on our way home from the airport. There's a flight in two hours you can catch if you leave now. Want me to book you?"

"Wait, what? You guys are back in Chicago?"

"Yeah. That's why we kept trying you. To see if you wanted to fly back with us."

"Oh. Um, I—"

"Why the hell are you hesitating? Connor's pop died. He's going to need you."

"We, um," I stutter, flabbergasted. Emotion crashes down on my head in waves and my ability to think clearly evaporates.

Zoe's voice returns to the line. "Harlow? Is everything okay?"

"We got in a fight."

"Okay. I understand. But I'm sure he'll still want to see you."

"I don't know."

Eli again. "Harlow, cut the shit. It doesn't matter, okay? Nothing matters except that Cameron died this morning. Whether or not Connor wants to see you is irrelevant, because he's going to fucking need you."

At the resolve in his tone, I finally catch up to the moment. To everything that happened, to the world that crumbled, to the man sitting in a hospital, alone and broken hearted, while I fucking slept. "Okay. Book me on the flight. I'm packing now."

"Good. I'll send a car to pick you up from the airport. It will take you straight to our home. See you tonight." He hangs up.

I sit on the edge of my bed and blink into the sunlight for a full minute before I spring into action, throwing necessities and random items into my suitcase.

Thirty minutes later, after leaving Jack a voicemail and scrawling a hasty note to my mom and Kent, I'm in the back of a cab, bound for LAX.

THE FLIGHT IS TORTURE.

Not because I'm sandwiched between a desperate mother, bouncing a wailing toddler on her knee and a drunk man hiccupping on my shoulder, but because my head is all over the place.

Was Eli right? Will Connor need me now? If he does, will we both just be settling for the moment, instead of hashing out what really needs to be said between us?

God, that's so freaking selfish. Connor just lost his dad. The last thing he's thinking about is our relationship.

Are we still in a relationship? It was one fight!

Was it even a fight? Did we break up? Did he end things with me and I don't know? Does he think I ended things with him?

Jesus.

When the plane lands at O'Hare, I hurry to the baggage claim and into the waiting car that Eli sent, relieved and petrified and coming undone at the seams.

The ride to Eli and Zoe's is short compared to the agony of the flight. The moment the car pulls into their driveway, I'm racing to their front door.

Zoe pulls it open before I can knock and I skid into her, wrapping my arms around her to keep her from falling back.

"Thank God you're here," she says the second I step out of our embrace.

"What? Why?"

She tips her head toward the living room. "He's been sitting in there for hours. Eli's with him, but so far I don't think they've spoken a word to each other."

"What are they doing?"

"Drinking."

I wince.

Zoe nods. "I mean, of course he needs a drink. But he's stewing. Turning things over and over in his head and as well as I know Connor, he's drawing some really negative conclusions."

Fear washes over me. "Do you think I should go in there?"

"You have to." Zoe pushes me in the direction of the living room. "I'll bring you a glass of wine and pull Eli out. Maybe then, Connor will finally start talking."

"Everyone grieves differently."

"I know that. I also know that bottling it all up is more harmful than helpful."

"Yeah." I take a large inhale, exhale slowly, square my shoulders, and push into the living room.

Eli's eyes flick to mine the moment I clear the threshold. His green eyes blaze with concern, his jawline tight. I sense his worry immediately, which is great if he's showing it so freely.

I step up to the man I love so much it hurts. Even more so now that I pushed him away just last night. Just hours before life TKO-ed him. "Connor."

His gaze meets mine, dark, bottomless, unreadable.

"Hey." I crouch in front of him, placing my palms on his knees.

He doesn't move, just continues to stare at me.

I hear a rustle behind me and know that Eli left the room.

The air crackles with our energy, the way it always does. But now, Connor makes no move to close the space between us. I don't press him. Instead, we stare at each other, wary, hesitant, like the individuals we used to be instead of the couple we've grown into.

A pang cuts through my chest and I press my cheek into

his jean-covered thigh, my arms encircling his waist. After several moments, his hand lifts and settles in my hair, his fingers threading through the strands and holding me against him.

I don't know how long we sit there, but the silence is oddly comforting. Shadows grow longer on the pale grey walls. My knees begin to ache, but I don't move a muscle.

Instead, I offer whatever tiny comfort I can provide and pray like hell that Connor accepts it.

24

CONNOR

Nothing.

I feel absolutely nothing.

Everything is numb. Dulled. Muted.

My senses. My thoughts. My emotions.

After I lost to The Bulldog, I never thought I'd feel so low again.

I was wrong.

But this isn't feeling low. This is feeling nothing. This is an agony that doesn't burn, a hurt too sharp to absorb, a loss too fucking great to understand.

Pop's face fills my mind. His eyes, nothing like mine, were blue and bright and glowing. His smile, nothing like mine, was enormous and freely given. He was a million times greater than the man I'll ever be, and now he's gone. And I have no clue how to carry on without him.

The pain is nothing like when my mom left. Then, I felt abandoned. Now, I feel obliterated. Like the strings keeping me tied to this world, to reality, have been cut.

Instead, I'm flapping out in the wind, untethered to logic, to anything that makes any kind of sense.

"Are you sad?" Maddie asks in her sweet voice. Her palm rests on my cheek.

When I glance down, I'm surprised to find her sitting in my lap.

"I am," I tell her.

Her eyes, too soulful for a three-year-old, fill with emotion. She seems to understand more than most adults.

"Then I am too."

"Why are you sad?" I nudge her.

"Because you're sad," she replies, like it's the most obvious reason in the world. Although, I stop to think about it, she does have a point.

"But I don't want you to be sad, Maddie."

She shrugs. "I don't want you to be sad either."

That earns her a small smile, which she returns before resting her head on my shoulder.

"Madeleine Ann," Zoe comes into the living room.

Maddie scurries from my lap quickly, shooting me an apologetic look over her shoulder before hurrying after Zoe.

I've been sitting in this chair for so many hours, I lost count.

"Connor? You hungry?" Harlow asks, her tiny frame shadowing the doorway. She crosses her arms over her chest, but the movement isn't defensive, it's protective.

Part of me wants to reach out and pull her into my lap. Last night flickers briefly through my head. Was it just last night? It feels like a lifetime ago. When the heaviest thing weighing on my mind was whether or not I fit into Harlow's world.

I chuckle, but the sound is harsh and Harlow winces.

Pop is gone. Dead.

"What are you doing here?"

She flinches and I silently curse myself. Why can't I ever

say the right things where Harlow is concerned?

"I came for you."

"I thought you wanted to spend time with your family and friends?" Jesus, I wish I didn't sound so defensive. Is she here out of guilt? Obligation? I don't want her to hang around, walking on eggshells, trying to piece me back together because she feels bad for me. I don't want anyone's pity.

Got that bit from Pop for sure.

Harlow shrugs, pushing off the doorway and stepping toward me. "Things change."

"Yeah."

"Are you hungry?"

I shake my head.

"You need to eat."

She touches my wrist. It's gentle. Compassionate. And it pisses me off because it's hesitant.

Like I'm going to fucking shatter. Like she isn't sure if she should be the one to touch me.

I crave her touch and detest it at the same fucking time.

"I'm fine right now."

"Connor, I—"

"You don't have to say anything."

She bites her bottom lip to keep it from quivering. "I'm going to head out now."

"Okay."

"Unless you want me to stay?" Is that hope in her tone? Or is it misery?

"Whatever you want to do."

She nods slowly, her eyes boring into mine. "I'll be back tomorrow, Connor."

She quickly strides from the living room, like she can't wait to get away from me.

Where's the girl who laid her head in my lap earlier? How

long ago was that? Could have been fucking days. But when I stare down at the outfit I wore when I boarded the flight from L.A. to Chicago a lifetime ago, I know it wasn't.

Ah, I can't blame her. I wouldn't want to be with me right now either.

"Don't do it."

"What?" I bite out, turning to see Eli standing where Harlow was a moment ago.

"Push her away."

I snort.

He plops down in the armchair across from me. "I'm serious, Connor."

Earlier today, we sat like this for hours, consuming copious amounts of alcohol. But no matter how much I drank, I could never reach the mental oblivion I sought. The numbness came, but not the ability to forget.

Tomorrow, I'll have a hangover that served absolutely no purpose.

Just like Pop's death.

It shouldn't have happened, and I don't understand why the hell it did.

"I know you," Eli continues. I glare at him. "Any time you're faced with the impossible, you fight your way out of it. Don't take up a fight with Harlow."

"Too late."

"She's not going to back down."

"Wanna bet?"

"Goddamn it, Connor." Eli leans forward, his expression menacing. "I know you're hurting, okay? I can't imagine how the hell I would react if my mom unexpectedly passed. But me, Zoe, Evan, Harlow — we're you're family. So you can sit here for as many days as you'd like and drink yourself stupid. You can swear and scream and fucking cry if you want. You can ice us out with your silence. You can pick every damn fight you want about whatever you want. But we're not going anywhere. Accept that. I'm going to sleep. Tomorrow, I'll go with you to make the funeral arrangements."

"You don't have to."

"I want to. Because family doesn't let family make decisions like that on their own. You're one of ours, Connor. And Harlow is too. Don't push her away just because you're hurting."

I don't say anything to that. It's easier to push everyone away and sit in this quiet spot and drink than it is to remember his laughter, the way he told me not to come back from California without Harlow. He really liked her.

Outside, darkness falls. Inside, the house stills.

I feel nothing at all.

Just numb.

POP'S FUNERAL is like nothing I ever imagined.

Mainly because I never allowed myself to consider such a possibility.

We bury him after a morning service. I'm surprised by the amount of people who show up to pay their respects. Friends of his from the union, veterans who served in Vietnam, guys from Shooters Pub who Pop used to shoot the shit with. My fighters from the gym, the same ones who were on the fence about starting over someplace new, now shake my hand and offer me their condolences. They all come, dressed in their Sunday best, with bowed heads and solemn expressions.

That's when the first crack fissures in my chest.

Father John offers a heartfelt graveside eulogy that leaves

the majority of attendees fighting to control their emotions. Pops oldest friend, Nicky "Kick" Kirkpatrick, dabs at the corners of his eyes with a handkerchief in Scottish plaid. The sight of him, openly weeping for my pop, causes the second crack.

Pop is lowered into the ground under the bright, blue sky of summer. He celebrated his birthday just last month, making him seventy-five when he passed. Birds chirp, trees thick with green leaves rustle, and sunshine gleams. The setting is all wrong. The day makes no goddamn sense. Nothing about Pop's death makes sense.

Kick drops a flower onto Pop's casket.

The third crack fractures.

My eyes latch onto Harlow. God, she's so damn beautiful, seeing her here hurts.

A trim black dress flirts just above her knees with tiny sleeves that barely cover her shoulders. A black purse hangs from her arm. Black heels cover her feet. But her mouth, her lips are painted a deep red. Scarlet. She looks elegant and classic. A timeless beauty.

Her green eyes glisten with tears, wide and vulnerable. Loss haunts her features and I know she's hurting, partly from the loss of Pop and partly for me.

The fourth crack explodes inside of me. I bite down, hard, until the rust taste of blood fills my mouth.

Father John concludes the burial ceremony. Friends pull me into handshakes and hugs. Words of sympathy are whispered in my ears.

The Church women have committed to a meal schedule to make sure I eat for the next week or two.

Eli's hand on my shoulder, heavy and settling. Evan's compassionate expression. Zoe's warm embrace. The press of Harlow's lips to the underside of my jaw.

Words.

I nod but I don't hear anything anyone says. Not really.

The cemetery empties out. Everyone returns to their lives. Their normal. Their wholeness. Errands and work and family dinners. Planning vacations and paying bills and exercising.

The fifth crack slams through me and I drop to my knees, grateful I'm alone.

A keening sound pierces the air and it takes me a moment to realize it's me.

Jesus. When was the last time I cried? Why does it hurt this fucking much?

"Let it out, son."

I turn, glaring at the person behind me but I lose the will to stay angry the moment I spot Kick.

"What are you still doing here?" I drop my head to scrub a hand over my face, hiding my tears.

"Not ready to say goodbye," he answers, his Scottish brogue thicker in grief.

I force myself to my feet. "Yeah. Me either."

Kick and I stand at Pop's graveside. We stare at the hole in the ground for a long time. Long enough that I lose track of time.

"Fancy a pint?" Kick's voice is quiet.

I glance at him, understanding the melancholy in his face, the longing to not return home. To emptiness. To quiet. To be left alone with your thoughts when you could be swallowed up by the rowdiness of a pub.

"Something stronger."

Kick nods and after a lingering glance at Pop, he turns and leaves the graveside.

I blow out an exhale and stare at Pop's casket. "Take care, Pop."

25

HARLOW

"He's not answering. Do you know where he is?" I ask Eli as I burst into his kitchen. I've tried Connor five times in the past hour and each time he doesn't pick up the anxiety in my throat crawls higher. Now, I feel like I'm going to choke on it.

"He's at Shooters."

"And you're here?" I point at him accusingly. Shooters is a pub that he owns, along with Zoe's dad.

"He's with Kick, Cameron's best friend. They're, you know, talking. I think he needs a minute. I'm going to pick him up when Joe calls me."

Joe is Zoe's dad. Even though he no longer works at Shooters due to his blindness, he still has a penchant for a pint and a chat. Especially if it's about football.

"Okay," I say, some of my concern dissipating since Eli doesn't look worried at all. "Where's Zoe?"

"She just put Maddie to sleep, and then Charlie called."

"Oh, she'll be awhile."

Eli snorts. "Tell me about it. I ordered Indian. Should be here any minute."

"Good. I'm freaking starving."

"Yeah. It was a tough day."

"The worst. How are you holding up?" I glance at Eli, knowing how close he was to Connor's dad.

Eli shakes his head, pinching the bridge of his nose. "Okay. It hurts. It fucking sucks. But Cameron wasn't Cameron this past year. His disease came on fast. It seemed like he was a different person overnight. I don't know. I guess I've been mourning the Cameron I knew for months and this was inevitable. It doesn't make it any easier, but it makes it a little more just. For him. Seeing him suffer ripped Connor apart. And Cameron was suffering."

"I didn't realize it was so…aggressive."

"Connor's had a shit year. Cameron's death is going to devastate him. It's like as long as he had his pop, he had something to work for, toward. Now, fuck."

The doorbell rings. As Eli stands to accept the takeout, my phone buzzes with a new message.

Helen: Great job at the premiere. A junior-level position just became available in the L.A. office. Could be a great opportunity for you. There's a short list. Your name is on it if you want to throw your hat into the ring.

My heart thuds, my hands growing clammy as I re-read Helen's message. A junior-level position? Wow. This is what I've been working toward ever since I became Eli's P.A. Of course I know my connection to Helen is directly related to my relationship with Eli. If Eli didn't encourage me to network the way he did, Helen wouldn't even know my name. But now, for her to consider me for a position at her firm? To have the chance to work for other celebrities, to build my client base, to expand?

"What's up?" Eli asks, placing the takeout bag on the island.

"Helen just messaged me. There's a junior-level position available in L.A. and I'm being considered."

Eli whistles before cutting me a grin. "That's huge, Low. Congratulations."

"Do you think I should try for it?"

"What do you mean? Of course you should try for it. This is what you've been working toward, isn't it?"

"Yeah, but you're not mad if—"

"Of course I'm mad," he says cheerfully. "Helen is trying to poach the best asset on my team." He grins, his eyes softening. "But you've been working toward more for a hell of a long time, Low. Plus, you impressed the hell out of Helen with the way you handled things for the premiere. She was short-staffed and asked if she could pull you into some additional work. I knew this was your shot, so…"

My mouth drops open as I hold up my phone with the message on it. "You orchestrated this?"

"I'll always support you, Harlow. This is the start of the career you always talked about."

"I know. I just mean, I just moved here and…"

Eli puts two and two together. "Connor."

I shrug, not wanting to voice that yes, Connor.

Eli unpacks the takeout and passes me a plate. As we pile our dishes with chana masala, butternut chicken, and rice, I watch Eli curiously, knowing he's considering his words. Once we're seated, I pop the tab on a Diet Coke and wait.

"If the position was located in Chicago, would you want to be considered for it?"

"Yes."

"So, you want the job? The scope of work? The professional responsibilities and opportunities that come along with the position?"

"Yes."

Eli takes a swig of his Coke. "If Connor wasn't in the picture at all…"

"I'd be focused on securing the position."

Eli looks at me, hard. "Harlow, you need to try for the position. Connor is my best friend. He's a hell of a guy. Even for you, and I hate almost everyone you date."

I smirk.

"But you can't put your life on the backburner for anyone. Especially not now, when you're just getting started."

"I just… I don't want him to feel like I'm abandoning him. Or jumping ship, the way so many of his fighters did after he lost that fight."

"I know. It's a tough spot to be in. But right now, Connor's not thinking straight. If he was, he'd want you to interview for the position. Just….if you get it, make sure you're here for the launch."

"Soul Sanctuary," I groan, smacking my palm against my forehead. "Do you think we should postpone?"

"No way. Connor's going to need something to funnel his grief into. And for the next week, the launch is going to be the only thing he has to distract himself from Cameron's loss."

I nod. Eli's right. Connor is going to need this event even more now than he did last week. "I'll connect with Moe, make sure everything is still ready to go."

"Yeah. And Low?"

"Hmm?"

"This next week, with Connor, don't take a lot of what he says or does personally. He's hurting. Real fucking bad. He has a habit of pushing people away when he's hurt."

Eli's words cut through me. I don't mention how Connor and I fought, how I pushed him away. Shame fills my stomach like a tree trunk, branches expanding into my chest, filled with leaves of guilt.

I twist my nose ring and clear my throat, lightening my tone. "Like someone else I know?" I force out, quirking an eyebrow at Eli.

He snickers. "We've known each other a long time."

"We have."

"That's why I know you need to go after this position with everything you've got. Don't back down from anything, Harlow. Especially not for a guy. Not even a guy as great as Connor."

I'M ALREADY in bed when the shrill ring of my phone cuts through the air.

"Eli?" I answer. "Is everything okay?"

"Lowwwwww," Connor slurs on the other end and even though I can hear the pain in his tone, his voice still makes me smile.

"What are you doing, Connor? It's late."

"Wanna come over. Now. Need you."

Need. Not want.

The word choice isn't lost on me and it causes some of the hurt from the weekend to evaporate as I embrace his need with both hands. "Tell Eli to drop you here."

"Take me to Harlow," Connor grumbles.

"Harlow?" Eli's voice comes over the line. "Are you sure? He's really sloshed."

"It's fine. Drop him off."

Eli sighs, "Okay."

I slide out of bed, tie on a robe, and go stand out front.

When Eli's SUV pulls in front of my apartment building, I hustle to the passenger side as Connor nearly falls out.

Eli swears, rounding the SUV, and pulls Connor's arm over his shoulder to maneuver him to my building.

"Your elevator better be fucking working," he grumbles.

"It is." I assure him, using my key fob to swipe into the building.

Connor murmurs to himself the entire time, senseless things that must make sense to him because they hold his attention until Eli pushes him onto my couch.

Eli cuts me a stern look. "You sure about this?"

"We'll be fine." I walk him toward the door. "Thank you."

"Yeah. Call me if you need me."

"Goodnight, Eli," I lock the door behind him and turn toward my living room.

My breath sticks in my chest as Connor's bloodshot gaze pierces mine. Seated, leaning forward so his forearms rest on his knees, he stares at me.

"You okay? Want some water?" I ask, moving toward the kitchen. His eyes follow me. I feel the heaviness of his gaze as I pour him a glass of water. I really need to invest in a Brita. When I flip off the faucet, I frown, "Hey, it's not leaking."

"Fixed it," Connor mumbles.

My head snaps up as I meet his gaze. "You did?"

He waves a hand dismissively, like he isn't watching out for me, taking care of me. The realization that he did something for me without telling me, without looking for credit, slams into me. I watch him for a long moment, hating how sad he looks. Hating that I don't know what to do for him right now. "Thank you."

"Was nothing. I'd do anything for you, Low," he murmurs, scrubbing a hand over his face.

"Here, Connor." I place the water glass down on the coffee table.

He stares at the glass for a long moment before his face crumples and he holds out his arms.

My chest constricts and I physically ache for him. At the loss etched into his features, at the vulnerability gleaming from his dark eyes.

"Oh, Connor," I murmur, striding into his outstretched arms.

He wraps me up and pulls me against his chest. I melt into him, clinging to him with as much ferocity as he shows me. He smells like a pub but with an edge of desperation that unsettles me.

"He's gone," he whispers.

"Shh." I hush, my fingers massaging the back of his neck.

At my touch, Connor's sob breaks free. I hear his pain as it bursts in his chest. I absorb his loss as he cries into my hair.

"Let it out, baby," I murmur, rubbing circles up and down his back. "Let it all out."

Connor holds me tighter as if his grip on me will allow him to check his tears. And he does. After a few moments, his ragged breathing travels over the column of my neck instead of his sobs.

"I got you, Connor. I'm here, baby." I tell him over and over.

His lips connect with the base of my throat and I freeze.

He kisses me again, his hand gripping my waist.

"Connor…" I trail off, not sure what to say. I want to help him through this; I want to be here for him. Any way he needs me.

I've missed his touch. I've craved it since he disappeared from my bedroom in L.A. four days ago.

But is this what's best for him? Is this really what he needs right now? Is he craving a connection or a distraction?

He leans back into the couch, pulling me over him as he nips at my shoulder.

My breath hitches. Connor does it again before pressing an open-mouthed kiss to the spot, soothing the sting.

"Connor, are you sure?" I ask again, trying to decipher what he needs.

"Please, Low," he says, sounding more sober than he has since he entered my apartment. His fingers untie the sash of my robe and it falls open.

Connor's eyes widen as he glances up at me, as if asking permission. His eyes are so dark I can't decipher his pupils from his irises, but God do they undo me. Brimming with vulnerability, swirling with desire, flickering with a need so strong, it's poignant.

I nod. Taking his hand in mine, I bring it up to my breast and place his hand there, curling my fingers around his.

He sighs, closing his eyes. Kneading my breast, he brings his face closer and drags his tongue slowly up the center of my chest. My nipples harden, the one pressing into the center of his palm. He brushes his nose back and forth, softly, as I sink lower on his lap.

His eyes glance up, holding mine as he moves his mouth to my other breast, pulling my nipple in between his teeth and sucking.

"Oh," I moan, my hand finding the back of his head and holding him against my chest.

He lavishes my breasts with attention, kissing and sucking and touching until my core is throbbing and I'm desperate for him.

Returning his mouth to mine, he turns us, laying me back onto the couch. He shifts and sheds his pants, losing his boxer briefs with them. His hand grips the base of his dick, running up his shaft, pumping slowly as he takes in my body.

I can't blink. I can't breathe. I can't tear my eyes away from the desperation in his.

Growling, Connor snaps my panties at my hip until I'm completely naked. Then, he hovers over me, running the head of his cock through my folds.

"Jesus," I clutch his shoulder blades, urging him closer.

Finally, he pushes inside and I drop my knees wider to accommodate him. When he bottoms out, he gathers me to his chest and kisses my temple. "I don't know what I'd do without you, Harlow."

My eyes close, emotion I'm unprepared for welling up inside of me.

Then, Connor begins to move. Slowly, reverently, passionately.

We make love as everything falls apart around us. Loss, grief, hurt, uncertainty. It all fades away as I hold Connor's eyes, drowning in their depths, and allow him to fully claim me.

To ruin me for anyone else. To mark me with the depth of his feelings.

And in return, I love him with all of mine.

26

CONNOR

I throw myself into my work.

All the work.

I hit the heavy bags when it's still dark outside. I run my fighters through their trainings at dawn. I spend the long summer days sweating my ass off at various construction sites. At night, I sit with Harlow and Moe, or Harlow and Zoe, or sometimes, just Harlow, and prepare, organize, hammer out details for the launch of Soul Sanctuary.

"Are you sure you don't want to postpone?" Harlow asks me for the third time.

"Are you serious? We're two days away from the launch." I look up at her, gesturing to the piles of papers and folders scattered across my kitchen table. It's late, already nearing 11PM, and I'm bone tired. Too tired to waste time having a pointless conversation.

"I know. I'm just worried you're pushing yourself too hard."

"I'll show you too hard."

For the first time ever, she doesn't snicker or even smile at my joke.

"What's going on?" I ask, bumping her shoulder with mine. I note the dark circles under her eyes. We're burning both ends of the candle and eventually, one of us is going to burn out.

She sighs again, placing down the schedule of events in her hand. "You haven't said anything about your dad since the night of his funeral."

"I've been busy."

"Busy avoiding."

So what? It sits on the tip of my tongue, desperate to burst out of my mouth. But that type of reaction will draw more questions, questions I don't want to answer on a good day and definitely not on a shit one when I'm ready to drop into my bed. I shrug instead.

"Distracting yourself," she continues.

"Grieving," I counter, giving her something. Grieving is supposed to be positive, isn't it?

"You can't push your grief away with work and sex."

"Watch me."

She huffs, exasperated. Her frustration is so potent, I can sense it. It fills my mouth like smoke. It perfumes the air like cheap cologne. She fixes me with a stare. "After the launch, promise me we'll talk."

"Sure."

"Connor, I'm serious. We still haven't even discussed everything that went down in L.A."

I close my eyes, rubbing at the space between them at the mention of L.A.

Seems like ages ago, and it hasn't even been two weeks. Worst fucking night of my life. Parading around with the fakest people on the planet, watching the woman I love morph into someone else while Pop took his last damn breath without me by his side.

"I'm doing my best, Harlow. I've got a million things going on right now." I bite out. L.A. is the last fucking thing I want to talk about. The launch is two days away. It's everything I've been working toward. It's the last thing about my life I shared with Pop.

It's something that sets my soul on fire.

For the most fleeting of moments, he understood. He knew. He was *proud.*

No way in hell I'm messing this up, or postponing, or doing anything that will detract from the success of Soul Sanctuary.

"I know. I just think we need to talk." Harlow mutters the words no boyfriend ever wants to hear.

On a different night, I may have *heard* the warning in her tone. I may have cared enough to choose my response carefully. But tonight is not that night.

"Can't we just chalk it up to a miscommunication? It was a bad night, okay? Do we need to rehash every little thing?"

"It's not some little thing if you're not going to at least try and understand my life, my world."

"Oh?" I push a pile of papers away and watch, my anger mounting, as they flutter to the floor. Turning my glare on Harlow, I bite out, "L.A. is your world now? You live here, in Chicago." I jab my index finger into the table.

"Not if I get this job in L.A.!" she snaps, smacking her hand against the edge of the table.

At her words, the tension between us explodes. The rubber band connecting us, constantly shifting with a little push, a little pull, snaps. An arctic blast whips through the kitchen, eating up all the heat.

"What?" I ask, feeling like I just got sucker punched. "What job?"

Her expression is frozen, panic edging out her irises. But

she takes a deep breath and allows her shoulders to drop. "I'm being considered for a position at Helen's firm."

I laugh. Staring at her, my mouth open and laughter pouring out, I can't believe how ridiculous she sounds. I asked her if Chicago was permanent or temporary. I asked her if we were doing this for real.

And now, what?

She's going to jump ship on this, on us, before we even have a chance because something better came along? Something flashier? Something more L.A.-esque? "Oh, this is good." I say to my freaking kitchen walls before fixing my focus on Harlow. "Are you kidding me right now, Low? When were you going to tell me?"

"I'm telling you now."

"Right," I nod. "Is that why you wanted me to love your damn city? Because you were planning on moving back?"

"No." She shakes her head emphatically. "No, I didn't even know the job was an option until…"

"Until?"

"The night of your dad's funeral."

"Ah. The night of Pop's funeral. And then you couldn't tell me because…what? I was too drunk to have a meaningful conversation? Or too selfish to understand that your life didn't stop just because my pop died? Or too wrapped up in my own grief? Which one is it?" I push back hard from the table. The chair legs scrape against the floor, the sound jarring. I catapult from the seat, nearly tipping the chair, before striding to the other side of the kitchen.

Desperate to add distance between me and Harlow, I lament the fact that my kitchen is too damn small. Bracing my arms against the kitchen sink, I hunch forward, hanging my head. This is bullshit. Insane.

Usually, my fingers are itching to touch her. My mouth

is hungry for hers. Normally, especially this past week as my loss bubbled into a hot air balloon, threatening to lift me off my feet and carry me away, I couldn't get enough of her.

But not now.

Now, I'm angry. I'm hurt. I feel... betrayed on a level I've never experienced before.

"I didn't want to hurt you," she whispers. "I didn't want to say anything that would cause you more pain."

I whirl toward her, hating the damn apology in her eyes.

"So you let me make love to you instead?" I shoot back. "Jesus, Harlow, that wasn't just fucking." I point to my bedroom as images, unbidden and torturing in their clarity, of all the positions I've taken her in over the past week fill my mind.

"I know. It wasn't for me either."

"Then how could you keep this from me? I thought we were past the distance and the pushing each other away. I thought we were for real."

"We are."

"No." I shake my head.

Harlow sobs, her hand covering her mouth.

"No. If we were real, you would have talked to me about this."

"Like the way you've talked to me about your dad?" she shoots back. I falter from the anger in her voice.

But I'm done. I'm too tired to fight and too emotionally drained to try. "That's not the same thing and you know it." I flip my chin to the table. "We're done for the night. I'd appreciate it if you'd still come to the launch. But I understand if you don't want to. After all, you have bigger clients needing your expertise." I grip the back of my neck. "Come on, I'll drive you home."

"Connor, stop. Don't be like this." She shuffles back half a step, her eyes wild. "Let's talk about this."

I pick up her bag and my car keys and start for the door.

She bristles behind me and I can feel her anger as she follows me out of my townhouse. The drive to her apartment is silent yet deafeningly loud. Tension builds between us as we both sit, seething with words we won't say. When I pull up in front of her building, she slides from my truck without a word and slams the door.

I swear, watching as she makes her way into her building. I sit and wait until the light in her apartment flickers on. Then I drive home, my anger mounting. By the time I step back into my townhouse, I'm nearly vibrating with fury.

Seething, I pace back and forth. Emotions I've never experienced bubble up inside of me, intense and over-whelming and real. Rage bubbles beneath my skin. My fingers shake with adrenaline, with a desperate energy to release everything swirling inside.

I hate it. I hate how I feel, like I can't control myself. I hate that I don't understand where the hell Harlow's head is at.

I hate that Pop isn't here to counsel me through it.

My hand clenches into a fist and my mind fogs over. It's only a matter of time before my fist collides with the wall, going right through it.

I stare at the hole, breathing heavily.

The smallest flicker of relief swells in my chest and I close my eyes.

Haven't I always known this would happen? She's always been too big for my world. I could never keep her here. Not when the pull of L.A. beckons.

I just didn't think she'd leave so soon.

"You're for fucking real?" Eli questions, his eyebrows pulled so low, they nearly touch.

I nod, reaching for the neck of my beer bottle and guzzling a swig.

"Man, come on. Think this through. You and Low, you guys were—"

"It's not going to work."

"Because she may take a job in L.A.? Connor, that's not fair and you know it."

"Because she didn't even tell me she might take a job in L.A." I glare at my best friend. "You know, you're supposed to have my back, right?"

"This isn't like that. You can't expect Low to turn down opportunities she's worked her ass off for. If your positions were switched, would you want her to ask you not to train for a big, career-changing fight because it would mean time away from her? Think about it, man."

I know he's right. Of course Harlow should interview for the position. Of course she should try for it. But right now, I just want one person in the damn universe to be on my side. To have my back. To put my needs first. The same way Pop did.

But now, Pop is gone. There is no one else.

"Yeah, well, the tables aren't turned. So basically, if I was still some hotshot UFC fighter, taking on a fight that was going to bring in bank, you'd want me to go for it. But since I'm a nobody, trying to plug holes on a sinking fucking ship, Harlow has no business waiting around, right?"

Eli's expression falls before a shock of anger blooms in his expression. "Fuck off, Connor. You know that's not what I meant. Jesus Christ, do you hear yourself?"

"Yeah, Eli. I do. I'm launching the most important thing I've done since ruining my career tomorrow. It's the last thing I swore to Pop that I'd do right. It's in less than twenty-four hours, there's a shit-ton of things to wrap up, and instead of concentrating on my *career* like Harlow, I'm sitting here arguing about her with you. Still putting her first."

"Uh, hey," Moe knocks tentatively on my front door, even though the upper half of his body is already wrapped around it. "Is this a bad time?" He looks sheepish, like someone who just caught people arguing do.

"Nah, we're all set." Eli decides, standing from the table. "Don't be an idiot." He points at me before making his way toward the door.

Moe steps into my kitchen, stuffing his hands deep in his pockets.

"What's up?" I ask.

"We've got a problem."

"Of course we do," I mutter. Can one thing in my life go right? Just one? I just want one sign that my whole life isn't turning to shit.

"Callie's ex, Daryl, is threatening to show up at the launch."

I groan, closing my eyes.

"It's a public event…" Moe continues, knowing we can't bar him from attending.

"Did Callie file a restraining order?"

"No. She was scared, embarrassed…"

I nod, knowing it's no use trying to figure out how to stop Daryl from coming tomorrow. Our time is better spent preparing for the fire he's going to try to ignite.

"He wants a payout," Moe whispers.

"Not going to happen." I glare at him, my fingers curling into fists the way they always do when I'm pissed. Right now,

I'm more than pissed. I'm fuming. "We're not going to give that piece of shit a dime. He wants to come tomorrow? We'll make him the damn poster boy for a wife beater. And I'll personally show him how I deal with boys like him."

Moe closes his eyes, the color draining from his face.

"What?" I snap.

"Daryl is the stepson of the Chief of Police."

"I wouldn't care if *he* was the Chief of Police. I'm not feeding into this. He shows up tomorrow, I'm taking him down."

Moe looks at me and nods. "You're right. Okay."

"Okay. Anything else?"

"Nope. I'll see you tomorrow."

"See you," I grumble. Standing from my chair, I pace around my kitchen, anxiety and anger and so much crap swirling in my veins, I don't know how to process it all.

Pop should be here.

What if Daryl blows up the event? How much damage control should I prepare for?

Why does it feel like when I clear one hurdle, I'm already tripping over the next one?

Hopping up onto my kitchen counter, I drop my head back until it hits the cabinets. Glaring at my kitchen ceiling and the stupid water stain there I need to get fixed, I think of Pop.

He would have loved this. The energy, the excitement, even the challenges of preparing for tomorrow.

He would have loved the concept of Soul Sanctuary.

Set your soul on fire.

The next chapter.

A purpose.

Isn't that what I'm trying to do? Isn't that what I am doing?

Screw Daryl. Screw all these missteps and mishaps.

Screw the fact that I feel physically ill inside that Harlow is leaving. Again. That she's running back to L.A. because Chicago, my life, doesn't hold a candle to the bright lights and fancy parties.

Didn't I always know this? Isn't it my own fault for thinking we could have a future when she was always destined for more?

I blow out a deep breath and slide off the counter.

Tomorrow is about the next chapter. My future. I only wish Harlow was going to be a part of it. But deep down, I know that's not going to happen.

It's time for me to let Harlow go. It's time for me to step up and throw everything I've got, every shred of myself, into Cyanide.

For myself. For my future.

For Pop.

27

HARLOW

"Thank you so much for considering me," I say, flipping my pen between my fingers.

"Absolutely, Harlow. You have impressive experience and come highly recommended. We're speaking with a few more candidates this afternoon and will reach out soon."

"Sounds great. Thanks again."

"Thank you. We'll be in touch."

"'Bye," I end the call, doing a little happy dance around my kitchen and living room.

I throw myself down on the couch, close my eyes, and try to hold onto my excitement. The good vibes pulsing around my chest are short-lived as Connor's image floods my mind.

Connor.

Two nights ago, we had a fight. A real disagreement that left with him shutting me out and me crying. We haven't spoken since. Now, I have no clue where we stand.

While other aspects of my life are falling into place, creating the type of harmony I've always strived for, my romantic life, as usual, is imploding.

I feel blindsided.

Tears prick the corners of my eyes as my stomach clenches.

I never anticipated Connor shutting me out because of one disagreement. Because I have an opportunity I can't pass up. Anger rattles through my veins as I think about how much I've supported him with Soul Sanctuary and how he shut me down now that my career is on the brink of advancement.

My phone rings and some of my frustration eases at Zoe's name.

"Hey Zo," I answer.

"How'd it go?"

"Great!" I smile, recalling my interview. "So much better than I thought. It was so natural, like a conversation. David, the guy interviewing me, is the person I'd be reporting to if I get the job. He was really open and straightforward. He's interviewing a few more people this afternoon so fingers crossed. I can't believe this interview happened at all, never mind this quickly."

"Wow," Zoe whistles. "That's amazing, Harlow!"

"I know. I mean, if I'm lucky, there will be a second round to prepare for, but I didn't expect the first call to be with David. You know?"

"I'm so happy for you! You deserve this, Low. You've worked so hard for so long, it's about time things start paying off."

"One thing at a time," I remind her and myself.

"Right. First, the launch."

I groan.

Zoe's sigh fills the line. "Have you told Connor about the interview yet?"

"No. The interview timing was so last minute, and we haven't talked in the past two days."

Zoe swears, and I swallow back my sob. My emotions are

all over the place, oscillating between excited and happy to heartbroken and desperate every other blink.

"Are you still coming today?" she asks.

"Of course," I respond, somewhat offended.

"I didn't mean, I just…Are you and Connor okay? Like, are you together?"

Her question, a valid one, rips me wide open. "I don't know," I admit, hating the uncertainty that fills me.

Are Connor and I together? Are we having a disagreement or did we break up? Why don't I ever know where I stand with him? Why do I keep letting him put me in this position? This *limbo*.

"You guys should talk," Zoe advises.

"Yeah."

"Maybe after the launch."

"Maybe." I say the words, but anguish fills my chest and I know I won't be able to wait that long. For a girl used to sliding into default mode and focusing on the work, I can't tear my mind away from Connor. I can't knowingly attend today's launch without knowing where we stand.

My phone beeps and I frown when Moe's name appears on screen. "Hey Zo, that's Moe beeping in. See you at the gym?"

"Yes, meet you there."

I click over.

"Hey, Moe! Ready for today?" I ask, forcing professional Harlow to outshine personal Harlow. At least where Connor isn't concerned.

"Hi, Harlow. I think so."

"What's wrong?" My heart rate ticks up at the worry in his voice. This isn't unusual. Most clients have some sort of a freak-out before their first event and small details tend to unravel in the eleventh hour.

Clicking my pen, I sit up straighter and balance the phone between my ear and shoulder.

"Daryl, Callie's ex, is threatening to come to the launch."

"Shoot. Does Connor know?"

"Yeah, I told him last night. I just didn't want to bug you so late."

I wait for Moe to continue as I click the back of my pen. In. Out. In. Out.

Just the thought of Connor has me on edge. Why didn't he call me? Is it because he's done with me? With us? Does he even want me to come to the launch today? Is he expecting me to skip it?

"He blew it off. Basically said he'll deal with Daryl if he shows up."

"Damn." I rub my forehead. I'm not surprised by Connor's dismissal. He knows he can take down a guy like Daryl, a guy who gets off on hitting a woman. In fact, Connor might even welcome it.

But the optics of a fight, a showdown, at the launch of a non-combat program for victims of violence looks bad. Really, really bad.

That old adage "there's no such thing as bad press" isn't entirely true.

Running through a mental list of ways to mitigate the escalation of a conflict, I start concocting a contingency plan. "Don't worry, Moe. I'm on it. The last thing he needs is more stress on his plate."

"Really?"

"Yes. We'll beef up security. I'll get Eli and Evan in on it," I blurt out. Eli's star appeal is always a positive, and Evan's reputation as one of Chicago's most bad-ass criminal defense lawyers is always useful.

"Okay, whatever you think is best, Harlow."

"See you in a few."

"Sounds good. Thanks."

I end the call, lean back in my seat, and take a deep breath.

Nerves still jumble in my chest from my call with David. Possibilities and what-ifs flood my mind before my thoughts drift back to Connor. He's the sun in my universe right now, and it seems like everything revolves around him. My thoughts, my feelings, my future plans.

I've made him my sun and I don't know if I'm a star or an asteroid in his world. The thought leaves me more unsettled, more anxious, more desperate for the truth.

I pull myself from my chair, checking my phone for the time. I need to get ready for the event. I want to be at Cyanide early to help set up and make sure everything is where it's supposed to be.

I hesitate, shuffling from one foot to the other as my mind screams with what I really want.

To see Connor. To know if we're okay. To have some answers I can base decisions off of.

I glance at the time again. If I hurry, I can catch Connor, come back to get ready, and still make it to Cyanide ahead of the launch.

I dress quickly. As soon as I look somewhat put together, I grab my purse and beeline to the nearest L stop. With each passing minute, my worry and anxiety grow.

Is Zoe right? Should I wait until after the launch? Is talking to him now going to make things worse? Will he be comforted by my presence the same way I am by his?

By the time Connor's townhouse comes into view, I'm a bundle of nerves. I feel unsteady on my feet, a ball of dread in my stomach, as if I'm waiting for the other shoe to drop.

I skip up his front steps and rap on the door.

He pulls it open, surprise crossing his expression when he sees me.

I gulp. Do not be distracted by his muscles. Do not be intimidated by his hotness. Do not—

"Low? What are you doing here?" he asks, adjusting the towel wrapped around his hips. Drops of water hug his naked chest and ripple in the indents of his stupid twelve-pack.

I push past him, partly because I'm jittery and partly because I'm distracted, which only unsettles me more.

"Okay," he says slowly, closing the door behind me.

Once I hear the latch catch, I spin around. "Whatever you do, don't fight Daryl today." My stomach twists tighter as I mentally berate myself.

That's what I started with? His fighting or not fighting Daryl isn't even why I'm here!

But it should be.

I want a career in public relations. I want the job at Frost & Heath PR. The launch of Soul Sanctuary is my first solo venture into the field. If I was professional Harlow right now, I would be focused on knowing where my client's head is at, not my boyfriend's.

Is Connor still my boyfriend?

He swears, pinching the bridge of his nose. "Moe called you?"

I regroup, pushing away my distressing thoughts. "He's worried about you. So am I."

Connor sighs, his expression softening. Some of the dread in my stomach dissipates.

I step forward. "I'm sorry."

"For what?"

I stare at Connor, drinking him in like I haven't seen him in years instead of days. Strong, resilient, and fierce, he looks like a warrior. But his eyes are shadowed and haunted like a man who has lost too much. Like a man who has nothing left to lose.

That worries me.

"I'm sorry we're fighting. I'm sorry I didn't tell you about the job in L.A. I'm just sorry that today is a huge day for you and our baggage or whatever you want to call it is hanging over everything. I can't do everything I need to for Soul Sanctuary right now when I have no clue where I even stand with you."

Connor frowns, shaking his head as he shuffles back. His shoulder blades collide with the door. He glances at me, his look distant and aloof. It pierces something in my chest. "Harlow, it's okay. You're not responsible for all of this. For me."

"I know."

"We can talk things through another time when—"

"I'm scared." I admit on a whoosh of air. My confession hangs in the air, a declaration that needs to be addressed before we can move on with anything else.

His brow dips, a flicker of concern blazing in his cocoa eyes. I'm so relieved to see real emotion there that I lean forward, closer to him. "Why? Did something happen? Are you hurt?"

His concern for me, for my well-being, causes emotion to clog my throat. "I'm scared for you. For us." I clarify.

"Low. Come on. I'm okay. You don't need to worry about Daryl," he responds, flashing a lopsided grin. He doesn't respond to my second fear, making it grow until my chest aches and my fingers tremble.

"I'm serious." I grip his arm. "Don't engage with Daryl today. Don't lose your cool. You can't."

His eyes harden. The compassion from a second ago has

fled the scene and now, a sharpness I was unprepared for stares back at me. "Harlow, I'm a fighter."

"Were. You *were* a fighter."

He shakes his arm from my grasp. "No. Cyanide is my gym. Soul Sanctuary is a program that I'm launching. This next chapter is everything I've worked for. I'm not going to jeopardize the success of this venture by letting Daryl, or any other woman beater, show up and start shit. There's too much on the line. The success of this program, the women it could help, not to mention Cyanide's future, and my own. There are sponsors, investors, prospective fighters," he ticks them off on his fingers. "I'm not looking to start with Daryl. But if he shows up running his mouth, I'm going to take care of him."

I lay it all out, baring my heart and soul. "I'm worried about you, Connor. About us. I love you."

My breath stutters in my chest and my body turns cold.

At my words, Connor's jaw tightens and his eyes narrow. I freeze at the sudden change in his demeanor. Why is my love not enough? It's supposed to be enough for *him*!

"I know you do," he mutters, his hand curling into a fist. His eyes shift to the floor for a long beat before he meets my gaze again. "You should apply for the job in L.A."

My heart shatters and a sob rips from my mouth, startling us both. I stagger back half a step, the heel of my palm digging into my sternum as I squint at him. Is he done with me? With us? Is this it? We have one disagreement, one unresolved argument, and he's ready to call it quits?

He watches me silently, his expression not changing, which is somehow worse.

Don't you even care? I want to hurl the words at him. Instead, I say, "I had my first interview this morning."

Surprise rocks through him and his head rears back. I feel

a ripple of satisfaction at his reaction. The fact that he had a reaction at all.

He clears his throat. "Wow. I didn't think it would happen so soon."

"Me either."

"They must really want you."

I shrug, miserable at the thought when only an hour ago, I was elated.

My heart thuds so loudly, I can hear it in my eardrums.

"How'd it go?" Connor leans against the door casually, like we're old friends having a chat.

His towel slips on his hips, giving a peek at the cut V below his abdomen.

My gaze tracks the line and I lick my lips. When I glance at Connor again, the right side of his mouth is tugged up in a smirk. Of course he caught me looking.

Even a nun couldn't avoid drooling over this man's body.

"It went well."

"Good. I'm glad." He pushes off the door and approaches me, stopping when we are nearly touching. His hands lift up and rest on my shoulders. "Look at me, Low." His voice is deep, raspy.

I look up hesitantly, feeling like I'm on the edge of a cliff. Will I fall or will I jump? Will I be alone or will he be at my side?

I swallow. I hate that I can't read his eyes, can't decipher his expression.

Our breaths mingle in the space, our eyes locked together as though in a trance. Fear churns in my stomach, traveling upward as I wait for his words.

"You're going to get the job," he murmurs.

"You don't know that."

"Yes, I do. Deep down, you know it too. You're just too

scared to hope for it. But you've been hoping and hustling for a long time, Low. You deserve this."

"Thank you."

He leans forward, his breath fanning across my forehead before he presses a kiss against my skin.

I shiver at his touch, leaning into him.

His fingers dig into my shoulders as he pulls back and offers me a sad smile. "We were never going to work, baby. It was a valiant effort. We tried. But you and me, we're from two different worlds. Two different realities. Other than wanting each other, I don't think we even want the same things."

"Wh-what?" I sputter, confusion slamming into me, injury hard on its heels. "You don't… you don't even want to try?"

Pain flares in his eyes, his expression twisting. But it's nothing compared to the agony searing my soul.

I expected this, didn't I? I knew it was coming…

So why does it hurt so badly?

I step out of his hold, putting one, two, then three paces between us. My mind tries to process his words.

He's breaking up with me.

We had one fight, one, and he throws in the towel? Because I want to pursue a job in L.A.?

If he can't support me in this, we never had a future together.

Yeah, that's what he's fucking telling you.

Oh, God.

Hurt flares through me, causing my knees to buckle. I reach out to grip the wall. Connor steps forward, but I swat away his touch. If he touches me right now, I'll break. I'm tired of breaking. Especially in front of him.

"Harlow, I'm sorry."

"No, you're not." I glare at him. "You don't even want to try. You don't even want to try to support me."

"That's not true. I want you to be happy. I want you to have the life you worked for."

Tears fill my eyes. Yeah, real fucking happy over here. "It's my mistake. I knew better than to trust you again." I say, wanting him to hurt the same way I am. I want him to know the pain slicing through my ribs, churning in my stomach, causing my heart to feel like it can't even beat.

He winces, his mouth thins and his eyes burn but he doesn't say anything.

Nothing.

Shaking my head, I step around him.

"Harlow," he murmurs my name but doesn't make a move to stop me.

"Good luck today."

"Are you coming?"

I glare at him as my hand closes around the doorknob. He looks desperate, helpless. He looks like he needs me. In the past, that look would carry me to him. The plea in his voice would have me pouring out my love. But not now.

I don't have much more love to give. Even if I did, it wouldn't matter. Because, obviously, my love is never enough anyway.

"Yeah, I'll be there," I whisper. "But not for you, Connor. I'm going for the program I made a commitment to, for the women Soul Sanctuary will help. I'm done doing things for you."

His eyes shutter closed and I pull the door open.

Stepping out into the sunshine, I fish out my sunglasses and shove them on my face. Not because the sun is blinding, but because I don't want anyone else to witness my tears, my shame.

28

CONNOR

"Thank you so much for starting this program." A woman I've never met says. She's younger than me, even a few years younger than Harlow. Except, there's a wisdom in her bright eyes, a haunting shadow that shouldn't be there. The discoloration along her jawline is a dead give-away that she's experienced violence, and the knowing look she gives me aches as much as it angers.

Men should never raise their hands to women. Ever.

It was something Pop drilled into me at a young age, especially on the nights when our street rang with angry shouts of jealous wives that were met with the back hands of their drunk husbands.

"It feels good to be part of something important," I respond, still unsure what to say to these brave, strong women when they confront me so honestly.

"It is important," the woman says.

"Hey, you met Callie." Salma, Moe's cousin, appears at my other side.

I glance between Salma and the woman, Callie, and the pieces snap together.

"Hey, sorry. I didn't know you were Callie." I extend a hand. "Connor."

She nods, taking my hand in hers. "I know who you are. I just didn't realize you knew…" She shakes her head, embarrassed. Salma slips her arm around her friend's waist and says something low in her ear.

"I'm glad you came today," I admit, clearing my throat.

"I'm going to talk." She juts her chin toward the podium where victims of assault and violence have agreed to share some of their stories.

"Good for you. Do whatever feels right for you and your story." I offer a smile before excusing myself.

"This is going so well!" Zoe grins, gripping my arm and giving it a shake. "I'm so proud of you for pulling this off, Connor."

"I couldn't have done it without you, Zo." I heave a deep breath, some of my nerves settling now that the event is underway. A lot more people than I anticipated showed up. While that sent me into a panic, Harlow arranged everything so flawlessly that the extra numbers were easily absorbed into the launch.

Large posters with statistics are on display throughout the space. Trainers mill about, engaging with the crowd. Jay is at the front desk, giving out vouchers for free classes and training sessions. The refreshment table is popping, compliments of Shooters Pub.

Eli is, as always, a huge celebrity. Today, he's relaxed, walking around and talking to people. I think he enjoys this part a lot more than he lets on, but it must feel good knowing your name alone can draw a crowd or attention to an important issue.

"Okay, everyone." Moe stands up and the crowd quiets down. People huddle closer to the podium, coffee cups and sliders in their hands. "Thank you so much for coming out today. We are so thrilled that you're here. Connor and I are excited to launch Soul Sanctuary, a non-combat program that will meet two mornings a week at Cyanide MMA. The objective of this program is to provide women who are victims of assault and violence with a safe space to congregate. Here, women will meet other women who have similar experiences. We will work on building confidence, growing stronger, and slaying demons."

A small round of applause circles through the crowd.

Moe grins. "We've got experienced trainers at your disposal. We've got a speaker series in the works. We've got resources for sure, but more than that, we've got the heart for a program like this. We are so proud of all of you for being here and hope that if you are a victim of violence, this program will provide you with an outlet. There's no need to live in fear. There's no need to be intimidated, or ashamed, or isolated. You are strong. You are bold. You are a survivor. And you are not alone."

Another cheer rings out.

"Connor and I decided to start this program after hearing Callie's story. Callie graciously consented to share her experience today so let's give her some encouragement."

Callie takes a shaky breath and steels her spine as encouraging words are flung at her. Moe gives her a hand up as she steps to the podium. She tucks her hair carefully behind her ears, sweeps her gaze over the crowd and begins. "Hello. My name is Callie James. A few months ago, my boyfriend beat me up for changing the password on my cell phone…"

My insides squeeze as Callie recounts her experience. A piece of shit boyfriend who stole money from her account. A password change to protect her finances. A night filled with too much vodka. Ugly words, hurtful, hateful things said in moments of extreme anger.

Broken ribs. A busted lip. Two black eyes. A fractured jaw.

Jesus Christ.

My insides twist so damn tightly, I can't breathe.

I scan the crowd. Most present have water filling their eyes or look like they're about to burst out of their skin in anger.

When my gaze collides with Harlow's, my lungs constrict. Her beautiful face looks heartbroken. Tears cling to her eyelashes and her lips are pressed together, pinned between her teeth, to control her emotion.

Regret, as large and intense as a tidal wave, crashes down on me. Harlow helped make my vision into a reality. I never could have pulled this off without her.

But her vision will never become a reality if she keeps herself chained to me. I'll only hold her back. She doesn't see it now but one day, when she's sunbathing on the deck of her mansion overlooking the sea, her three-carat diamond throwing the sunlight, she will.

"Thank you," I mouth to her.

A tear spills onto her cheek and she looks away.

"You lying bitch!" A roar from the crowd has me swinging toward the noise.

A man staggers forward. He's unsteady on his feet and it doesn't take a rocket scientist to deduce he's three sheets to the wind.

I propel myself forward, ready to rip his fucking face off when Harlow, Eli, and Evan close ranks and remove Daryl from the crowd before I have a chance.

What the hell are they doing?

I spin around to see Moe reassuring a shaky Callie and escorting her away from the microphone.

The crowd seems frozen, their mouths open in shock, their eyes narrowed in disgust.

Zoe takes the microphone and redirects everyone's attention while Moe assists Callie and Harlow—where the hell is Harlow?

Jogging out of Cyanide, I turn the corner to witness Daryl slinking away, his head bowed, his feet faltering. A white Hyundai Sonata pulls up beside him and he collapses into it before it speeds away.

"What the hell was that?" I bite out, my glare accusing as it swings from Harlow to Eli to Evan.

"That was us keeping your name clear," Evan explains, walking toward me. He tosses me a grin as he passes. "You're welcome."

Eli chuckles, slapping my shoulder as he follows his brother.

Harlow stops several feet in front of me. She looks gorgeous in a blue dress and nude heels. Her hair is pulled back in a low bun, several curled tendrils framing her perfect face. But she's sad, and I hate myself for making her feel anything but happy.

"Are you okay?" I ask her.

She crosses her arms over her chest. "Sure."

I grip the back of my neck, squeezing hard. "I'm serious, Low."

"So am I. I am physically fine." She sweeps her hand down to indicate her body.

I close my eyes, surmising what she's not saying... that emotionally, she's broken. "I told you I'd fuck this up."

"That's not a good enough excuse, Scott. In fact, I'm tired of your excuses."

My eyes snap open at the venom in her tone. She's glaring at me. I stare back, absorbing her hate and her hurt, knowing I deserve it. The least I can do is take it.

"Thank for you today, Harlow. I couldn't have done it without you."

She nods once and moves to sidestep me.

"Low." I reach out, my hand closing around her upper arm. I don't even know what the hell I want to say, but I know I don't want her to walk away from me. Not like this.

She shakes off my touch. "Congratulations on today, Connor. I truly believe Soul Sanctuary is going to help a lot of people. I also think this launch is going to save Cyanide." She offers me a half-smile. "I hope it sets your soul on fire."

She walks back toward Cyanide. I watch her walk away, yearning for all the things I'll never deserve.

I DON'T SEE Harlow again for the rest of the event, but I feel the weight of her emotional anguish. No matter my intentions, I hurt her and that's something I swore I wouldn't do.

"Thank you again for doing this," Salma grins at me as Moe heaves the final trash bag from clean-up on his shoulder.

"Thank you guys. I'm really excited about this." I step up to take the trash bag from Moe, but he moves it out of my reach.

"I got this," he says. "You better close up quick if you're going to fix things with your girl."

"What are you talking about?" I scan the gym again for Harlow.

Did she leave? Did something happen?

Moe's eyebrows pull together. "She didn't tell you?"

"Tell me what?" I ask, starting to lose my patience. Where is Low?

"She got a call about two hours ago. Something about an interview in L.A., the day after tomorrow. She's probably at the airport by now."

"What?" My eyes connect with Eli's over Moe's shoulder.

Eli shrugs, his expression hard as I glare back.

Moe smacks me on the back as he and Salma move toward the exit. "Buy a ticket, man," he advises, shouting out a farewell to Eli and Zoe.

The second Moe and Salma leave, I turn to my best friend. "She's running?" I holler.

Eli shrugs again, his expression infuriatingly calm.

"What the hell, Eli? You weren't going to tell me?"

"I was," he says, "as soon as you asked."

Blowing out a deep breath, I pinch the bridge of my nose. "She made the next round of interviews."

"Yes."

"She's at the airport now?"

"Yes."

"She's going to get the job."

"I fucking hope so," my best friend mutters.

I nod, a quick snap of my neck. "I got the rest of this," I gesture to the few things still needing to be tidied.

Eli gives me a hard look, "Doesn't have to be this way, Connor."

Ignoring him, I fold up one of the refreshment tables. "Yeah, it does."

29

HARLOW

Z oe: *Good luck! You're going to rock this interview.*
      Me: Gah! I hope so. I'm so nervous.
   Zoe: When's your flight?

   Me: In an hour. I'm already at the gate. How did the rest of today go?

   Zoe: Great! Connor was asking for you…

   Me: …

   Zoe: There's still unfinished business between you guys.

   Me: Always…

   Zoe: I hope you work it out.

   I sigh, not knowing how to respond to Zoe's message.

   Part of me hopes more than anything that Connor will appear before me like an apparition and we can travel back to where we were two weeks ago.

   Some wishful thinking, that is.

   Me: I'm tired of always being the one to hold us together. I should have known better… nothing's really changed. I thought my being in Chicago would make things better, but it turns out our issue wasn't the long distance between us after all. It's us.

Zoe: I'm so sorry, babe. Let me know if you want to talk about anything.

Me: XO

The flight back to L.A. is long. By the time I arrive in baggage claim, I'm physically exhausted, emotionally drained, and so heartsick I ache.

"Harlow," I hear my name right as I pull my suitcase off the baggage belt.

I turn to see my brother Jack standing in front of me with his arms wide open.

I drop into them and he holds me close, his embrace filled with so much reassurance, so much comfort, that I start to cry.

"I'm sorry you're hurting," he whispers.

I cry harder.

Around us, people collect their belongings and head for the parking garage or taxi stand. But I remain in the middle of LAX and sob onto my brother's shoulder for a long time.

When my sobbing turns to sniffles, Jack gathers me under his arm and grabs my suitcase. "Come on, we're going to get you good and drunk."

"But my interview," I sputter.

"Isn't for two days. Tonight, you can mourn your relationship. Tomorrow, you can sleep off your hangover. And on Monday, you can begin a new life after you get the job offer you deserve."

I snort, half a cry, half a laugh, and let Jack lead me to his car, to our favorite bar, to the tequila shots waiting for me.

"My heart hurts," I say simply, polishing off my third shot.

Jack's voice is soothing. "I know, Harlow. But you're going to be okay."

I close my eyes against the whirl of the bar. It's a hole in the wall pub that Jack and I have been frequenting for years. At first, it was because they didn't really ID so we could drink underage. But over time, it became our place. A spot no one would recognize us in, a little corner of peace where we could speak the truth without eavesdropping ears. Here, we aren't the son and stepdaughter of a famous producer. Here, Jack isn't an up-and-coming Hollywood actor and I'm not the host of "that TV show." We're just a brother and sister slamming back tequila and lamenting my current heartbreak.

"You know, Connor fed me tequila shots after Bryce..." I trail off, tears welling in my eyes again.

"Harlow," Jack squeezes my arm until I meet his gaze. "You are the strongest, most independent woman I know. I mean that even more so because I know your mother."

I snort.

"I'm serious," Jack continues. "I like Connor. He's real and cool and—"

"You're not supposed to like the boys who hurt me, Jack."

"I think he loves you, Harlow. I don't think he meant to hurt you. Not like this."

"Now you're going to be rational?" I hiccup, anger causing my cheeks to burn. "When I told you I wanted to marry Bryce, you said—"

"Bryce is a fuckwit." Jack scoffs. "Connor fucked up. I'm not making excuses for him, but I still think he loves you and cares about you."

"He has a funny way of showing it," I huff, gesturing to the bartender for another shot.

"He does," my brother agrees. "But you don't need him or any other man to create the life you want, Harlow. This job interview is going to change your life. It's the chance to build the career you've always talked about. Even as a kid, when you pretended to represent your stuffed animals—"

I laugh, some of my tears drying.

Jack grins. "I always knew you were meant to shine bright in L.A. This is your shot. Don't let a break-up ruin what you've earned."

I nod, staring at my brother.

"You get tonight to drink your face off. That's it. Tomorrow, you sleep it off. You shower and wash away the hurt. You let all this shit go, because your future is waiting for you."

I wince, his words sounding so much like Connor's after Bryce's infidelity scandal broke. An unsettling sense of déjà vu washes over me, and I grip the underside of the bar.

"I know this is selfish, but I'm happy you're home. I missed you." The truth underlining his words eases some of my hurt.

"I missed you too," I confess. "I didn't even make any new friends in Chicago."

"To be fair, you weren't there that long."

"I know, but I just fell back into my comfort zone. Eli, Zoe, Evan, Connor…that's it."

"At least you gave it a shot."

"I might be going back."

"No way. I know you're going to get this job. Especially after seeing how passionate you were about the Soul Sanctuary launch."

At the reminder of Connor's project, my smile dims.

"None of that." Jack raps his knuckles against the bar. "How did it go today?"

I blow out a deep breath and clear Connor from my mind. Focusing on the logistics of the event, on Callie's speech, on the energy in Cyanide this afternoon, I smile at Jack. "Really great!" Then, my entire day pours out of me. When I'm done talking, Jack smiles.

"See? You're passionate about this, Harlow. That's what's going to show in your interview. The fact that this work fills you with excitement, it feeds your soul."

I pause as Connor's voice fills my head again.

Find something with a bigger purpose, something that sets your soul on fire.

"I hope so," I murmur.

"Trust me," Jack says. "I haven't been wrong yet. And I'm not wrong about Connor either."

<hr />

THE FOLLOWING MORNING, when I wake with cotton mouth and a throbbing headache, my brother's words play in my head.

I haven't been wrong yet. And I'm not wrong about Connor either.

I swipe my phone off the bedside table. My heart sinks when I realize there aren't any messages from Connor – just a slew of notifications of photos I've been tagged in from the premiere and one from Jack last night at the bar.

"This time you're wrong, Jack." I tell no one as I slip from bed and throw myself into a hot shower.

After a long shower and a hot cup of coffee, I feel human enough to venture out to the backyard where my brother and some of his friends are goofing off in the pool.

"You're awake!" Jack slow claps for me as I make my way to a sun lounger and collapse into it.

"Barely," I say but I'm grinning.

"You look beautiful, Harlow!" Jack's best friend Bryan, says.

My brother shoots him a look, and Bryan and I laugh.

Bryan has been hitting on me for years. At some point, it turned into this big joke just to piss Jack off. But today, his words give my dead confidence a little boost that I'm grateful for.

"What are you guys doing?" I ask, closing my eyes as the sun beats down, warming my skin.

"Just hanging."

I cluck.

"I'll take you to lunch at Shark if you give me a smile!" Bryan calls out.

"Leave her alone," Jack grumbles.

I open my eyes and point at him. "I'm taking you up on that, Bry!"

Bryan's face lights up, his boyish good looks brightening. "See?" he nudges my brother. "Told you I'd wear her down eventually."

Jack snorts. "I'm coming too."

"I'm going to change." I announce, standing.

Tomorrow, I'm going to rock my interview.

Today, I'm going to forget about Connor and enjoy hanging with Jack and Bryan, two guys who have always had my back and can always make me laugh.

30

CONNOR

"She got the job," Eli tells me as I bite into a burger at his kitchen island.

He catches me off guard and I jerk back, swinging my gaze to his.

He smiles.

I take a few extra seconds to chew and swallow my bite as I process this information. Of course she got the job. She deserved the job. She earned the position.

"I'm happy to hear it." I say, taking a swig from my water glass.

"Oh come off it, Connor. You're just going to let her go? Just like…this." He gestures at me.

"She seems to be doing okay to me."

Eli's eyes narrow. "What's that supposed to mean?"

"You haven't seen her social media?" Evan laughs, walking back into the kitchen and slipping his phone into his back pocket. "Ollie's spending the night at his friend's." He explains the phone call that pulled him from the kitchen moments after our burgers arrived.

"I don't check social media," Eli explains. He lifts an

eyebrow in my direction. "And I didn't even think you were on any social media platforms."

I shrug. The truth is, I'm not. I don't have any personal accounts. But Cyanide MMA is on every social media platform and, idiot that I am, I gave in and checked Harlow's handles.

"Our Low is celebrating," Evan elaborates, cutting me a look. "As she should, since she landed her dream job."

"Right." I take another bite of my burger.

Eli chuckles. "You're jealous."

I glare at him.

"Of course he is," Evan says, bumping his shoulder against mine. "Who wouldn't be?"

"What the hell are you talking about? I'm not jealous. I'm…fine."

Evan and Eli laugh and I flip them off, causing their laughter to grow louder.

"Man, I gotta tell you something," Evan says after a beat, his expression turning serious.

"What?" I ask, wiping my mouth with a napkin. I brace myself for some irritating comment at my expense.

"Low came over for dinner a few weeks back."

"She did?"

A sheepish look crosses Evan's face. "The day she popped by, I was in a shit mood. Things were falling apart on this case and I missed Ollie's school pick-up, having to rely on one of his friend's moms." He sighs, waving a hand as if that's not important. "Anyway, Low asked me about Charlie —"

Eli groans.

"And I said something off the cuff, something about making sure this life is enough for her."

Eli groans again, and I narrow my eyes at Evan.

"I'm sorry, Connor. I didn't even think about the words I said because truthfully, I was talking about me and Charlie. But I guess you guys too. I said that your life is here, in Chicago, like mine. And that she needed to figure out if this was going to be her life too because it wasn't for Charlie and, Jesus, man I'm sorry."

I shake my head, letting the anger whoosh out of me as quickly as it built up. "Nah, it's not your fault. You were just being honest."

"Or bitter," Eli supplies.

Evan sighs. "She was all in, Connor. I could tell by the look on her face. She wasn't thinking about anything except you and that *you* were enough for her."

"Maybe at the moment." I shake my head again. "But it was never going to last."

"You guys are the worst," Zoe announces, breezing into the room. The softest swell of her stomach is visible beneath her shirt and the way she keeps covering her bump with her hand brings attention to it.

"You feeling okay, Violet?" Eli asks, rushing to her side. The nickname stuck even after Zoe dyed her purple streaks brown.

"I'm fine." She glares at Evan and me. "But you two are on my shit list. You have two beautiful, talented, amazing women trying to give themselves to you and all you do is muck it up at every turn." She sighs, swinging her gaze to me. "Connor, Evan's right. Harlow was all in."

"She ran," I deflect. "Just like last time."

"Because you pushed her away. Just like last time." Zoe flips her chin at my cell phone. "You think last time you pushed her into Bryce's arms?" She snorts. "Well, her social media platforms are blowing up. She's being tagged left and right in photos with guys clamoring for her attention. And that's on you." Zoe punctuates her sentence with a finger jabbed in my direction. "And you..." She turns to Evan but I tune her out.

I pick up my phone and activate it. I check Harlow's Instagram first. In her stories is photo after photo that friends have tagged her in.

Her taking shots. Her hanging off the frame of some guy named Bryan who has an arm wrapped around her waist. Her laughing as she dances on top of a bar.

My stomach twists, an emptiness I've never known scraping at my ribs.

This is what you wanted. For her to move on. For her to have the life she deserves. The mansion. The built-in pool. The flashy diamonds.

My throat tightens and my muscles clench, locking down in frustration.

Isn't this what you fucking asked for?

I glance around the kitchen, my wild gaze connecting with Eli's. He's staring at me curiously, his mind turning over questions I already know I don't want to answer.

I knock my knuckles against the top of the kitchen island and stand from my seat. "I'm heading out."

Eli nods, like he was expecting this.

Zoe stares at me for a long moment. "She's flying back into Chicago next week to pack up her stuff and ship her furniture."

Nodding, I head for the door.

Once I'm in the safety of my truck, I grip the steering wheel so hard, it seems to bend under the pressure.

What the hell did I do?

It's for the best, isn't it?

We were never going to work.

The thoughts run through my mind on a loop, but they're

accompanied by all the images of Harlow's social media showing her partying, drinking, laughing. She's already rebounding, and I'm mourning her like she's some void in my life. Like a ghost. Like Pop.

I drive aimlessly for what feels like hours before I find myself parked in front of Pop's house.

I stare at my childhood home, a slew of memories crashing over me like a wave. Finally, I pull myself from my truck and enter Pop's home. As soon as I cross the threshold, I breathe in deeply, holding the unique scent of his house, of my childhood, in my lungs. One day, I won't be able to breathe it in anymore because it will cease to exist, kind of like the man who once lived here.

I walk through the house, running my hand over the photo frames collecting dust on the mantle, over the recliner where Pop religiously watched rugby, over his favorite mug.

It's been several months since I've been here. I moved him into the living facility over five months ago, but this never stopped being his home. I know I need to pack it up and probably sell it. Right now, though, I don't have the heart to move any of his belongings.

I'm walking out of the kitchen when something catches my eye.

Turning slowly, I peer at the white envelope in the center of the kitchen table, weighted in place by the saltshaker.

I step closer, noticing the yellow post-it note attached to the envelope.

Connor — your pop asked me to drop this here. He said you'd find it when the time was right, when you needed to hear his words the most. Be well, son. - Kick

I plop down on one of the kitchen chairs and pull the envelope toward me. Removing Kick's note, I press the adhesive to the top of the table and turn Pop's letter over and over in my hands.

I'm not sure how much time passes while I debate whether or not to open the envelope. Is this the right time? Do I need to hear Pop right now?

Yes.

I tug open the flap, gently remove the folded paper, and smooth it out. At the sight of his handwriting, tears fill my eyes.

My dear boy,

Writing this to you is the hardest thing I've ever done in my life. Even harder than playing that rugby match with a fractured ankle.

I snort, rubbing my eyes.

This letter is most likely the last thing I'll ever write. My memories are fading, my mind is slipping, and some days my damn fingers don't work. I know I don't have a lot of time. It's a goddamn shame, Connor, because watching you grow into the man you are has been the greatest joy of my life. I wish I could be here to witness the rest. To see you walk down the aisle, hold your first baby in my arms, teach him or her to love rugby the way you love MMA.

I smile again, even as tears stream down my face.

I'm sorry I'm going to miss it. I'm sorry I'm not going to be here when you need me the most. I'm sorry I'm letting you down, son.

I thought the day your mother left was the hardest of my life. I was wrong. Watching you lose your dream career was harder.

That night, I told you to find something else. Discover something bigger, something that set your soul on fire.

I know you will find that next thing, Connor. You have so

much passion running through your blood, you just need to channel it into something else.

But the secret I never admitted to you is that raising you, YOU, is what set MY soul on fire. You filled my life with purpose, you filled my heart with love, and you gave me the greatest gift any person can ever have — a life well lived, brimming with experiences, and rich with laughter.

The night you lost the fight, I saw you pull out that magazine. The one with Harlow Reid on the cover. The one where she's smiling a secret smile. I saw the expression on your face when you looked at her and I knew, I know, that she sets your soul ablaze.

If you love her, son, you better fight for her.

Because the only fights that really matter are the ones for love.

Don't let her go. Don't give up on yourself. Fight for the life you want. And I promise you, I will fight to the end to be your Pop.

I love you, Connor. I hope you love as fiercely as I did.

Pop

A sob rips from deep inside and shatters the quiet. I drop my head to Pop's kitchen table and cry, careful not to let tears fall on his words that are now more precious to me than anything else in the world.

Righting myself, I fold the paper up when a postscript catches my eye.

P.S. When you're ready to make Harlow yours, your nana's engagement ring is in my sock drawer. It was once a ring of a true love story with a fairytale wedding. It was crafted with love and forged in devotion. If you want it, it's yours…Harlow's.

Blowing out a shaky breath, I stand from the chair and walk

to Pop's room. I open his sock drawer and find the small square box. I pry the lid open and inhale sharply at the sight of the ring I haven't seen in years but that Pop kept safe all this time.

A sapphire stone set amid diamonds shimmers inside. I pluck it from the box and sink to the bed. Holding the ring, my future, in my hand, Harlow's face fills my mind.

Her sunshine feeds my soul.

31

HARLOW

"You sure you can't stay longer?" Zoe asks me outside the airport.

I grin at her as I pull her in for another hug. "I wish I could, but my new job starts Monday. I want to be unpacked and know that my furniture is on the way before I lose myself in work."

Zoe chuckles, "Not like last time? Waiting around for a couch."

"Exactly. It was so good to see you, Zo. I promise, I will visit so much more often."

Zoe steps back and places a hand on her belly. "You better."

"And Eli—"

"He's fine, Harlow. Of course you are irreplaceable, but he will find someone to manage his stuff less successfully than you."

We both laugh.

I grab the handles of both my suitcases. "I can't believe how much stuff I accumulated in such a short time."

"Call me when you land."

"Okay. See you soon, Zo!"

"Good luck Monday!" she calls after me as I step into O'Hare International Airport.

I wave goodbye one last time before heading to check-in. Once I have my boarding pass and make it through security, I buy an iced latte and collapse near the boarding gate.

Taking a sip of my drink, I relax and people watch, letting my mind wander.

It seems ridiculous that just two weeks ago I was sitting in this same chair, at the same gate, waiting to board a flight for my interview. Now, I'm leaving Chicago for good and starting a new chapter in L.A. with my dream job. I chuckle to myself, hardly believing how crazy this summer has been.

A lot of ups and downs, that's for sure.

Movement flashes in my peripheral vision. I turn just in time to hear, "I knew you would get the job. Congratulations."

I look up at the shadow looming over me, surprise exploding in my chest.

"What are you doing here?" I glance around the airport, as if expecting TSA agents to tackle Connor at any moment. But no one is paying us any attention.

Clad in ripped jeans and a simple black t-shirt, Connor looks as sexy as ever. But his eyes are tired, his expression defeated.

He shrugs. "You didn't say good-bye."

The hurt in his tone scrapes at my heart and I steel it, willing myself not to go back down this road with Connor. We've been here too many times. At the end of all the roads, I end up broken-hearted. Alone. Empty.

"I thought we said everything that needed to be said."

He sits down next to me. "You don't believe that," he

refutes, tilting his head to the side. He runs his hand through his hair, causing it to stick up at odd angles. He looks delicious, as usual. I want to wrap myself around him and never let go.

I glance at the floor. "I need to believe that."

"Harlow," he sighs, lifting my chin until my gaze locks on his. Regret swirls in his irises. "I'm sorry."

I close my eyes, knowing his words come too little too late. "Why do you keep doing this to me, Connor?" I force my lids back open so I can read his face.

His skin pales, his lips thinning as if he finally understands, sees first-hand, just how much he's hurt me in the past. Yes, fine, I've hurt him too. But Jesus, if we haven't gotten it right yet, shouldn't we stop playing this game?

"I don't deserve you, Low. I never have."

I turn away.

His hand settles on my arm, gliding down to my wrist and linking with my fingers. "But I see you. And you're more than enough. It's time for me to be enough for you. For real. I know I pushed you away. I know I was unfair. I fucking hate myself for hurting you. But I swear, Low, I thought I was doing right by you. My head's been messed up since Pop…"

I glance at him from the corner of my eye, feeling myself soften as his voice cracks.

"Since Pop died, I haven't been myself. I know it, you know it. It's a fucking awful excuse, but it's the truth. Baby, please, let me prove to you how much I want this to work. How badly I want to support you the way you've always supported me."

"What are you saying?" I ask, my heart galloping.

"I'm saying I want this. You. Us. I want it so badly that I'm not willing to walk away. Not ever again."

"Why should I believe you?" my voice cracks on the question and Connor winces.

"You don't believe me, do you?"

I shake my head, a tear spilling onto my cheek. I brush it away with the back of my hand.

Connor inches closer, twisting his body so my tears are hidden from view. "Then let me prove it," he demands, a thread of steel wrapping around his words.

"Prove what?"

"How much I love you. That my love is enough for you. That I can be the man you deserve."

My eyes close at the solemnity in his voice, at the desperation behind his words. Can I give him another chance? How many chances are too many?

My throat burns and my body feels ready to burst with the hope, fear, love, and uncertainty coursing through my veins. "How?"

Connor's breath fans across my face as he presses a kiss to my cheek. "Let me catch you, Harlow. Let me hold us together. I swear to you, I won't ever let go."

His eyes are serious, his expression so earnest it unnerves me.

"It won't be easy," I warn him.

"Nothing worth it is ever easy."

My gaze holds his, weighing his words and wondering how much I can trust them.

"Now calling passengers for flight 5301 to Los Angeles," an airline representative's voice rings out.

Connor's dark eyes remain locked on mine. Unblinking, just feeling.

I know, in my heart of hearts, that he *sees* me.

Around us, passengers stand and stretch, gather their coffee cups and shoulder their carry-ons. A line forms several rows away, and a hush of silence falls over the seats we occupy.

"Please, Low," Connor tries again.

I stand slowly, picking up my purse. "I start my new job on Monday."

"I know." His smile is so radiant, so unexpected, it blinds me. I blink against it. "I'm so proud of you."

"Connor..."

"Section A of flight 5301 is now boarding," the airline representative announces.

Connor fidgets, pulling a boarding pass out of his back pocket. "That's us, Low."

My mouth drops open. "You bought a ticket?"

He picks up his backpack. "Of course. How else could I get to the gate?"

"Wait, you're coming to L.A..?"

"Packed in my carry-on."

"Connor..."

"Harlow."

"I don't know what to say."

"Then don't say anything. We have hours to chat in the air." He flips his boarding pass to me, grinning. "I got the seat next to yours."

I sigh, shuffling from one foot to the next.

"My pop wrote me a letter," he says.

"What?"

"He left me a letter."

I reach out and touch his hand. "Oh, Connor."

He flips it and holds onto my fingers. "He knew. He knew that you were it for me. I know I fucked up, Harlow. I don't have any excuses but to own it and tell you the truth. But my pop knew how much I love you. He knew that your love redeems me. Please, Low, please, give me one more chance. I swear to you I won't fuck it up this time."

"Sections B and C of flight 5301 are now boarding."

"I don't just need your words or your actions, Connor. I need both. And they need to be in sync with each other," I tell him earnestly, my heart splintering at the determination in his expression.

"I know."

I roll my eyes, finally nodding and offering him a small smile. Not because I trust everything he said to me. But because I truly see his effort, his desire to try. And I want to believe that this time, he means it for the long haul.

I step toward the line of passengers. "Come on."

Connor sidles up beside me, reaching out to hold my hand. "I want you to show me all of L.A. Your favorite places to eat, the things you do on a normal day. I'd really like to meet your friends. Oh, and we're having brunch tomorrow with Jack…"

"*Connor.*"

He glances at me, his lopsided grin pulling up one side of his mouth. "You make me a better man, Low. All this time, it's been you. And there's no way I'm letting us burn out, baby. No fucking way." He passes our boarding passes to the airline representative and guides me toward the plane.

When we step onboard, he chats with the flight attendant before gesturing to our seats. "We're these two," he says, stowing our carry-ons.

I roll my eyes again, sliding into the window seat.

Connor plops down next to me and takes my hand.

"Don't make me regret this, Connor Scott."

"Not a chance in hell, Reid. I got you, baby."

WHEN I WAKE the following morning, Connor is seated in the chair next to my bed.

Shirtless, messy hair, and the warmest chocolate eyes I've ever seen. I debate pinching myself to see if I'm dreaming.

"You're really here," I murmur, wondering if yesterday was some freaky dream.

My new job offer, my whirlwind twenty-four hours in Chicago to pack up my apartment, the airport, Connor's apology, him being here now, it's all too much. It's a sensory overload I'm unprepared to deal with, especially first thing in the morning. Without iced coffee.

"I'm really here," he confirms, springing off the chair. He drops next to me on the bed and tucks some of my hair behind my ear. "Thank you for letting me come."

"You didn't really leave me much of a choice, Scott."

"That was intentional, Reid."

I manage a smile but the truth is, I don't really know how to handle his being here. Why now? What's changed?

"I know I have a lot to prove to you, Harlow," Connor says, his fingers continuing to sweep through my hair. "But I swear to you, I'm up for the challenge. In the past, my walking away had nothing to do with you and everything to do with me. Me not thinking I was *enough* for you. Me not wanting you to sell yourself short. Me not giving you enough credit to know your own heart."

I quirk an eyebrow. His words warm me from the inside out, but I need more and he knows it.

"Let's have the L.A. weekend we should have had during the premiere. Let's lose ourselves in the fun and enjoy being with each other. I promise to be myself."

The intensity in his gaze speaks to the truth of his words. God, I'm desperate to believe him. To believe in us.

"This is your last chance, Connor."

"It's the last one I'll ever need, Low."

I pull myself up from under his frame and stand from the bed. "Okay," I agree reluctantly. Something on my bedside table catches my eye and I pause. "Peonies."

"I know you like them."

I breathe in the delicious scent of the bouquet. Half-joking, I say, "You haven't won me back yet."

"They're congratulations for your new job," he says . "Plus, I know you need a vase."

I drop my gaze to check out the unique white vase decorated with colorful polka dots. The sweet gesture causes some of my attitude to melt away. I do need a vase. I laugh. "Thank you. They're beautiful."

"You're beautiful."

I groan and he chuckles.

"I need to shower."

"I know. We're meeting your brother and friends for brunch in an hour." He stands, drops a kiss to my cheek, and smacks my ass, "I'll race you to the shower."

I snort as I trail him into the bathroom.

He's already stripped down, stepping into the hot steam when I enter. Immediately, I drink him in and feel all my tough girl resolve weaken.

Connor lifts an eyebrow. "No go, babe. We'll be late meeting your friends."

I pull my sleep shirt over my head and toss it to the floor. Connor retreats behind the door as I step out of my panties. The moment I enter, his arms are waiting for me.

The second he touches my skin, my head quiets and my heartbeat quickens. I fall into his embrace as easily as I did the first time, so many years ago. Without reservation, without hesitancy, without a second thought.

Connor kisses me hard on the mouth as the hot water beats down on our heads.

His touch is sure, his gaze imploring.

I blink, narrowing in on the sincerity pouring from him. He lifts my chin, captures my lips again. Heat shoots through my veins, warming every cold place, filling every empty crevice until I allow my soul to free fall with Connor Scott's.

32

CONNOR

We're forty minutes late to brunch, but no one seems to care. Not even Jack.

In fact, when Harlow's friends or acquaintances or whatever you want to call them meet me, they do so with wide smiles and genuine interest. I'm surprised, unnerved even, but I don't show it. Instead, I let my guard down and invite her friends to grill me, demonstrating to Harlow that I'm one hundred percent in.

"Wait you guys are going to do long distance?" One of her friends, a willowy blonde named Aubrey asks, wrinkling her nose.

Harlow shoots me a look of panic, but I don't return her gaze. Instead I shrug, placing my hand on the back of Harlow's chair. "That's the plan for now."

"So, you'll commute from Chicago?" Dina, a petite woman with block braids, asks skeptically.

"I'll do whatever I have to until I can move out here, permanently."

A sigh travels through the table. Another of Low's

friends, Juan, grips his heart. "That's love right there," he whispers to his boyfriend.

Harlow's eyes remain trained on the side of my face, but other than sliding my hand from her chair to her thigh, I don't make eye contact.

I want her to know that I'm serious. Sincere. All in. This time, I pray like hell she believes me.

After several rounds of mimosas and Bloody Mary's, our boozy brunch comes to an end. I hug Low's friends goodbye as she finishes up a conversation with Aubrey. When it's just us, she slips her arms around my waist.

"You were a hit," she reassures me, her face open and happy.

"I'm relieved to hear it. I want your friends to like me, Low."

"They more than like you. Especially Juan."

"That's good to know." I curl my arm around her as we head toward the car. "But I'm more interested in what you think."

She glances up at me, her green eyes bright. "I think that was a great first impression. Even though I wish you'd made it weeks ago. Hell, *years* ago, I'm happy you're making the effort now."

I squeeze her tighter, dropping a kiss to the top of her head. "I'm going to figure my stuff out, Harlow. The most important thing I realized this year is that I don't want to live my life without anyone in my corner. And the only person I want in my corner is you. For the longest time, I resisted anything outside of Chicago because it was my home. It was the only place I could see myself, the only place I ever thought I'd fit in. But now, none of it matters except you. You're my home, Low. I want to be with you, wherever in the world that is."

"I want to be with you too, Connor. More than you can understand."

"No." I stop walking, placing my hands on her shoulders and peering into her eyes. "I do understand. I understand perfectly. I got you, baby. And you got me. We've always been us, Low. This time we're just making it permanent."

Slowly, a smile spreads across her face until she's beaming at me.

I lean forward, kissing her sunshine and letting her warmth fill me up.

Harlow is home.

And home is the best damn place to be.

———

I PACE back and forth next to the pool.

"Dude, relax," Jack calls out from his perch on the diving board.

"She hasn't messaged yet," I reply, staring at my phone like I've done every ten seconds for the past ten minutes.

Her first day should have wrapped by now. Did she love it? Was she overwhelmed? Is it everything she hoped it would be?

"Oh, Connor. You're back," Mrs. Reid-Kinsley says, stepping out onto the pool deck.

I turn and smile at Harlow's mom. Last month, an interaction with her put me on edge. But now, things seem easy. I'm not here for her. I'm here for Low. It doesn't matter if her mom likes me or hates me. It only matters that Harlow loves me. Harlow's love is more than enough and I shouldn't have wasted so much time and energy trying to fit into her life when I fit perfectly with *her*. "Hey, Mrs. Reid-Kinsley."

"Call me Debra, dear."

"Good to see you again, Debra." I turn back toward my phone.

"What are you and Jack up to? Where's Harlow?" she asks, glancing at Jack.

"Just hanging. Low's at her first day of work."

"Oh, that's right. Well, I'm sure she made a great impression." There's a glint in Debra's eyes and a sharpness in her tone when she adds, "You know she's not returning to Chicago, right? That was just temporary."

"I know. I'm really happy for her. She deserves this."

Surprise flickers in Debra's expression. "Long-distance relationships are difficult."

"Relationships in general are difficult. The only ones that work are the ones people make work," I point out.

Debra clears her throat. "Harlow's a vivacious, spirited young woman." She changes tactics and I smirk at how obvious she is. Does she think I don't know who Harlow is? That her outgoing nature and high energy aren't some of the reasons why she's so easy to love?

"Harlow is everything, Debra. You raised an incredible woman."

At the compliment, some of the harshness in her expression softens. She stares at me for a beat before nodding in agreement. "Yes, well, since you're still here, we should celebrate Harlow's new job, her first day."

"I'm sure she would love that."

Her mother lifts an eyebrow at me. "Tonight."

"Sounds good."

Debra nods again before turning on her heel. Before she clears the pool deck, she glances at me over her shoulder. I can tell she has no idea what to make of me.

Once she's back inside, Jack's laughter rings out.

"What?" I ask him, walking closer to the diving board.

"Man, you confused the shit out of Deb," he chuckles. "Good for you. Compliments go a long way with her."

"I figured." I glance at my phone for the umpteenth time.

"Dude, come on. She'll be home soon enough, filling us in on every little detail of her day."

"I know. I know. I'm just… God, I'm nervous for her."

Jack jumps off the diving board, straight into the clear pool water below. When he surfaces, he shakes out his hair like a wet dog and swims to the side. "You really love my sister?"

"I really love your sister."

He grins. "I know. I knew it the first time I met you. I knew it two years ago when you broke her heart."

"How?" I ask, curious.

"Because you always put her first. Her needs, her opportunities, her experiences. They always came at the expense of your happiness. I knew that one day, if you guys could just get out of your own damn way, you'd be together. Today's that day, Connor." He nods once before tacking on, "Don't fuck it up again."

"I won't." I jump in the pool.

As soon as I clear the water, the most beautiful woman in the world walks into the backyard. My eyes latch onto hers and I drink in the happiness blossoming in her expression.

"Well?" Jack asks.

She lifts her hands above her head, her green eyes glittering like emeralds. "I had the best day ever!"

"Hell yeah!" I cheer, climbing out of the pool. Beelining for my girl, I don't care that I'm soaking wet. I don't care that she's wearing a dress that probably costs more than my monthly mortgage payment. I don't care that she's a million light-years out of my league. I pick her up and twirl her in my arms.

She giggles breathlessly. "Connor!"

Holding her against me, I run to the edge of the pool and jump in the water. When we break the surface, Harlow is sputtering water, her eyes wide with shock, her hair a mess.

"Connor Scott! Are you crazy?"

I chuckle, pressing a hard kiss against her lips. "You used to like spontaneity,"

She rolls her eyes, wrapping her arms around my shoulders. "I used to like you, too."

I snort. "You're writing your new chapter, Low."

"I'm writing my new chapter."

"And I'm making an appearance?" I ask the only question that matters.

"You're making much more than an appearance."

Holding Harlow close, I kiss her in the pool, in front of Jack, in her parents' backyard. I don't care who's watching. The only thing that matters is the woman in my arms.

As she pulls back, her eyes are sparkling, her smile wide, I know she feels the exact same way.

EPILOGUE

ONE YEAR LATER

Harlow

I spot him the second he steps into the arrival's hall.

"Connor!" I lift a hand in greeting.

His face breaks into a grin the moment he sees me and he strides toward me, lifting me in his arms and kissing me like a soldier returning from war instead of a man who hasn't seen his girl in a week.

"Missed you, Low." He settles me back on my feet.

"It's been five days."

"Five days too many."

I nod. "How long can you stay?" I ask, biting my lip as I note his backpack and lack of a suitcase.

"Long enough." He tosses an arm around my shoulders and steers us toward the parking lot. "Thanks for picking me up."

"How'd everything go this week?"

We step out of the airport into the bright California sunshine and the symphony of honking car horns, blaring radios, and shouting.

"Everything went…"

I glance at Connor, dread sinking in the pit of my stomach.

"Awesome!" He squeezes me against his side and drops a kiss to my cheek. "Soul Sanctuary is expanding so quickly, it's unreal."

"I'm proud of you."

"I'm proud of you too, my little badass."

I snuggle into Connor's embrace. Over the past year, we've managed to maintain a long-distance relationship. It hasn't always been easy, but the truth is, it's always been fun. Of course, I've flown out to Chicago every opportunity I had, which was more than I originally thought due to my still working for Eli, although now it's as a publicist on Helen's team. Connor spends as much time as he can in L.A. So much so that we picked out a new apartment to be our California home base.

To keep things fun and fresh and a little bit spontaneous, we also met in the middle, visiting scenic places like The Grand Canyon, Lake Tahoe, and Mount Rushmore. It's been a year filled with adventure, firsts, laughs, and so much love my heart feels like it could burst at any moment.

I unlock my car and toss the keys to Connor, knowing he prefers to drive. He drops his backpack in the backseat as I slide into the passenger seat. Within moments, we're easing into L.A. traffic.

"How was your flight?"

He rests his hand on my thigh and grins at me. "I slept."

"The whole way?"

"The whole way. I'm ready for whatever you've got in store for me tonight." He wags his eyebrows and I swat at him, laughing.

"I'm going to pass out tonight. I've been in the office

early every morning this week so I can take Monday off and be with you."

"I think we're going to be really busy."

"On Monday? Why?" I wrinkle my nose, not wanting to have to share him with anyone. By anyone, I mean my family and friends. Jack and Connor have a legit bromance. Kent thinks he's great. Even Mom has come around and started asking Connor for his opinion on her home gym and her new trainer's workout routines.

"I need to scope out a few gyms," he responds.

"Gyms?"

Connor nods, grinning at me. "It's happening, baby."

"What's happening?" I ask, too scared to give in to the hope rising in my chest.

"Soul Sanctuary is coming to California."

I gasp. "What?"

Connor's smile widens as he changes lanes. "I'm moving out here. Permanently. With you. Forever."

I lean over the center console to kiss his cheek. "Are you serious?"

"I'm serious," he replies, taking the next exit.

"Wait, where are we going?"

"Just gotta do something else to make it official."

"Make what official?" Did he already sign with a gym? Is he leasing space somewhere?

Connor ignores me, his eyes focused on the road. Several minutes later, he pulls up to the beach and parks the car. Biting his lower lip, he tilts his head. "Take a walk with me?"

"Okay," I drawl, unlatching my seatbelt. "Are you meeting someone?"

"You'll see."

I step out of the car as the heavy salt air rushes to greet me.

Connor rounds the car and slips his hand in mine. We walk toward the rolling waves as I glance around, waiting to see who we're meeting.

For the most part, this stretch of beach is empty.

I turn toward him. "Connor?"

He stops walking and smiles at me, waiting for my question.

"What are we doing here?" I ask.

"I'm glad you asked."

I quirk an eyebrow.

Connor tilts his chin toward the roaring ocean, the waves crashing on the shoreline, throwing foam into the air.

"Many moons ago—"

I snort.

"My grandad, Colin, took a beautiful woman, my Nana Aileen, to the shores of The North Sea. It was a blustery morning, grey and cold. But my grandad always said he was sweating, more nervous than he'd ever been in his whole life."

I stare up at him, trying not to laugh.

Connor pushes my hair back from my face and offers his lopsided grin. "I'm sweating, Low," he chuckles. "Anyway, my grandad walked with my Nana for a bit, working up his courage and practicing the words in his mind, wanting to get everything right on the first try."

"Connor—"

"But then a squall came and my Nana Aileen jumped and started talking about heading back. In that moment, he realized that in life, you need to seize the moments you have. Nothing is ever going to be perfect. Ever. But some moments come as close to perfection as possible and being with you Low, is pretty damn perfect."

My heart thuds, my hands grow clammy, as I note the

seriousness in his gaze. My hands wrap around his forearms and he offers me a shaky smile.

"Grandad Colin got down on one knee," he explains, dropping to his knee in the sand.

I gasp, letting go of his arms as I stagger back a half-step, one hand lifting to my mouth.

Connor smirks. "Don't go too far away." He reaches out and pulls me closer. "And he presented my nana with this ring." From his pocket, he fishes out a beautiful sapphire ring set in the center of a row of diamonds. "It's not three carats, it's not a flawless diamond, it's not princess cut. But when I found Pop's note mentioning this ring, I knew it belonged on your finger, Harlow. The same way I've always known that I belong to you."

Tears gather in the corners of my eyes.

Connor's expression softens, his eyes so tender I lose myself in his gaze. He takes my left hand and holds out the ring.

"I'm going to stop with Grandad Colin's story now because I think my version is better."

I laugh.

"Harlow Reid, I've loved you for years. You are pure sunshine and I don't want to know what it's like to spend one more day without you by my side. Please, baby, make me whole. Marry me, Low?"

I nod, tears streaming down my cheeks. "Yes," I say, dropping to the sand and throwing my arms around Connor.

He chuckles, the sound reverberating in his chest as he grips my arms. Pulling back slightly, he slides the ring on my left ring finger and grins. "Perfect fit," he murmurs. His lips capture mine as my eyes flutter closed. The wind whips around us, the sea crashes in the background.

Right now, in this moment, I let myself drown in

Connor's touch. I lose myself in his kiss. My heart sings in my chest and my soul bursts as I live my real-life fairytale, the one I've wished for for so many years.

"I love you, Harlow Reid."

"I love you, Connor Scott."

Connor grins, clasping my cheeks and dropping his forehead to mine. "I got you, baby. Forever."

"Forever," I repeat. This time, I'm one hundred percent certain that I am more than enough for me, for Connor.

For us.

THANK you so much for reading Connor and Harlow's story! If you want more second chance vibes and single dad romances are your jam, don't miss Healing My Heart! Evan and Charlie have off-the-charts chemistry!

HEALING MY HEART

Chapter One - Evan

The sight of Ollie, my son, placing an ornament on the Christmas tree brings a smile to my face.

I lean back in the comfortable chair in my brother's living room and lift the bottle of beer to my lips. Taking a sip, my shoulders drop, some of the tension and stress I've been carrying around for what feels like eternity receding.

"Do this one, Maddie." Ollie lifts a snowflake ornament from the box and passes it to my three-year-old niece.

"Ooh, it's so sparkly," Maddie breathes, as if the sound of her voice will disrupt the glitter. She takes it gingerly from Ollie's hand and hangs it on the tree.

"They're the fucking best," my brother Eli chuckles next to me, taking a large swig of his beer.

"Can't believe you've got another one on the way." I glance at him.

He shrugs but I don't miss the way the corners of his mouth curl up.

My little brother is really something else. He's the person

I'm most proud of in the world. A reckless teenager with a chip on his shoulder, he managed to turn his life around. He moved out to L.A., the stars aligned, and now he's an A-list Hollywood actor with a beautiful wife, an amazing little girl, and a baby on the way. His eyes gleam, content with the certainty that is his life, as he watches our kids decorate for Christmas.

I used to have that look in my eyes. Once upon a time when I was a happily married, new dad, the holiday season brought wonder and joy similar to when I was a kid. Even the damn snow blanketing the streets seemed magical instead of a giant pain in the ass.

But that was before.

Now, I'm just grateful to be Dad to the world's most awesome kid. A boy who is growing up too fast and asking too many questions about his mom and my lack of a dating life.

I drain my beer, an unbidden image of Charlie Adams filling my mind. If there was one woman I at least imagined a future with after Sophie left, it was Charlie.

Long, blonde hair, sparkling blue eyes, and a personality that outshone the sun, Charlie made me feel things I hadn't felt in years, made me yearn for things I forgot, and made me believe in things I know better than to want. But of course, I messed that up, too.

Our whirlwind romance ended as quickly as it began. I couldn't commit, not the way she deserved. We broke up, endured a year of intense awkwardness every time our paths crossed, and then, she skipped town. She moved all the way to New York City for an advanced design program, and I threw myself even more into my workaholic tendencies. Most days, the only thing within my control seems to be my career, and I cling to it, even if I'm beginning to resent the long hours.

"Who wants hot chocolate?" My sister-in-law, Zoe, who also happens to be Charlie's best friend, pushes into the cozy living room holding a tray with steaming mugs.

At the same time, my brother and I jump to our feet to help her. She laughs as Eli takes the tray from her hands and moves it to the coffee table.

Ollie whoops as Maddie's eyes grow round. "With marshmallows?" Maddie asks.

"A whole handful," Eli quips.

Ollie snickers and grabs a bunch of marshmallows, dropping them into his and Maddie's mugs. "Thanks, Aunt Zo."

Zoe's expression softens as she gazes at my son. "You're welcome. You're getting too grown-up, Ollie."

Ollie blushes, ducking his head. "I'm almost eleven."

"Eleven?" Maddie asks. "You're old."

I laugh along with Eli and Zoe, but the truth is my son is growing up too fast. A strange sensation squeezes my chest as the realization hits me. In seven years, Ollie will be heading to college, and I'll be an empty nester. All alone in a big home that Sophie picked out and I worked countless hours to pay for. That's all I'll have to show for the soul-sucking grind I've flung myself into.

Disappointment streaks through me. I have a great life—a life people are envious of. A well-paying job, a well-behaved son, a brother I admire.

The fact that it doesn't feel like enough rubs me the wrong way. Like I'm too selfish to count my blessings.

But sometimes, I wish for more. For me and for Ollie.

Sighing, I swallow back my frustration mixed with beer.

"Oh!" Zoe exclaims, her eyes glued to her phone.

"What is it? What's wrong?" Eli narrows his gaze in concern, his hand flying to her belly. "Is it the baby?"

She shakes off his touch and smiles. "Charlie landed early."

Charlie?

I sit up straighter in my chair but keep my expression unreadable.

"I thought she was coming tomorrow," Eli says.

"Me too." Zoe nods, tapping out a message on her phone. "I told her to come by before she goes to her mom's. If she heads straight home, I won't see her for days, considering how much Mama Adams misses her baby."

Eli snorts and holds Maddie's mug while she takes a gulp of hot chocolate.

"Charlie's coming?" My son's face lights up, and I feel a pang of guilt slice through my stomach.

Even though Ollie never knew what went on between Charlie and me behind closed doors, Charlie was a constant fixture in Ollie's life before I messed it all up. As Zoe's best friend and Maddie's godmother, she was at every family event and weekend game night, sometimes even filling in as babysitter when I was in a bind. When I pushed Charlie away, I didn't just shove her out of my life but out of Ollie's life too. The fact that my son still misses her only intensifies my guilt.

Heat rushes through me as I realize that in thirty minutes, I'm going to come face-to-face with the woman I never forgot for the first time since she moved to New York eighteen months ago.

Eli taps his knee against mine and I glance up.

He narrows his gaze at me, as if asking where my head is at, asking if I'm cool.

I offer him a half-smile and dip my head to let him know I'm good. Everything is fine.

Just because Charlie and I aren't a thing anymore doesn't mean I can't be polite and cordial when we're in the same room. We played the charade well for the year-and-a-half after we ended things and before she moved. It was easier to avoid her at a big family event than it will be tonight. But I don't want to avoid her anymore. Especially not during the holiday season.

Especially when she makes my son beam.

"Merry Christmas!" Charlie waltzes through the door, and I have to physically force myself not to step toward her.

I hang back while Zoe, Maddie, and Ollie rush her, but my mind explodes with a million memories.

The way her blue eyes dazzle and how her hair falls around her shoulders like an angel's halo is exactly the same. But there's something different about her. Confidence grips her shoulders, keeping her posture erect. She has an air of maturity, of wisdom, that didn't exist when she walked out of my life more than three years ago, and I let her go.

I let her go.

Charlie Adams is fucking beautiful. She always was. But the woman standing in Eli and Zoe's foyer now is just that. A woman. A self-assured, confident, stunning woman with a smile that could grow a garden and a laugh that could tilt the Earth off its axis.

"Merry Christmas!" Ollie exclaims, throwing his arms around her waist.

My chest tightens as I watch her wrap her arms around

Ollie, her eyes closing, her smile widening, with no hard feelings, no judgement, nothing but admiration for my son.

My throat dries as she turns her attention toward our goddaughter and spins a squealing Maddie in a circle before placing her on her feet.

Zoe wraps an arm around Charlie's waist, and Eli presses a kiss to her cheek and she beams. Caught up in her homecoming, she gives off the same genuine energy, the same warmth, from years ago but with a sophistication that's new.

The Christmas lights twinkle around her, laughter rings out, and I try to get my bearings as an unexpected wave of emotion swells inside of me.

Nostalgia.

Charlie is home. She's here. And it feels…right.

"Welcome home, Charlie," I manage to say as she glances up.

Her gaze connects with mine, and even though her expression never slips, her eyes darken, azure like the sea.

Energy zaps between us as she offers me a quick hug, the scent of her perfume so familiar it causes my lungs to ache. "Thanks, Ev. It's good to be back."

I nod as she steps away. Ollie and Maddie overwhelm her immediately, pulling her into the living room.

"I can't wait to see your tree!" Charlie exclaims.

"We have hot chocolate, too," Maddie informs her.

"And marshmallows," Ollie adds, the excitement in his tone reminding me of when he was younger.

Zoe trails after them.

I suck in a deep breath as Eli's hand comes down on my shoulder. "She's back."

"She's different."

"She grew up," my brother explains like it's the most obvious thing in the world. "You okay?"

I nod, not voicing how not okay I am.

Eli chuckles, muttering under his breath. He leaves me in the foyer, staring after the whirlwind I was once too scared to be swept up in. Now, all I can do is wonder how different things would be if I gave in then.

Would I be as fulfilled as Eli? As happy as Zoe? As sure of myself as Charlie?

Would I be the family man I always thought I'd become instead of the guy who can't seem to get out of his own damn way?